EVERYTHING SHE EVER WANTED

A DIFFERENT KIND OF LOVE NOVEL

LIZ DURANO

OTHER BOOKS BY LIZ DURANO

DIFFERENT KIND OF LOVE: TAOS

Breaking the Rules

Where She Belongs

Other Side of Love (Prequel)

DIFFERENT KIND OF LOVE: NEW YORK

Falling for Jordan

Friends with Benefits

Lucky Charm

LOVE BEACH EVER AFTER

Summer with a Navy SEAL

Merry with a Tycoon

Spring Break with a Bodyguard

CELEBRITY

Loving Ashe

Loving Riley

WORTH IT ALL

Worth the Risk

Worth the Wait

Worth the Fight

To Sara

Maybe what you need is a better kind of love
One that you could only dream
Maybe it will take all the sorrow away
And let you feel free

- Brendan James, *Different Kind of Love*

CHAPTER ONE

Harlow

If someone had told me six months ago that going off-grid would make the perfect vacation, I'd have considered them crazy and crossed them off my friend list.

Off-grid meant off-everything. Away from civilization, cable TV, and worse, Wi-Fi. All right, I'm exaggerating because I do have Wi-Fi, even if it's very spotty. And none of my friends picked this place out in the middle of nowhere; I did.

But still, how on earth was I supposed to know how my patients were doing? Were their donor kidneys getting used to their new bodies? What about the antibody counts? Were their sodium-potassium levels balanced? What about their blood pressure?

But that was six months ago, back when the only thing that mattered to me was being one of the top pediatric kidney transplant surgeons in the country who authored countless medical papers and took wide-eyed doctors on rounds at Miller General Hospital, a top medical and research facility in Manhattan.

I take a sip of my wine and lean back in my chair, gazing out at the wide expanse of sagebrush outside the double-pane glass windows. It's dark outside my sustainable home-away-from-home, and all I see are the moon and the thousands of stars in the sky. It's a breathtaking sight, one I hadn't seen before I came up here, not when I've lived most of my life in the big city with most of my waking hours spent inside the hospital treating patients or holed up in my office typing away research papers.

I can't remember now what possessed me to stay on the outskirts of Taos, New Mexico, but here I am anyway, away from it all, just the way I'd planned it—or not planned it. At least, the part where I'm sitting alone in the dark, drowning my anger and grief in my third glass of wine.

It had started with the newspaper announcement that Jeff was getting married in three weeks. Friends back home were so shocked by the latest development that they forgot themselves and just had to call me.

Was the divorce even final?

Good question. But I wasn't about to tell them anything, not when I couldn't call a single one of them a friend, definitely not after they showed me just how much more important their reputations were the moment things fell apart in my marriage.

Of course, they had to pick the Director of Transplant Surgery at Miller General Hospital, and not his unstable wife, even if she happened to be the Assistant Director of Transplant Surgery.

This is what I get for not venturing outside of our old

circle of friends. I should have worked harder at making friends on my own, especially after Jeff filed for divorce.

But it's too late to worry about such things now, not after the *friends* had already made their calls, pretending to act concerned about how I was taking the news of his impending nuptials.

Did you know he's getting married to his secretary? And she's pregnant with his baby! And hadn't Jeff and I been trying to have a baby for the last five years, and even after all the IVF treatments and acupuncture, nothing happened? Nothing that meant a successful pregnancy, anyway?

Learning Leilani was pregnant definitely hurt, especially when I knew it was the one thing Jeff had always wanted—a child, preferably a son who would carry his name. And for five years, after every implantation and their corresponding failure, I finally accepted that it had to be my fault like he always insisted.

After all, I was hitting forty, and the old eggs must have long shriveled up, even though all my medical training told me it wasn't possible, not when my estrogen levels and other numbers were fine.

But that's all part of the past now. The venerated transplant surgeon, Jeff Gardner, M.D. filed for divorce eight months ago, and life went on.

Unfortunately for me, it meant life inside the same hospital where we both worked as transplant surgeons until one of us had to leave. And it certainly wasn't going to be the Director of Transplant Surgery. Nope, not in a million years.

I slip half a teaspoon of rich fudge between my lips

and chase it with a long sip of red wine. It's something I learned during my first and only trip to Napa Valley so many years ago and being a chocolate girl, it's a habit that stuck, especially when I'm stressed. And boy, am I so stressed that I'm despondent. I don't know why, or that's what I tell myself because I do know why I'm feeling this way.

I'm a fucking failure.

I take another sip of wine, forgoing the fudge this time, and then another before I pick up the gun next to the half-empty bottle of Bordeaux. I rise from the couch, feeling the room sway around me. I take a deep breath and stare straight ahead, determined to finish what I'd started.

With the glass of wine in one hand and the gun in the other, I make my way toward the front door with its tempered glass insert, probably useless in a zombie invasion, and stare at the darkness beyond it.

For a moment, I can't figure out how to open the door with my hands full. Still holding the gun, I set the wine glass on the floor next to me and pull open the door, step outside and turn around to pick up the wine glass. Hell if I'm wasting any of this wine. At two grand a bottle, the landlady can use the rest of my deposit to cover the cost.

I make my way to the fire pit area, ignoring the gravel cutting into the bottoms of my feet. I'm too numb to feel it, and soon I'll be too dead to feel anything else.

I take another sip of the wine, though this time, I spit it out, feeling it dribble down my chin. From the way I'm wobbling on my feet, I've had enough of it even though I'm not quite there yet. I still need one more glass to drown out the rational part of my brain that's begging me to think my decision through, telling me that things aren't that bad; that despite what Jeff told me over the phone this afternoon, it was a terrible idea to kill myself out in the middle of nowhere.

Who'd find my body out here? Would the coyotes get to it first? Is that why I picked the field of sagebrush to do the deed while I'm still standing, where no one would notice my body till after the vultures would circle the area days later?

I just wish I'd put on some footwear before I'd come out here because that damn gravel is really starting to hurt, breaking through the veil of numbness that I hoped would keep me till the very end.

But even as I stand out here, my thoughts are getting discombobulated, the rational—albeit drunk—part of my brain begging the emotional, fucked-up part of me to please, please reconsider.

You're just letting Jeff win. And he will win the moment that bullet enters your brain, you know. And what a smart and beautiful brain it is, too, wasted over a man who's so intent on making up for his tiny dick that he pisses over everyone, even the ones who helped him get to where he is now. And honestly, Harlow, do you really want Little Dick to win? Do you? Do you?

I laugh out loud, my laughter lost in the surrounding darkness. Behind me, the Earthship I'd rented for the next three weeks stands gloriously lit up with solar lights, like a beacon in the night. It's one of those weird-looking sustainable homes one sees off the highway just outside of Taos, built with its back against a hillside, or bermed as the landlady, Anita Anaya, told me.

Built from re-purposed materials like crushed soda cans and old tires packed with earth that make up the heavily insulated walls and fences that surround the property, and multi-colored glass-bottled walls that filter sunlight into the rooms, it's like something out of a *Flintstones* movie. Solar panels and wind turbines generate more than enough DC power for the whole Earthship, stored in several types of deep cycle batteries next to the garage.

There's also a cistern inside the utility room that gathers water from the rain and nightly condensation, which is then filtered, so it's good enough to wash my dishes and do my laundry as long as I used organic detergents. That way, that waste water is then filtered through the indoor vegetable garden and from there, it ends up as the brownish water in my toilet.

There's so much more to the Earthship christened the Pearl, like the beautifully carved woodwork that draws the eye at every turn, accents that only a master carpenter could have made. But that's as much as I had time to notice during my quick tour yesterday before I said, *yes, I want it for three weeks*, and paid in cash.

I just hope Anita checks up on me before the three weeks is up. To be fair to her, it's why I'm out here surrounded by buzzing mosquitos instead of inside the Pearl. It would be such an inconvenience to kill myself in such a beautiful place when I had all the outdoors to blow my brains out while I was drunk and beyond caring.

Unfortunately, as another sharp piece of gravel cuts

into the skin of my foot, I'm not past that beyond-caring stage yet. But I also don't want to drink another glass of wine to get to that point because I'd probably end up puking my guts out, and that would be so messy. I hate messy. I yawn, not even bothering to cover my mouth since my hands are full, anyway. Crap, now I'm also sleepy.

Ah, screw this.

I turn away from the sagebrush and make my way back to the Pearl, pausing at the door. With one hand holding the wine and the other, the gun, I'm not quite sure how to grasp the handle and turn it open without shooting myself. And wouldn't it be a hoot if I shot myself by accident this time?

To think I'm a damn pediatric surgeon, able to transplant donor kidneys into my young patients yet here I am, Dr. Harlow James, unable to open a simple door. I feel ridiculous. But the moment I step inside and shut the door behind me, I realize I don't care how I feel (drunk) or look (probably terrible). I just want to go to sleep and pretend this craziness never happened.

I stagger toward the couch and return the wine glass to the table. I rest the gun on top of the note I'd written, barely remembering what I'd scribbled earlier through all my tears.

I feel more foolish now than when I started this drinking binge hours earlier, but at least, I'm still here, still breathing, and my brain is still in one piece. And really, who cares if I can barely remember what started this whole thing about killing myself in the first place?

But if there's one thing I know, I'm going to have a hell of a hangover in the morning.

CHAPTER TWO

Dax

I WAS NEVER into fairy tales.

But discovering a real live princess in my house at three in the fucking morning when all I want to do is crash after a long drive from Flagstaff reminds me of the story of the three bears and that blonde chick who breaks into their pad, eats all their food, and sleeps in their beds, too.

Just like the one that's in mine right now.

At first, I was afraid she was dead, but the gentle rise and fall of her chest told me that she was just passed out, probably from the half-empty bottle of Bordeaux in the living room that she must have enjoyed all by herself for there was only one wine glass next to it.

But of all the wines she had to pick from the cellar, it had to be the 2005 Château Lafite-Rothschild Bordeaux I had been saving for a special occasion. Two grand down the drain, courtesy of Goldi-fucking-locks here, who's not only passed out cold, but she's also naked.

Thank her lucky stars the sheets cover her hips,

though it doesn't cover her torso, her gorgeous full breasts on full display. I have to stop and stare for a few seconds even though my mind tells me to look away. I'm a man, after all, and not a dead one at that. And her tits are real, not those fake ones that I see all the time just about everywhere.

I adjust myself before walking out of the room and shut the bedroom door quietly behind me. Just because I own the place doesn't mean I can crash it anytime I want, and certainly not with Goldilocks snoring on my bed.

Once in the living room, I pull out my phone and scan my calendar. *Did I agree to have the place rented out this month?*

My calendar app appears on my phone screen, and the next three weeks are shaded in red to indicate that Nana did rent the place out at the last minute. I check my text messages, and sure enough, she sent me a text message yesterday telling me that the new tenant had paid in cash. She even left a message on my voicemail.

Too bad I didn't check any of my messages because that would have certainly saved me a trip. But I'd been too busy the last two days finalizing custom orders.

I exhale and sit down on the couch, picking up the bottle of Bordeaux and taking a sip. I might as well find out what two grand tastes like. I doubt she drank it straight from the bottle, so I'm not worried about cooties at all. And even if she did, that's no big deal.

The big deal is sitting right in front of me, sharing the same space with the wine and a jar of half-eaten fudge.

A gun.

I sure hope she brought it for protection. A woman

traveling alone in the outskirts of Taos is not exactly a good thing, not when the Pearl, the name I'd picked out for the Earthship I mostly built on my own, is off-grid and about a quarter mile away from the nearest highway.

The only people who rent the Pearl are usually individuals and families curious about sustainable living, and small groups who taught yoga and meditation. But maybe I'm going about this all wrong, assuming only the worst.

Maybe the woman is expecting company. It wouldn't be unusual for one party to arrive early and the rest coming later. Still, the gun bothers me, especially when it's resting on top of a note that begins with five words.

I'm sorry I failed you.

I take another sip of the wine before I set the bottle down. I never was a wine drinker. I'd bought it to impress some woman I was madly crazy about many years ago. Madison Dane. That's what I get for snagging a fashion model for a girlfriend. Even her name sounds like a clothing brand, but it works for her because now, it is a damn clothing brand.

Better than Madison Dane Krakowski, she told me when I helped her set up her clothing line years ago, just before we broke up. *And when we get married, I'm not taking your name either. Drexel. Isn't that the tool brand thingie?*

That's Dremmel, babe.

Oh, same thing, she had shrugged, flipping her blonde hair like she always did. *Nope, Madison Dane it will be for me.*

We never did get married even if she'd dropped the

hint more than a few times. Sure we had fun together, and damn if the sex wasn't amazing, but that was about it. I wasn't what she wanted anyway, definitely not a woodworker from Taos.

Even if my work had won one award after another and my company, based in Flagstaff with a showroom in Manhattan, was now making millions, I was still a carpenter. Besides, we barely saw each other, not with her jetting off to some exotic location for her modeling shoots every week, and me flying from one client's home to another to assess what they wanted me to build for their homes.

Two years later, I hear Madison snagged herself some Los Angeles Kings hockey player and was living the life in Manhattan Beach, California.

To each his own, babe. Nice knowing you.

I push thoughts of Madison away and pick up the gun. A Gen 4 G19. Damn, but this is one serious piece. The only reason I know this is because one of my friends, Neil Alvarez, is a cop, and he always likes to tell me about them. So either Goldilocks knows her guns, or she knows someone who does.

I turn my attention to the letter, the choice of whether she brought the gun for protection or for something else heavily depending on what's on that piece of paper.

For a few moments, I debate reading it, not wanting to be nosy. I have no business poking into my guests' affairs, but at the same time, there's no denying the fact that there's a gun inside my property sitting above something that looks suspiciously like a suicide note. So technically, if ever there was a need for an intervention, it was now.

I pick up the letter, not needing to turn on any lights to read its contents. That's one of the things about Taos and living off-grid away from the city lights.

It's why I bought the property and built the Pearl—for the stars. You see millions of them on clear nights like this, and it's a breathtaking sight, enough to remind you of how little you are in the grand scheme of things. Sometimes I sit here alone with that view in front of me and think. Sometimes I remember the woman I built it for.

I get up from the couch and walk along the pathway flanked by an arrangement of vegetable and flowering plants and even medium-sized fruit trees. It leads to the south-facing glass panels overlooking the property, sloped to take in the sunlight as it rises in the East and sets in the West. It also serves as the perfect nightlight with the stars illuminating the tear-streaked sheet of paper in my hand.

I'm sorry I failed you.

I'm sorry I didn't stop chasing the dream, the accolades, and the prestige that came with being one of the best in the country. I'm sorry I ended up putting other things before you, foolishly telling myself that you were going to be okay, and that in the end, all my struggles to be the best would be worth it. I'm sorry for being so wrong, for even with all the accomplishments, I realized too late that none of it was worth the price - not when the price I paid was you. I'm sorry for saving everyone else when all this time, the one I needed to save was you.

A lump forms in my throat as I read the letter again. Damn, if this isn't a suicide note then I don't know what is.

It surely isn't a fucking poem one writes for the heck of it. I return the letter to the coffee table, resting the gun on top of it just the way Goldilocks had left it. As long as she didn't sign it with her name, she'll be Goldilocks to me. After all, I need to put a name to the face—and the tits.

I sit back down on the couch to think. In an hour, the sun will rise, and I'll have a front-row seat, but I know I can't remain sitting here like I own the place, even if I do. Nana always said that once the place was rented, I was supposed to stay out of the way like the good land-lord that I am.

But the very idea that someone considered killing herself in my sanctuary grates at me. Restless, I get up from the couch and walk to the kitchen, checking the refrigerator to see it fully stocked. She'd shopped enough to feed herself for a week or two, which is a good sign.

It means she had planned to stay longer. I know I'm being too optimistic but at the moment, I don't have much choice. Either that or I'll need to call the cops and have her removed from the Pearl before she can do anything stupid, maybe get some mental intervention set up for her to help her out. It's not like I've never been in a dark place before, though it was never bad enough that I'd pull out my gun and write some note of apology to someone I couldn't save.

Save.

The word nags at me. That and the fairy tales that featured damsels in distress and their knights in shining armor coming to save them. I'm certainly no knight in shining armor, definitely not to damsels in fucking distress.

I'm not even close to being anyone's Prince Charming, not when every girl I'd been with has called me an asshole more than once, and other names much worse than that, especially after I dumped them for someone else. Even supermodel Madison Dane.

But still, a part of me wants to give my guest the benefit of the doubt. Mama always told me that there was more to a person than meets the eye and that sometimes, not everything is what it seems.

Yet even though it's plain as day—Goldilocks *was* planning on killing herself, *and in my sanctuary of all places*—Mama also said that there are no accidents, that sometimes Fate works in the strangest of ways. Sometimes we're meant to be where we're supposed to be. And maybe that's why I'm here right now, two weeks ahead of schedule.

Goldi-fucking-locks sleeping on my bed or not, I'm where I'm supposed to be.

CHAPTER THREE

CRAP, I need to pee again, which means I have to get out of bed again and make my way to the bathroom.

Whoever designed this place must have been on crack because it doesn't make any sense. Because of the so-called grey-water system, the water pipes that supply the bathroom faucets all go along the south-facing wall opposite all the bedrooms, where a supply of clean water is kept warm via solar heating.

Whatever, when you're hung over, the specifics don't matter. When you gotta go, you just gotta go.

But right now, even as my eyes remain shut and I cover my face with a pillow, there are a few other facts that I need to face. First, I've got a pounding headache that's like a marimba band working overtime inside my head.

It reminds me of the lightweight that I am when it comes to alcohol since I usually don't drink more than a glass of wine during dinner, if at all.

Second, I feel like an idiot for even considering

killing myself last night, all because my bigger idiot of an ex-husband told me I was so ugly and frigid that I might as well hang myself.

Ugly? Who does he think he is to tell me that I'm so ugly when I'm not? At least, I know I'm not. And frigid? But then, it doesn't help that I'm such a nerd that I haven't even been with anyone else but Jeff.

The tears slide down the sides of my face, and I tell myself to stop it, that it's just me playing the *woe-is-me* card. I shouldn't let the words of a bitter man bother me, but I guess no matter how old someone is or how mature she thinks she is, insults still hurt.

Jeff didn't use to be that way. We used to be happy; two ambitious Fellowship candidates with big dreams, who did everything together until one day, we started competing with each other and didn't even know it.

I can't even remember how or when it all began, the motivation to be among the best pediatric transplant surgeons in the city, and then later, in the country.

Maybe it was how we channeled the desperation that comes with wanting a child so badly by distracting ourselves with work, the accolades and the achievements piling up one after another until we lost sight of why we were together in the first place.

All I know is that by the time I realized that I was competing with my husband, it was too late. Jeff didn't want to go into counseling to save our marriage and afterward, I didn't see the point of it either.

After three failed implantations and one stillbirth later, the marriage was over. The only thing left were the assets, accumulated after six years of marriage between two successful surgeons.

And now here I am, hung-over after almost killing myself over an angry man who wanted me to sign the quitclaim deed to the house we both owned in the Hamptons, and so he needed to know where I was because he was having the documents couriered ASAP.

As if signing such documents were that easy! We're in the midst of a damn divorce as it is! And even if I knew where the hell I was, I wouldn't have told him.

It was then that he said what he thought about me—*ugly bitch, frigid, good-for-nothing ice queen. You're not even half the woman as my Leilani. Why don't you do the world a favor and just hang yourself, Harlow?*

The venom in his voice chilled me. How Jeff hated me. Ever since little Marcus—that's the name I had given him before they took his little body away—emerged forever sleeping, Jeff hated me. It was all my fault, he said. *Your eggs are all shriveled up, and soon you will be, too!*

It was the last thing I needed then—his hatred—but it was the only thing I got. That, and everyone's pity; and more of the same pity when he filed for divorce less than a month later.

Mercifully, I didn't fight it. I had no strength left in me then, too lost in my grief to care who got what. I left everything up to my lawyer to negotiate for me, even when I knew the man played tennis with Jeff at the country club. I had my work at the hospital, and my patients, and that was all I needed to get me through each day.

Until the day came when I had neither.

Though never done formally, one of the Board members told me in confidence that the Board of Directors thought it would be in everyone's best interests that two doctors in the midst of a nasty divorce no longer work together in the same hospital. He claimed that the longer I stayed at Miller Gen, the worse Jeff would treat everyone, maybe even the pediatric patients.

I remember thinking then that there had to be a silver lining somewhere, and there was. After packing my life away in a storage unit and making sure Kathy Pleshette, my office manager, updated me on my patients via secure email, it was time to see the rest of the world.

But instead of flying to exotic locales and having the adventure of my life, I decided to take the convertible and go *Thelma and Louise* on the open road. Only there would be no Thelma on this trip—just me—which meant, hopefully, there'd be no trouble. I stayed at the best hotels along the way, and I kept to myself.

When I ended up in Albuquerque last month, I met Andrea Martin, a doctor who ran a community clinic in the South Valley. We hit it off immediately, and while staying in a quaint hotel in Old Town Albuquerque, I consulted with her patients for free, most of them suffering from kidney failure as a consequence of hypertension and diabetes.

When she suggested I visit Santa Fe and check out the Georgia O'Keeffe museum and other things she knew interested me, I jumped at the chance and even saw my first outdoor opera. From there, I remember someone telling me about these strange structures off the highway in the outskirts of Taos, and I was off, wishing I could shut my eyes as I drove over the Gorge Bridge.

This time, even though I could have stayed at one of the nice hotels in town, somehow, I chose the Pearl.

Anita Anaya, the little old lady who met me at the door of the Pearl, told me that it belonged to her grandson and that she was in charge of renting it out to small groups and families while he lived in Flagstaff.

She wondered if I was expecting anyone else since every occupant had to be in the rental agreement, and when I told her no, she was clearly surprised. She worried that a city girl like me wouldn't last more than a day out here alone surrounded by sagebrush, with coyotes yipping at night.

For the first few hours as I sat alone with my gun next to me, afraid of everything that moved beyond the glass, I feared she was right. Then I saw the full moon aglow amid the thousands of stars in the sky, and that's when I knew I'd be okay.

Until the damn phone call from Jeff that sent everything to hell.

I should never have answered his call yesterday. It would have saved me from this hangover, or worse, actually pulling the trigger out here in the middle of nowhere. I had no idea just how hearing his voice for the first time in months could still throw me off-kilter, hurtling me back into self-doubt and self-loathing. Worse, Leilani is 21 years his junior, for crying out loud.

I scream as loud as I can, my headache responding like an explosion going off inside my head, but I don't care. I'm not even upset that Jeff is with someone so young. I'm angry that she can give him the one thing that I can't, and for that, I just need to let it all out one way or another.

But first, I need to pee.

An hour later while drinking my coffee and reading yesterday's paper on the patio, I spot a silver-hued truck turning into the private road leading to the Pearl. As I stare at the dust clouds trailing behind it, my heart begins to race.

Is that the courier with the quitclaim deed? How did Jeff find me?

But even if it is, it'll be a waste of time for the courier to have driven all the way up here for nothing. After last night's bawling session, there's no way in hell I'm giving up the house in the Hamptons.

As it is, Jeff already got the Upper East Side apartment when I signed away my share shortly after Marcus was born. I don't even remember why I did it, only that I couldn't stand knowing that there was an empty nursery waiting for a baby who would never come home.

But for Jeff to want me to do the same for the Hamptons property borders on insanity. Does he really think he can intimidate me into giving up the vacation home, too?

I may have had a moment of weakness last night when I almost blew my brains out because of his latest tirade, but after a long shower where I probably wasted half the water supply in the Pearl, I'm feeling more like myself.

I even ripped my pathetic suicide note to shreds and put the gun away, vowing that I'd never allow myself to feel that vulnerable ever again.

This version of myself is more familiar to me, even if I'm in the unfamiliar territory of Taos where everything around me seems barren, like my womb. But this is the version of me that is self-assured, before the time when I felt like I was good for one thing only, having Jeff's babies.

What if I could never have kids? Did that make me any less a woman?

Scientific facts alone tell me that the answer is no. Plumbing-wise, I'm still a woman, and no one, not even Jeff can tell me—or make me feel—otherwise.

Not anymore.

CHAPTER FOUR

Dax

Oh, good. Goldilocks is dressed this time, and alive.

Well, that second part, I was sure of, but the first part —the naked part—that was up in the air for a while considering I got to see Goldie buck naked running to the bathroom just as I was about to leave at five in the morning. She better be careful walking around naked like that, even in her own Earthship.

My neighbors have been known to have their telescopes trained here because of the damn yoga retreats throughout the year. Even in their yoga pants, the women looked as good as naked to some of my neighbors who had nothing better to do but peep into other people's houses and smoke their ganja while discussing the latest developments on sustainable living.

I sometimes hang out with them, and did so more often when I was still building the Pearl with their help and guidance, but these days, I'm usually holed up in here designing something new.

Even a man like me needs some solitude now and

then although my desire to be by myself for the next three weeks has been ruined by a messed-up schedule (my fault for not checking my messages before coming up here) and my inability to stay away from Goldilocks.

I park my truck behind her dusty Beemer, wondering why she doesn't have it parked inside the attached garage and save it from all the dust and sun. But at the same time, it's none of my business. It's her car, after all.

Goldilocks is wearing a beige cardigan over a t-shirt and jeans, and designer canvas shoes. A straw hat covers her head. She's curvy, with tits I'd recognize anywhere, and as she comes closer, I force my gaze back up to her face. Any more staring at her chest and my dick will be poking a hole through my jeans—and that would be rude. It doesn't help that it's been a while since I've been with a woman, all of two months.

It's not like I don't have them calling me all the time. I do. But with my production schedule on overdrive, it's amazing how fast time flies when you've got custom work to complete for a Hollywood mogul with a house in need of a grand wooden staircase in Big Sky, Montana, leaving one hardly any time for pussy.

Pretty much, I'm horny as hell, and seeing Goldie's tits this morning did not help that sad predicament. It's not like I'm ruled by my dick—I sure hope not—but there's just something about Goldie here that makes my stomach feel all tingly, and the damn feeling goes all the way down my dick.

It also doesn't help that I got to see her naked as she stumbled to the bathroom when I was heading toward the door. Her with those perfect tits and a perfect body.

Fuck, it does things to a man where it shouldn't be doing things.

That's why I didn't even wait for her to come out of the bathroom and introduce myself. I simply snuck out and drove to Nana's house for a cold shower and some sleep—and to review her rental agreement.

She's supposed to be some big-shot doctor from the East Coast, traveling around the country on her own. It explains the gun, but it still bothers me considering the note it was sitting on, though that bit of information I kept from Nana. She would have panicked if she knew what I'd seen, or in the case of the note, read. So I have to talk to the good doctor and figure some things out.

She may not like what I've got to say, but then Dax Drexel was never known to be subtle.

She meets me halfway between the unpaved driveway and the Earthship, her hands on her hips. I haven't even begun to introduce myself and already she looks pretty pissed off to see me.

"Miss Harlow, I'm–"

"That's *Doctor* Harlow James to you, young man," she snaps, glaring at me. "So what is it now? Are you the courier? How did you find me? I'm afraid you've wasted your time coming here because I am not signing any papers unless I have my lawyer with me. But if you think all you have to say is jump and I'll say how high, think again. The lawyer will have to wait until I get back to New York."

I almost tell her that I'm not this courier she's falling all over herself to meet and that either way, she may not like the papers I carry in the brown envelope I've tucked under my arm. *Well, almost.*

"That's a shame because you do have to sign these papers, Doctor Harlow James, and I'm not leaving until you do. In fact, I don't plan on leaving at all."

She crosses her arms in front of her chest, and her chin tilts up. I don't even care if her eyelashes are those extensions women are into these days, but they do a fantastic job at framing her beautiful big brown eyes. She's fiery when she's angry, and I like it.

"And what if I don't? What are you going to do about that?" She glances toward the house, probably wondering if she should run right about now, and get her gun.

"Nothing. I'll just bring my lawyer so you'll sign it and agree to my terms or leave–"

"Jeff's lawyer, you mean?" Suddenly she's right in front of me, poking her finger in my chest. Startled, I step back, but she takes a step forward.

I bring my hands up in mock surrender. "Damn, Goldie! Chill!"

She doesn't even hear me. She continues poking me with that finger of hers like I'm her personal push-button remote. "That prick couldn't even be bothered to tell me that he's sending you over here, and now, you're threatening me with *your* lawyer? Since when did couriers need their own lawyers, anyway?"

Alright, game over.

"Since they don't happen to be the courier you're expecting me to be?" I counter, hating that I got her this riled up. She's breathing hard, and her nostrils are flaring. If people shot daggers from their eyes, I'd have been dead a long time ago. That, and her damn finger against my chest. She'd probably dented it by now.

Harlow frowns, and for the first time, her face registers confusion as she takes a step back. "What... so... who the hell are you?"

I extend my hand. "I'm Dax Drexel, and I own the Pearl. Anita is my grandmother. I apologize for having misled you to believe that I'm–"

"That was not funny! You have no right pulling stupid shit like that on just anyone whenever you feel like it." She storms toward the house, and I follow after her, not wanting her to shut the door although there's another entrance I can use if she refuses to let me in.

The Pearl has six bedrooms and can accommodate up to 10 people. And with a wall dividing the east and west wings, it can also be rented by two separate groups.

"Wait! Look, I'm sorry. I shouldn't have done that." I race in front of Harlow, blocking her way. Damn, but she smells good. I detect a hint of rose oil as the wind whips her brown hair in front of her face and she tucks a lock behind her ear with her fingers. "Look, we need to talk. Apparently, there's been a little mix-up."

"About what?"

I cock my head toward the Earthship. "I'm scheduled to stay in the Pearl for the next three weeks–"

"The hell you are!" She pushes me to the side and continues to make her way to the front door. "I paid to rent this place alone, in cash, and I have the agreement to prove it."

"I have a copy of the agreement right here, and it allows the owner of the place or in the case of the manager, Nana—I mean, my grandmother—access should there be any extenuating circumstances," I say, waving the envelope in front of me. *And isn't that gun an extenuating circumstance?*

This isn't looking good, but I'm determined. Goldilocks is one stubborn woman, and I can't blame her. But I'm quite disappointed in myself as well. Somehow my charms have no effect on her, whatsoever.

She barely even looked at me. Well, she did, but that was only because she was trying to poke a hole in my chest.

I'm so distracted wondering why my charms don't work on Goldilocks that I don't realize she's stopped walking and has turned to face me until it's too late.

I barrel right into her, and we both topple to the ground.

Amidst the exclamations of *Oh shit* (mine) and *holy cow* (hers), I let go of the envelope so I can grab her by the waist with one arm and with the other, I cradle her head just as we hit the ground.

One thing about living off-grid: there are no paved driveways, just gravel, tiny little shits that are now cutting right through the skin of my arms as I break her fall. I just might need to rethink that design flaw and pave the damn thing all the way from the highway.

As Harlow clutches her head, I panic. I hope she didn't hit her head and suffer a concussion or worse, die on me. Great, she survived the night with a loaded gun, but certainly didn't survive meeting me and my big mouth.

"Are you alright?" I cautiously turn her head to make sure that she hasn't cut her scalp on the rocks, not when my arm took all brunt of it, and it's bleeding all over the gravel. It stings like hell, too.

"Oh, God, my head!"

"What about your head? Are you hurt?"

"I'm hung-over, that's what!" She groans, then freezes to stare at me, her eyes widening and her mouth forming a shocked O as her gaze moves down. It takes a second for my brain to register what's going on, and why she's looking at me like I'm the most hated man to walk this earth.

Then it hits me.

I'm lying right on top of her, between her legs, and right at this moment, the feel of her legs right alongside my hips sends shock waves through my body.

And my dick.

"Oh, shit! I mean, I'm sorry!" I scramble off her just as she pushes me away. I get up, offer her a hand, but she ignores me, getting to her feet without any help and dusting the gravel from her cardigan.

Who knew the scent of a woman could do things down south so fast that my brain didn't even register it? I turn away from her so she won't see just how hard I am. The Villier brothers better not be peeping with their damn telescope right now.

"Oh, look! Your precious agreement's all over the place, by the way," she says dryly, and as I turn to face her, all ten pages of the rental agreement for the 6,400-

square-foot Earthship blow past me and out to the sagebrush.

I manage to snag two sheets, but I know it's useless to chase after them and look like an idiot. I'd have better luck driving back to Nana's house and printing the whole thing out again, even with her twenty-year-old dot matrix printer that gives off a death rattle with every pass.

The sound of the front door slamming shut brings me back to the present. I don't even make an effort to rush to the house, not when it's too late for me to do anything.

When I do turn to look, Goldilocks, or rather, Doctor Harlow James looks at me from inside the slanted glass, one hand on her hip and the other with that all-popular raised-finger sign that matches the look on her face that says, plain as day, *Fuck you.*

CHAPTER FIVE

Harlow

THANK GOD, the kid actually has some brains. After picking up his dignity, he gets the hint that he's not welcome on my property and leaves.

But as I watch him drive away, there's no denying that I'm still in shock—not from the fall, but from the fact that I gave someone the finger for the first time in my life.

I gave someone the finger.

It feels like such a momentous occasion that with trembling hands, I dig out a hardbound leather journal from my purse and write it down. *I gave some guy the finger today! How I wish that were Jeff I was giving the finger to.*

But as I look at the words I'd just written, the last sentence gives me pause. That's certainly a good point, isn't it? Why hadn't I given Jeff the finger after the many times he fucked up? If I knew how raising one's middle finger could make someone feel this good, why didn't I?

Was it because I was more worried that such a childish action would put me in a bad light professionally, or was I so focused on maintaining my reputation even after my life fell apart that I suppressed everything else, even the urge to fight back?

I close the journal and toss it back into my purse. Whatever triumph I had felt at giving Dax the finger is now gone. I sigh and pick out a piece of gravel caught in the weave of my cardigan. As I roll it between my thumb and index finger, at least, there's one thing I can't deny.

Dax Drexel is one fine-looking young man. Definitely easy on the eyes, or as I've heard people say, *a tall drink of water*. I can't get over how good it felt—that split second that he held me in his arms—one arm around my waist and the other just behind my head, cradling me. That he had managed to move so fast surprised me though the hardness I felt pressing against my belly surprised me even more.

I've never considered myself beautiful. Outcasts didn't win popularity votes in high school, not when they were too busy burying their noses in biology books and talking about the nature of farts.

People like me simply didn't even register on anyone's popularity radar, although my brain got me places I would never have gotten as a foster kid moved from one home to another.

That and my heart. I cared too much for my young patients, probably more than I cared for myself especially when my marriage was falling apart. I sat with them after their surgeries instead of going home to an empty house, the nursery still intact but without the baby it had been lovingly built for.

Oh, great, there I go again. *Think of happier things,*

Harlow! I take a deep breath and force myself to think of other things... like Dax Drexel.

It's a nice name, and it sure goes with a handsome man. Where does that name come from anyway? It's sexy as hell, suiting the man who bears it. Dark hair, dark blue eyes, a trimmed beard. He smelled really good, too. He was probably wearing one of those colognes formulated with pheromones to arouse a woman's desire.

Before I can laugh out loud at the idea of me analyzing my reaction to a man, I force myself to remember how it felt to have him holding me for that split second. It's been a long time since I've seen a man responding to me like Dax did. That sure wasn't his phone pressing against my belly.

But who am I kidding? For all I know, Dax Drexel could get hard at the sight of a tree.

The sound of my phone ringing from the bedroom snaps me back to reality, and I'm so distracted by thoughts of Dax that I answer without glancing at the phone display.

"Dr. James! Finally! After only emails for so long, it's so great to hear your voice after all this time! Where are you right now?"

For the last five years, Kathy has been managing the office that I share with two other doctors, and I wouldn't know where I'd be without her. Nearing sixty, she's smart as a tack and knows the ins and outs of health insurance more than anyone I know. She's like the mother I never had, always making me something to bring home with me like a casserole, homemade mac 'n cheese, or apple pie, and reminding me constantly that if ever I need someone to talk to, she's there.

At first, I'm reluctant to tell her where I am. But then, wasn't I about to blow my brains out in the middle of nowhere? And what if Dax turns out to be some serial killer? I need someone to know where I am so they can send out a search party in case I disappear.

"I'm in New Mexico. Taos, which is nice," I blurt out.

"My, that's quite far. Are you having fun?"

"Yes, I am," I reply and in the background, I hear the sound of a phone ringing and Melody, one of the medical billers, answer the call. "So what's up?"

"Penny was just here," Kathy says, and that's all she needs to say for my chest to tighten.

Penny is Penelope Kingston, the youngest daughter of Senator Leon Kingston, who was born with polycystic kidney disease, a genetic condition characterized by multiple fluid-filled cysts that grow on the kidneys, rendering them useless. She was the last transplant I performed before hanging up my medical scrubs at Miller General for good, a special request by her father after Jeff, the original surgeon assigned to the transplant, lost his patience with Penny during a consultation.

From what I learned, Jeff didn't exactly shout at her; he just looked annoyed at something she had said during one of their consultations. Maybe Jeff was just having a bad day then, but I don't think he's ever forgiven me for accepting the Senator's request that I head the transplant team instead of him, and definitely not since I became Penny's favorite doctor, and by default, the Senator's latest addition to his guest list.

"What about Penny? Is she okay?" I ask.

"She says hello," Kathy replies. "She doesn't know what happened at Miller Gen, but she was hoping to see you during her maintenance visit with Dr. Rowe today."

Addison Rowe is my business partner, a nephrologist with whom I share my medical practice with.

"How is she? Is she stable?" I find myself wishing I'd stayed in town longer to make sure she had recovered from her surgery and that her medications didn't cause terrible side-effects. But I'm not her pediatric nephrologist; like Jeff, I'm the transplant surgeon.

"She had nasty side-effects from one of the anti-rejection meds, but Dr. Rowe substituted it with something else," Kathy said as I close my eyes and rub my temples, my headache returning. I feel concern for my young patient growing although another part of me reminds me that I need this time for myself. Grief didn't have a fixed universal deadline.

"How are you holding up, Doc? It's been five months since you left New York and we miss you," Kathy says as I open my eyes to see the landscape of Taos before me beyond the glass windows. It's dry and hot outside, so far from the New York that I know where Kathy is now, sitting in her office talking to me.

"I'm all right, Kathy. Thanks for asking."

"I'm here if you need someone to talk to," Kathy says. "Don't do anything rash now, okay?"

I chuckle at the memory of last night's stupidity, of the sight of myself standing outside in my bare feet with a gun and a glass of wine, cursing at the darkness. "I won't. I'm doing fine. Really, I am. Taos is beautiful."

"If you ask me, you're in a better place in Taos than over here, what with everyone talking about the upcoming nuptials," Kathy says. "Gardner must have sent announcements to everyone in town, even the local papers. But if I recall correctly, your divorce isn't final yet, right?"

"Right."

"Oh boy, that's going to be complicated, isn't it?" Kathy says, laughing though I don't respond. "By the way, Penny wishes you'd be back in time for her birthday, which happens to be the same day as the wedding."

I curse under my breath, my close call with death last night coming back to me. *How could I forget Penny's birthday?* I had promised her that I'd be there. She'd always feared she wouldn't make it to ten, and I assured her that she would. Unfortunately, she wouldn't be able to socialize with too many of her friends because her immune system wasn't ready yet, not for a few more months.

"Tell Penny I wouldn't miss her birthday for the world," I say, thinking of Dax and the contract he'd brought over. Maybe he'd get what he wanted after all, but that's only if I decide to take my time driving back home, the same way I took my sweet time leaving it. But back then, I had no birthdays to attend. I only had one birth to forget.

"I will," Kathy says before I say goodbye and hang up. Even though I haven't talked to Kathy in five months, our correspondence limited to emails, it feels good to hear her voice, and I'm glad I answered the call. I can't very well shut out the only person I trust in my life now that I've come back from the brink of almost ending it.

After making sure that Dax hasn't come back with another set of rental documents, I open the door and step outside. A warm breeze whips my hair about my face, and I tuck a stray lock behind my ear. I catch the scent of sagebrush and take a deep breath, letting it fill my lungs before blowing the air out through my mouth.

I remember someone in town saying that sage was used for healing. Healing what exactly, I don't know for I didn't stay long enough to find out. But as I look around me, I can't help feeling tranquil for the first time since last night's woe-is-me session. There's nothing to look at but the sagebrush and whatever else grows out here on the outskirts of Taos. It's barren, like my womb. But I also know that it's no accident why I'm here, and why I'm not about to let some arrogant kid like Dax Drexel bully me into leaving on *his* terms.

I'm here to start over, let Marcus go, and move on with my life. And that's exactly what I'm going to do.

CHAPTER SIX

Dax

IT'S BEEN two days since my run-in with the good doctor and I'm restless. I need to get into my workshop on the other side of the damn Earthship, so I can get some of my latest ideas down or head back to Flagstaff.

But ever since I breezed through town the last time I was here and barely got to hang out with my grandmother, I'd made a promise to stay longer the next time I came back. And Earthship or no, I will, even though the wait for it to be available for me to use it is killing me.

I can't believe how fast the ideas are flowing. It's why I stay at the Pearl whenever I come back to Taos. It rejuvenates me more than anything I've ever known, from the view of the sky and its billowy clouds and the mountain range where in the winters, one can find me skiing my heart out.

Out there, no matter the season, it's just me and the sky, and the ideas that come to me of handcrafted furniture made from hardwoods like wild cherry, mango, big leaf maple and English walnut.

With a list of pieces that clients have paid me to design and create for their custom-built homes, from staircases to cabinets and even bathtubs constructed out of sustainable and exotic woods and finished with a transparent composite barrier, my manufacturing schedule is filled for the next two years.

Still, I need the time to decompress, and that's what my hometown is for. It's where I dream up new designs.

But none of that vision is happening, not when silence eludes me from the shrieks of children arriving at the daycare first thing in the morning, and my older sister yelling at my nephew, Dyami, to get ready for school.

Nope, silence eludes me on this trip, and I should just get back into my truck and make my way back to Flagstaff. But I can't, and it's not only because of my promise to Nana that I'd stay longer this time.

I've tried, but somehow, I can't just leave Harlow James alone, not with that gun still in her house and that suicide note that she'd written. The words haunt me. *I'm sorry for saving everyone else when all this time, the one I needed to save was you.*

Who wasn't she able to save?

But it's not like I'm going to knock on her door and ask her that question. Hell no, not unless I want another dent on my chest from that damn finger of hers.

So for the past two days, I've hung out with the Villier brothers, Todd and Sawyer, who live nearby. We play video games for a few hours and whenever I could—without being too obvious—I'd look out toward the Pearl to make sure Harlow was still moving about.

And she was.

Funny what guilt does to a man. Harlow had called Nana to tell her that some guy had stopped by with a lease agreement—something about certain circumstances that would somehow force her to share the Pearl with him. That's when Nana stopped being Anita Anaya, the woman who managed my properties whenever I was out of town and became my no-nonsense grandmother.

Mi abuela.

It doesn't matter to her that I'm 27-years-old or that I've won furniture design awards the past two years; I'm still her grandson. In this case, I'm her grandson who fucked up.

She could sue you for trespassing, mijo, she said after she calmed down. *Sometimes you don't think with that pretty head of yours but with something else and honestly...*

She had eyed me with a look that told me not to say anything smart-alecky back at her before she sighed, shook her head, and returned to the kitchen where she'd been making tamales. But I already knew what she would have said, especially this time of year when everything about the house would seem emptier than any other time.

Ay, mijo, you remind me so much of your mother...

But I'm glad she didn't say it out loud, not when it would have made her sad to remember Pearl Anaya-Drexel, the daughter she'd lost to cancer five years ago. Fuck, it made me sad, too.

Why else did I bury myself in my business since she died, moving to Flagstaff so I could design furniture and then, for weeks at a time, drive back to Taos so I could build the Earthship that would bear her name with my bare hands? Even Dad had to pick up the slack by flying from New York to oversee production and the company's books while I was gone.

If it weren't for the Villier brothers, most of all Sawyer, who dragged me kicking and screaming from the pit of despair I'd allowed myself to fall into and then helped me design and build the Pearl, I'd have drunk myself to death in my grief.

Today, while the brothers and I sit outside their Earthship talking about installing more solar panels for the Pearl, I see Harlow drive away, her car leaving a cloud of dust behind her in the fading light. She shouldn't be out and about this late, even though I've outfitted solar lights alongside the road leading to the Pearl, but I can't very well impose a curfew on my tenants.

I thank the brothers for letting me hang out with them for a few hours before getting into my truck. I've actually considered staying at a hotel for the next few days so I can sketch out my new designs, but I know that if I do, I'm going to offend Nana. She always looks forward to my visits, knowing that even though I'd spend hours at the Pearl sketching and working on scale mockups of my latest designs till I got my vision right, I can always count on her for food. She knows exactly what I like, and always has it ready to go in containers and if she could, have me over for dinner every night and feed me.

And she's done just that every time I visit Taos and I've had to make extra trips to the gym just to make sure the pounds don't creep up on me.

The sight of the Beemer parked in the driveway

catches me by surprise when I arrive, and I have to do a double take to make sure that it's Harlow's. With the New York car plates, there's no doubt that it's hers. But what the hell is she doing here?

Then it hits me.

No. Nana. Did. Not.

I linger outside the house for a few minutes, my hands deep in my pockets as I pace in front of my truck, kicking gravel with my boots. I can smell the food and hear voices drifting outside through the security door.

I really should go inside, but the thought of facing Harlow after our first encounter has my stomach tied up in knots. I have to apologize for that stupid stunt, even if I still believe I had a valid reason to stay there with her.

I mean, wouldn't that gun and the note be considered extenuating circumstances? But then, it's not like I announced that little fact to anyone, so it's just my word against hers.

Then my stomach growls again, reminding me that I'm starving. I'm sure if it could do more than growl, it would probably tell me that I'm being such a damn coward standing outside when I could be inside.

Alright, dude, so you made a mistake. Be a fucking man and own it.

Besides, I want to own some of that green chile stew, too.

"You forgot, didn't you?" Sarah calls out from the dinner table the moment I step through the door before turning to look at our grandmother. "I told you he forgot. He was probably playing video games with the Villier brothers again."

"So what if I was? I'm on vacation," I mumble as I take the only available seat between Nana and my sister's on-and-off-again boyfriend, Benny Turner, and father of their eight-year-old son, Dyami. Benny works for the Bureau of Indian Affairs as an environmental protection specialist on climate change as it affects the tribes in the region.

After a round of *hi's* and *hello's*, Nana finally introduces me to our guest, who's sitting right in front of me, flanked between Sarah and Dyami.

"Hello, Dax," Harlow says as I mutter something that sounds like *Hi*. "Nice to see you again."

She's wearing a pink top that plays up her key assets —her flawless skin, pert nose, and big beautiful brown eyes. And then there are her full lips that she just now licks, and as my eyes drift lower, my gaze lands on her perfect tits.

Focus, Dax. Look up.

"Oh, so you've both met?" Benny asks as I tear my gaze from Harlow's tits to her face and meet her big brown eyes. God, she's beautiful.

"Yes, we have," Harlow says. "Dax came by two days ago to say hello."

"He did? That was sweet of him," Sarah says, smiling as she ignores my scowl and I know she's going to torment me all throughout dinner, and there's nothing I can do about it. Not in front of a guest. "I never realized he took the time to say hello to any of his renters."

"Stop it, Sarah," Nana says. "Why don't we say grace and eat before Dyami sneaks another piece of fry bread when he thinks no one is looking."

"You guys didn't have to wait for me," I say sheepishly as soon as Nana finishes saying grace and begins to dish out the stew in bowls, handing each one to Sarah to pass around the table.

"And since when do you turn off your phone, *mijo?*" she asks, handing me a bowl of stew. "We've been trying to reach you for the past hour to remind you to be here before our guest arrived."

I pull out my phone from my back pocket and place it on the table. "Turn off my phone? Why would I turn off my..." I pause, noticing that it's dead. "Oh, shit–"

"No cussing at the table, and you know my rule about phones during dinner. *All of them, off,*" Nana says as I return the phone into my back pocket, as does Benny who makes a guilty face.

"So, were you working at the Pearl?" Benny asks as Harlow takes a warm tortilla from the serving plate in front of her. "Want a beer?"

"Sure," I reply as he twists one open and hands it to me. "Nah, it's currently rented, in case you didn't know."

Benny shakes his head. "Nope, guess I didn't know that. I always thought you stayed at the Pearl whenever you're in town."

"Not right now," Sarah says in a sing-song voice as she grins at Harlow, ignoring the glare I'm shooting her way.

"Unfortunately, I'm renting it right now," Harlow finally speaks, and I pray she doesn't mention anything about my little visit. I continue eating my stew, biting into the tortillas that Nana makes from scratch. I can't wait to have some fresh fry bread for dessert. "I didn't realize that Dax uses it for work. If I'd known–"

"—you'd still stay according to your original plans," Nana says before glaring at me. "And don't you dare let my grandson bully you into leaving early."

"Dax? Bully you into leaving? Say it ain't true?" Sarah teases, watching me squirm before she turns to look at Harlow. "Is it true?"

I stuff a tortilla in my mouth and pretend I don't hear a word they're saying. Sarah is eight years older than I am and has always loved teasing me since we were kids. She knows how much I hate it, and so she does it every time we see each other. If I glare at her, she'll only keep doing it, but I'm not about to let her bully me into silence either, even if my mouth is full.

"I id not bully a-wone in-o leaving."

"Don't speak with your mouth full, *mijo*," Nana says as Benny chuckles.

"Yeah, don't talk with your mouth full, Uncle Dax," Dyami chimes in just as Benny raises an eyebrow at his son.

"And you, too, young man."

"Look, I'm sorry," I blurt out as everyone at the table suddenly becomes quiet. I know they're watching me as I take a deep breath and look at Harlow. I'm sure it's no accident why Nana has me sitting right across from her. "I'm sorry I came over that day, Dr. James, but I swear, I was not trying to get you to leave early."

"Call me Harlow," she says, smiling before she pins her gaze on me. "So why did you come over?"

I open my mouth to speak but stop myself. Mentioning the suicide note and the gun would only tell her that I was there that night, and that's the last thing I want anyone to know. "Does it matter now? I got my weeks wrong, that's all, and that's why I'm apologizing right now. And I don't care if you forgive me or not, but I'm sorry."

"Don't you have your stuff over there?" Sarah asks. "Why don't you just get them and do your work here?"

I shrug. "That's alright. I figure I'll head back to Flagstaff tomorrow and come back in two weeks. That should make everyone happy."

"YOU'RE LEAVING?!"

It's a chorus of voices that catches me by surprise, just as I see the hurt expression that crosses Nana's face. I see her glance at me and then at Harlow just as I look away.

"But you can't leave! You just got here, Uncle Dax!" Dyami exclaims. "Please stay! I still need to beat you in Minecraft."

I actually had no plans of leaving but for the first time, the crowd around the table is getting the best of me, and I hate it. But it's not their fault. Sure, I may look like my sister's easy target but she's just Sarah, the hospice nurse who sees so much death that she has to balance all that sadness out with something or she'll go crazy. It's one of the other reasons I look forward to coming home because when there are no guests around, I dish it back to her just as good.

No, it's not them. But the woman sitting across from

me is making me nervous. She even makes the butterflies in my belly flutter, and right now, I'm not happy about that.

She's a beautiful woman, and so out of my league, but I haven't been able to stop thinking about her since I first saw her on my bed that night. It's not even about the damn gun and the damn note anymore for she's apparently changed her mind about killing herself, and now here she is enjoying my grandmother's cooking.

No, this is about me and my damn knight in shining armor act, wanting to save every fucking damsel in distress. Only this time, it's different, and I can feel it in my bones.

With Harlow James and her damn tits, I'll be the one who'll need the saving.

CHAPTER SEVEN

Harlow

"So Dax tells me you're a doctor," Benny says as he takes the empty bottle of beer in front of me and replaces it with another one, fresh from the refrigerator. It's my second one, and I tell myself, it's my last one, too, or I won't be able to drive myself home—not when I have to cross the Rio Grande Gorge Bridge in the dark and I'm always afraid I'd fall right in.

Thank God I'm so afraid of heights that it didn't even occur to me that it would have been so much easier to end my life that way that night. But I push the thought away for as I watch the family around me bicker and tease each other playfully, I can't help thinking that I would have missed all of this if I had ended my life then.

Not only that, but I would have missed sitting at the most beautiful table I've ever seen. It's uneven as if it had been cut directly from the tree. There are no sharp lines anywhere. Instead, it's graceful and fluid. And where there's a groove that widens to the other end, it's secured by two large butterfly joints, with the hollow that widens filled with white pebbles and rocks of varying shapes. Coated with resin to protect the whole table, it gives an illusion of a river bed. It belongs in a New York show-room, not hidden in Anita's dining room.

"Yes," I reply, clearing my throat as Benny gets up to get another beer for Sarah. Except for Dax, we're mostly done with dinner now and after a casual round of conversation about how everyone else's day went, apparently, it's my turn.

"What kind of a doctor are you?" Dyami asks.

"I'm a surgeon. I specialize in kidney transplantation for children."

"Is that similar to a urologist?" Benny asks, "one who checks your prostate?"

"What's a prostate?" Dyami asks.

"No, I think she specifically said, 'surgeon.' Something about kidney transplantation. Like nephrons and stuff," Dax says.

There's a movement underneath the table, and I suspect Sarah just kicked her brother before she speaks. "Really? And what exactly are nephrons, Dax? I bet you don't know."

"Bet you ten bucks I do," he says, grinning as he holds his palm out to his sister. "I do know how to use Google, you know. I looked it up."

Sarah giggles. "Oh, really? Now, why would anyone want to look up nephrons, of all things? Is someone having *kidney* issues?"

Before Dax's face turns completely red, I step in to

save the poor kid. "Well, urologists and nephrologists both treat kidney problems. Urologists can do surgeries dealing with kidney and urinary tract disorders, while nephrologists usually prescribe nonsurgical treatments for similar problems. I'm a surgeon, and my specialty is pediatric kidney transplantation."

"So what do kidneys do… exactly?" Dyami asks as I see Dax glare at Sarah from the corner of my eye. "I know in karate; they tell us not to hit the kidney area, which is right about here." Dyami reaches for his side.

"And they're right. You shouldn't," I say. "Kidneys clean out your blood. They absorb certain stuff back into the body, like sodium and potassium but only what they need. The rest, they discard, and all that ends up in your pee. But sometimes, when kidneys don't work at all, I get called in to replace it with a new one from a donor."

Dyami's eyes grow wide. "Whoa! Just like that game, *Operation!*"

"Yeah, but there's no kidney in *Operation*," Dax says before he frowns. "Wait, is there?"

Though I never owned the board game when I was Dyami's age, I remember seeing it when I was in college. And no, there were no kidneys in the game. "I'm afraid not."

"Why not?" Dyami asks.

"Probably because you can only access the kidney from the back," I reply. "And did you know that you don't need two kidneys to survive? One healthy one is enough to do the work of two."

"What happens when both don't work?" Dyami asks. "What cleans the blood then?"

"Then the person will need dialysis—that's when a machine cleans out their blood for them instead of a kidney. And hopefully, as long as there are no complications, they're on a list for a kidney transplant as well."

"And that's when you come in," Benny says, grinning. "That's pretty impressive if you ask me. I mean, just the idea of how far medicine has come since the old days. It's mind-boggling."

"It certainly has come very far. Technological breakthroughs happen everyday, yet one thing remains constant. Our bodies remain pretty much the same," I say, noticing how serious everyone has gotten. Great. Me, and my excellent conversation skills. Why can't I talk about something else that's not related to medicine? Why do I have to be such a nerd?

"So if the kidneys don't work anymore, can a person still pee?" Dyami asks, his brow furrowing.

"Well, if their kidneys aren't working, then most likely they're on dialysis, and if they are, then their urine output may be lower, or in some cases, hardly any at all," I say. "But don't quote me on it. It depends on how long they're on dialysis and what the cause of their kidney failure is."

"Wow," Benny says, whistling. "You sure know your stuff."

"I sure would hope so, especially if she's about to transplant someone's kidney into someone else," Anita says, chuckling. "And if I ever end up in that scenario, I'd like someone like you to take care of me."

This time, it's my turn to blush. "Thank you, but I'm not exactly doing it anymore, not at the moment. I'm...

I'm on leave." I wish I don't stammer, but I do only because Dax is studying me.

"Why's that? I noticed your car plates. You drove all the way from New York to New Mexico, and that's quite far," Sarah says as I hear a scuffle under the table and Dax glares at her.

"That's right. It is far, but it's been a beautiful drive. Beats writing my 35th paper on reducing transplant rejection rates or long-term pancreatic allograft survival," I say and this time, I take a swig of my beer, a long one, hoping someone else will say something and divert the conversation away from me, or I'll bore them all to sleep.

"You drove all the way from New York by yourself?" Anita asks as I place my beer back on the table.

"I did, yes, and it's been a fun trip. I'm having a great time."

"How great a time, exactly?" Dax asks. The way he looks at me draws me in. It's an intent gaze that makes me wonder if he knows something that I don't.

"I'm sorry. What did you say?" I ask.

"How great of a time are you having so far? Are you enjoying your stay at the Pearl?" he asks again.

"He built it, you know," Benny says though I barely hear him. "And all the woodwork that you see—that's all award-winning craftsmanship right there. If it weren't so out of the way and so out of the ordinary...being sustainable and all, I'm sure it would make it onto the pages of the best architectural magazines."

"I'm having a very good time," I reply. "Thank you for asking."

"Dax won the highest awards in woodworking two

years in a row, though he's too humble to say it to anyone," Sarah says, and I barely hear her either for Dax's gaze hasn't left my face. "And did you know this dining table is built with no nails or bolts whatsoever?"

"I think it's called mortise and tenon joints," Benny says, turning to look at Dax. "Right, Dax?"

"Then stay for as long as you want," Dax says, his gaze unwavering and I almost feel like I'm under some spell. That, or maybe the beer is stronger than I thought.

I smile. "Thank you, Dax. I plan to."

"So, like, if a guy can't pee anymore, can he still use his penis for, like, doing the nasty? You know, sex?"

We all sputter our beers or whatever else we may have had in our mouths and turn to look at Dyami. Sarah and Benny stare at him in disbelief while Anita covers her mouth though I can't tell if she's shocked or amused. Dax rests his elbow on the table and presses his knuckles against his mouth, fighting the urge to laugh. But Dyami's face is serious. At the very least, he's curious.

I look to Sarah and then Benny and hope I'm doing the right thing. "May I answer his question?"

"Please do," Sarah says before she covers her mouth and there's that scuffling sound under the table again. Benny just nods his head before taking a swig of his beer.

"The answer is yes, he can. That's because the system that makes pee and the system that makes babies," I pause to look at Sarah and Benny and they're nodding their heads, "aren't connected at all. They just share the same tube at a certain point. But just because someone can't pee anymore because their kidneys aren't working doesn't mean they can't, um, have sex."

Dyami opens his mouth to ask something else when Anita suddenly gets up, the legs of her chair loudly scraping the floor. "Who's in the mood for ice cream? I think ice cream sounds good just about now, *si?*"

And judging from the sight of everyone's hands raised up in the air, I guess everyone else is in the mood for one, too.

An hour later, I've had a total of three beers, and I don't even argue with Dax when he says he's driving me back to the Pearl. He'll drop my car off in the morning and get one of the Villier brothers to pick him up.

"Why have someone else drop you off when I can do that tomorrow?" I say as he opens the door for me and I get into the passenger seat. "It's not like I won't have my car by then."

He shrugs. "Okay." And then he shuts the door, walks around the cab and gets in behind the wheel. On the front porch, Anita, Sarah, and Benny are watching the whole thing, grinning. I wish they'd go back inside, but they've insisted on seeing me off, complete with hugs and kisses like I'm one of the family. I wonder if they're like this with all their tenants or only the ones that Dax managed to offend.

As Dax turns the key in the ignition, I wave goodbye to the farewell party on the porch, laughing as I do so. I haven't smiled this much in months, where my cheek muscles ache. And why not? They've just had a hell of a workout tonight, and I loved every minute of it.

They would have let me sit there and do nothing after dinner and ice cream, but I was having none of it. I can't help it, but I feel both happy and jealous at the same time. Happy because they're themselves, and there's not an ounce of armor between them, but I'm also jealous because I wish I'd had something like this in my life, even the teasing they bestow on poor Dax who takes it like a champ though I suspect he enjoys it. Unlike Dax who apparently was the apple of everyone's eyes, life as a foster child hinged on hope and most times and if not all times, nothing else.

I have no memories of happy conversations around the dinner table or a unified effort by family members in getting things done. Neither were there any playful nudging of feet and legs under the table, or sitting in the living room with the TV on but no one is watching what's on because we're all busy getting to know each other.

I learn that Benny's mother is Navajo, and his father was Caucasian, an engineer who lived and worked in Roswell. Benny was six when his father died, and from then on, he was raised on the reservation or the *rez* as he called it, with his mother and her family.

He met Sarah while they were both studying at the University of New Mexico in Albuquerque and they've been together ever since. I don't understand why they're "on-again, off-again," which was how she had introduced Benny to me before dinner, but I figure it's none of my business. They all look like one big happy family, and that's what matters. You don't need a ring to prove to the world just how much you loved someone. My unhappy marriage proved that theory.

But there is something that I just learned, too. Families—happy families like the one that raised men like Dax Drexel—really do exist.

And I want one.

CHAPTER EIGHT

Dax

HARLOW IS quiet during the drive to the Pearl though I see her grip the car handle when we go over the Gorge bridge. I can't blame her. Even in the dark, it can be scary knowing you're driving on the seventh highest bridge in the United States, rising 565 feet above the Rio Grande. It doesn't help that besides being a popular tourist destination, it's also become popular for suicides.

Five minutes later, I turn into the Greater Earthship Community, the truck's high beams illuminating the road ahead. Out here, it's living in the middle of nowhere, even if I can see the lights of the closest Earthship, where the Villier brothers live, and another one in the distance which is mostly a single rental for most of the year, and right now, it's vacant. The path to the Pearl is lit up by solar lights that line the driveway all the way to the outdoor patio with its central fire pit perfect for roasting marshmallows. I had wanted it to look like a pearl in the middle of nowhere, and it sure does.

Living off-grid means residents have to be self-sufficient the best they can; that's why I installed solar panels for energy (and need to install more), grew vegetables and fruit trees in the indoor garden, and built a reservoir and filtering system for water. But because it's been quite dry the last few years, and with the Pearl hosting yoga and meditation groups, sometimes we end up having water trucked in at a few cents per gallon. If anything, it teaches anyone wanting to live here the importance of self-sufficiency.

But for the life of me, I have no idea what a city doctor like Harlow James is doing out here when she could be staying at the resort spa in town, complete with room service, a heated pool, and in-room massages.

"Thank you. I really appreciate this," Harlow says as I park the truck by the side of the Earthship and turn off the engine.

"No problem."

"Would you like to come in?" she asks. "Sarah said something about your tools being in here, and I thought..."

"I don't plan on loading any of my tools in the cab right this minute—"

"Come in, anyway," she says, cocking her head toward the front door. "Show me around."

"Didn't my grandmother give you a tour?"

"She did, but I'm sure it'll be different coming from the man who built it. It is beautiful, and I'm sure you're very proud of it."

My throat tightens. "I am. But I'm hardly ever up here as it is, and that's why Nana thought we could rent it out."

She doesn't say anything as she watches me. Then she smiles. "So show it to me, anyway, unless it's past your bedtime and you're expected to be back home by now."

Was that a challenge? "Nana might get away with telling me not to talk with my mouth full, but no one can tell me when to go to bed."

Harlow pushes open the passenger door, and I can't help wondering what she's up to. She's had three beers, and her guard is down. "So come on in then, unless you don't want to."

"Twist my arm now, why don't you?" I joke though I don't miss the playful glint in her eyes, and boy, am I in trouble now.

She laughs. "Can I be any less obvious? Consider it a curated tour."

It takes me close to an hour to give Harlow a very personal tour of the Pearl. She asks me so many questions that I have to rein myself in from boring her with every minute detail that went into building it, from its foundations built with earth-rammed tires and beer cans donated by the Villier brothers to the way the colorful bottles in the walls were put together. She listens intently as I talk about the inspiration behind certain pieces of furniture, like the slab dining table made of Dutch elm (my first big project under my mentor) and the rationale behind having an indoor fruit and vegetable garden that has nothing to do with zombie invasion preparations (self-sustainability). We even harvest a few fruits and vegetables, filling a basket that Harlow retrieves from the kitchen just before I show her what Sarah has playfully christened Bluebeard's secret room—minus the dead ex-wives hidden inside.

Instead, hidden behind the only locked door in the Pearl is my man-cave minus a big-screen TV or mini-bar. Just a drafting table, and a solid cherry slab with a planing stop where I get to design and create my pieces, though when I'm here, they're just scale pieces. There's a simple shelf at the far end where I keep pieces of wood for carving, and right now the shelves are mostly empty, the only thing remaining is one of my first creations, a small display cabinet constructed without nails or glue. Spartan at best, Dax's Man-Cave Deluxe is also the coolest part of the Pearl on hot days, bermed by soil on all three sides. The south-facing doors slide open to the rest of the residence, and it's perfect on days when I'm here all by myself.

While computer software and 3D printers are all the rage these days, I still use hand tools to create my pieces, starting with a *sumisashi*, a bamboo pen, and an ink pot and string line called a *sumitsubo*. It's the last thing people expect when they meet me, at first glance just another kid from New Mexico who knows his Japanese terms as well as the ancient art of Japanese joinery. I even speak it fluently, thanks to the Japanese American carpenters who work with me in Flagstaff and New York. I spent five years as an apprentice to Takeshi-san, a well-known Japanese craftsman who settled down in Santa Fe fifteen years earlier.

Under his tutelage, I learned everything I could about Japanese joinery or *sashimono* before he died of lung cancer four years ago. Unlike Harlow and her many years of medical school, I never went to college; a high school diploma is as far as I've gotten, and whatever I learned from Takeshi-san. But then, none of my clients require me to have a specialized degree to craft them a cabinet or a dining table, unlike patients who come to Harlow needing a kidney.

But we don't talk about medicine or *sashimono* the moment we step into my sanctuary. We don't speak at all. Sure, I could tell Harlow all about carpentry, but I don't, not when watching her walk around the room admiring everything tells me more than words can say. There's a reverence in the way she touches everything, and the way she studies the drawings left on the drafting table, of impossible staircases that have since won awards, and bath tubs made of wood. So far, they've all been completed, the drawings just reminders of my last brainstorming session here.

She takes a long deep breath as she runs her fingers along the sides of the small wood cabinet sitting on the shelf, closing her eyes as she takes in the smells of local and exotic woods that still linger in the room since I was last here three months ago.

"I love the smell of wood and earth. In the city, you don't get this much although there is Central Park. But even that place gets crowded," she says. "But this, the Pearl, is very grounding, and most especially this room. It almost feels like a... a womb. A place where ideas are born."

"Thank you. And yes, it is grounding. It was built for that reason."

She smiles wistfully. "Your family grounds you, too. They love you."

"They do, just as much as they love picking on me, too," I say, wondering what she's getting at. Behind my smile, there's a fight going on. A part of me wants desperately to close the distance between us and feel her in my arms as I kiss her while the other part chastises me to behave. But Harlow has been setting my nerves off-kilter since dinner, and now that we're alone in the one place I feel the safest, even more so. Except for family, no woman has ever set foot here before, not even when the Pearl was rented. It's always been locked until I come to town. Yeah, just like Bluebeard's special room.

If I can't hold her in my arms and kiss her, I might as well be close enough to drown myself in her big brown eyes before I apologize to Nana and tell her that I'm driving back to Flagstaff tomorrow. I'll just have to come back after Harlow leaves. It won't make her happy, just as it won't make the employees happy either to have their grouchy perfectionist of a boss back. But right now, I don't have any options.

"I was just thinking about what you said during dinner..." she begins softly as I stand in front of her.

"Yes?"

"If you need to work in here," she says, looking around the room, "then, by all means, you should."

"You don't need to—"

"I insist. The Pearl is over 6,000 square feet, isn't it? It's clearly too big for one person, and if you just need to do your work in here, you can do that without bothering me all the way on the other side."

"I can't do that."

"Think about it," she says, shrugging. "Doesn't this place accommodate up to six people? As it is, I'm just hogging the place, and there's no reason for you to drive back to Flagstaff just because I'm here. There are vegetables needing to be harvested and the kumquats, too. I can't do all that on my own."

I chuckle. "So you need a farmhand."

"No, I need company and even when I do harvest all the tomatoes and the garlic and eggplant and whatever else is in the garden, where's the fun in eating all that alone? Even when I drop off the vegetables at Anita's, whatever I keep..." She pauses, shrugging. "Whatever. I'm just putting it out there that you can stay here if you want."

"But I thought you came here to be alone." I can't stop thinking of the gun and the note.

"So? Let's say I changed my mind. You don't have to entertain me or anything, nor I, you. But if you need the place to design such gorgeous tables like the one your grandmother has or whatever it is you do in here, then, please. Don't let me stop you."

"You didn't think so three days ago."

She crosses her arms in front of her chest, her left eyebrow arching. "Three days ago, you made me believe you were a courier sent to have me sign some legal documents I wasn't keen on signing. Not only that, you tried to talk me into signing an amended rental agreement–"

"I said I was sorry about that."

"I know." Harlow takes a deep breath and shrugs. "Like I said, think about it. You don't have to give me your answer now. I know you planned to go back to Flagstaff, but I'd feel bad if the reason is me."

It is you, I almost say, *and sharing the same space with the woman who sends the butterflies in my belly fluttering like crazy is, well, crazy.*

"If I take you up on it, I'll have to insist on reimbursing you whatever you paid."

"And I'll have to insist you don't," she says, shaking her head. "You're just here to use this room and maybe some parts of the general living areas, and nothing more. So just bring your amended rental agreement tomorrow stating that I agree to share the Pearl with you, Dax Drexel, for the purpose of work and nothing else."

I frown. "You mean, no wild parties?"

She shakes her head. "Nope."

"You drive a hard bargain, Dr. James."

"Call me Harlow."

"Alright, Harlow," I say, stepping out of the workspace and waiting till she follows me outside before closing the doors and locking them. "I'll think about it."

"You can always say no, Dax."

The way she says my name sends a tingle down my spine but I tell myself to behave. I don't dare look back at her as she follows me to the front door and watches me head back to my truck. I pull open the door and pause, my heart thundering inside my chest.

"Thank you for dropping me off tonight, Dax, and for the tour," she says as she leans against the door frame, watching me.

"Anytime," I say, a part of me not wanting to get behind the wheel just yet. "I'll drop your car first thing in the morning."

"Take your time." I make a move to get into the cab but pause. *It's now or never, dude.* "Harlow, have you ever been to Bandolier National Monument? Over by Los Alamos?"

Her eyes widen. "Is that the one with the cliff dwellings?"

"Yup."

"No, I haven't. But I was planning to go there this week. I was just searching online for directions this morning."

"Want to come with me tomorrow?" I ask. "We can take in the views and revisit history. Just a day trip and then we'll be back before evening."

From where I stand, I can see her eyes light up. "I'd love that."

"We have to get there early to avoid the crowds and the heat," I say. "So you'll need to be ready before six—"

"I'll be ready," she says, smiling and I have to catch my breath. The good doctor is even more beautiful when she smiles.

"Six it is then," I say as I force myself to get behind the wheel and shut the door. Then I start the truck as casually as I can muster even though deep inside, I'm screaming like a prepubescent boy about to go on his first date with the most popular girl in school.

Harlow

Holy cow! I can't believe I flirted!

Worse, I flirted with a man who's way too young for me. I can't exactly explain why I did it, not in a way that would make sense to the surgeon in me other than it's all his cologne's fault—and his man-smell, if that is even a word. It's not body odor, like someone who just came from the gym—no, this is just his smell—pheromones at work—and it's so delicious it made my belly do flip flops in the passenger seat of his truck, and I had to squeeze my thighs together and grab hold of the door handle.

How can a man do this without touching me? He was minding his own damn business driving and here I was, sitting next to him, imagining him on top of me, making love to me. No, not making love. *Fucking me.* Oh, my God, and I even said the word, *fuck.* Not only have I given someone the finger in the last week, but now I'm saying a word I never say. Am I so desperate to have sex with the first man to cross my line of vision that I'm already acting like a whore?

To make matters worse, I asked him to give me a tour of the Pearl again and then told him he could stay if he wanted to! Sure, I meant during the day, but that would mean I'm still sharing what I'd intended as my sanctuary with someone else!

I slip my phone from my purse and scroll through the names in my directory. I want to talk to someone—*anyone* —about what's going on. I want to scream it to the heavens that I just flirted with Dax Drexel. Even his name exudes sex.

I could call Dianne, or maybe Barbara, both of them friends I hung out with at the country club. But as I'm about to call Barbara, I stop myself. They're both also Jeff's friends, which means that if I breathe just a word of my latest shenanigans out here, it's going to get back to Jeff, and the last thing I need is for Jeff to know that I'm so hard up for a man that I'm ready to pounce on the first male I come across.

It doesn't hurt that I know Dax likes me. I felt it the first time we met although just because a man gets a hard-on when they fall on top of you doesn't mean they like you. It just means the plumbing works just fine. Too fine in Dax's case, since I've allowed my gaze to drift down the front of his jeans when he's not looking, and boy, but is he pretty well-endowed.

I take a deep breath and sit down on the couch facing the garden before burying my face in my hands. I can't believe I even asked him to harvest vegetables! What was I thinking? Could I be any more transparent?

I sit for a few minutes in silence, forcing my breathing to calm down. But even as my nerves settle, there's one thing that isn't settling at all, and it's frustrating the hell out of me. Not for the first time, I find myself wishing I'd stayed in the resort spa in town, with all its amenities including a gym. I'd be working out by now, the restlessness I'm feeling quelled by an hour on the treadmill or the elliptical climber even as my dreams would still leave me wanting.

This is what happens when you haven't had sex in over a year, girl—hell, almost two years! Jeff hadn't touched me since we started the last round of IVF treatments that led to Marcus. There's nothing romantic about IVF, not when they sedate you to retrieve the eggs after a round of hormone therapy injections with the perfect match between egg and sperm done in the lab. After ovulation, the embryo is then implanted into the uterus and then the waiting starts. Only, my wait this time ended in a stillbirth, even after everything I'd done. With beautiful Marcus, the horizontal scar above my pubic bone is a sad reminder that I'd failed him.

Snap out of it, Harlow! You promised yourself you'd move on.

I get up and pace the floor for a few minutes before I finally decide to go to bed. The beers did relax me tonight, and though I could easily blame them for my behavior around Dax, I can't fool myself anymore than I already am.

Before tonight, I was always Harlow James, Doctor of Medicine, and Assistant Director of Transplant Surgery. I held onto that identity even in my personal life as wife to the Director of Transplant Surgery himself, and I had no other friends but the people we both worked with.

Even the medical team who attended to me during Marcus' delivery were the very people I passed orders to, and afterward, I could no longer look them in the eye knowing they'd seen me at my most vulnerable, when Jeff couldn't even bear to stay with me and walked out of the delivery room.

But something happened the day I met Dax Drexel. From the moment we toppled to the ground the first day we met to tonight when his family treated me like I was one of them, I was no longer Dr. Harlow James—not even when I talked about kidney functions and dialysis. I'd become just Harlow James, a woman. Though right now, she's a woman in the middle of nowhere in dire need of a vibrator.

Dax arrives at 5:45 the next morning, pleased to find me ready to go. I'm dressed in khaki pants and a deep pink tank top under a light shirt and hiking boots. The fact that I had packed hiking boots on my cross-country drive seems to impress him, but he doesn't spend too much time saying so. He simply makes sure we've got everything we need—sunscreen and a wide-brimmed hat for me and bottles of water and a packed lunch for both of us —and then we're off.

He hands me a Thermos filled with piping hot black coffee, with the half and half in a smaller container and a few packets of sugar stored in a plastic sandwich bag.

"My favorite coffee shop doesn't open till 6:45, but I stock up on their signature blend, and it's the best out there," he says as I inhale the aroma and sigh. Along with the intoxicating smell of his cologne mingled with soap and water, my current state is pure heaven.

"You didn't have to," I say as Dax slows the truck to a stop along the side of the road so I don't spill coffee all over myself. He waits until I pour the coffee into a travel mug and add the creamer before closing the lid. As soon as he's sure that I'm not about to burn myself with the coffee, we're back on the road again. I like how he takes charge of certain things, like a boy scout. Always prepared.

"I've got some breakfast burritos, too," he says, pointing to two coolers behind our seats. "Your side has breakfast, and my side has lunch."

Okay, too prepared. "You didn't have to, Dax."

"I know you're not vegetarian since you ate the chile last night, but are you okay with *chorizo?* It's one of Nana's favorite recipes, chorizo with eggs, potatoes, cheese and green chile–"

"Please tell me Anita didn't wake up early to cook this."

"She wakes up at five every morning, rain, shine, sleet or snow. And whenever I'm in town, she makes sure to make me my favorites, so stop worrying," he says, glancing at me before returning his attention to the road. "Just have fun for a change, Dr. James. Take it easy."

"I'm not on call right now, so please call me Harlow."

"Sorry," he says. "So, what kind of music do you like to listen to, Harlow? You get to choose, and if none of the songs in there are to your taste, we can stream the music although it might get spotty down in the canyon."

He hands me an iPod Touch filled with all kinds of music, from Euro techno, house, rock, to classical. Even country music and folk, if you're into those. I don't know what I was expecting, but I don't find any boy bands anywhere. Instead, I smile when I see James Taylor and Jim Croce, as well as the Sex Pistols, Eagles, and Queen.

"What about the Eagles?"

"Perfect," Dax says as I press *Play* and the music plays on the cab stereo speakers. For the next few minutes, I sip my coffee in silence, listening to Glen Frey telling me to take it easy as I take in the landscape in front of me. With Bandolier located southwest of Taos, it's less than a two-hour drive with the sun to the east of us, and I can't help but thank my lucky stars he'd asked me to come along. I've been behind the wheel for so long that I can't remember when I let go of directions and itineraries and let someone take over for a change. And right now, with Dax in the driver's seat and taking control, it feels good.

We arrive at the Bandolier National Monument in less than two hours. As we drive into Frijoles Canyon, Dax tells me that for several years, the park was closed to the public and that scientists working on the Manhattan Project and military personnel were housed in the Bandolier lodge nearby. He tells me that his mother used to take him here when he was a little boy, and it was one of their favorite hikes. She was an archaeologist, special-izing in Puebloan pottery, although she let that go shortly after he started school.

"I wasn't exactly the most well-behaved kid," he says, making a face as he parks the car in the lot. "Turns out, I was dyslexic, and so I wasn't keeping up with everyone else. I got into fights a lot with kids who'd tease me. That's when she quit her job to spend more time with me and round out my education with day trips here and there. This was one of her favorite places."

"She sounds like an amazing woman."

His Adam's apple bobs as he swallows and nods. "She was."

We'd been mostly quiet during the drive, and if we did talk, it was about a particular song or artist, and sometimes a bit of impromptu karaoke—on his part, not mine for I pretty much sounded like a strangled chicken when I tried. It was the perfect ice-breaker, listening and singing to songs that dated me and made it all the more obvious just how much older I am compared to him. But there's also nothing like the power of music to bridge the gap, for he knew the lyrics to Jim Croce, Johnny Cash and Journey's songs just as well as I did.

After packing our lunches in a backpack that he insists on carrying, we hike down to the Visitor Center on the Frey Trail, a switchback path to the canyon floor. Along the way, he points out certain structures, like Tyuonyi, the remains of an Anasazi village, and the cliff dwellings.

At the Visitor Center, we walk through the Bandolier museum exhibit where I get to learn all about the park and its history. Afterward, we pick up a map at the gift shop where four siblings excitedly talk about earning their Junior Park Ranger certificates, and to my embarrassment, Dax asks the Park Ranger if I can get one, too, if we complete the trails.

He's definitely right about arriving early, for the air is

still cool when we make our way to the Ancestral Pueblo dwellings and further along, the Alcove House, which can be reached only by wooden ladders. We continue along the Falls Trail, which Dax says will take us to Frijoles Canyon's Upper Falls. He points out the box elders, Apache plums, and ponderosa pines that surprisingly smell like vanilla.

"Doesn't *frijoles* mean beans?" I ask as we find a shady spot to sit and have some lunch. It also has the perfect view of the Upper Falls.

"Yup, so it's called Bean Canyon, but honestly, I think Frijoles Canyon sounds so much better," he says as he adjusts his baseball cap. "There's less correlation to passing gas."

I chuckle. "I agree."

There's such youthful enthusiasm in everything Dax says and does, made even more evident the moment he slips off his denim shirt and ties it around his hips and I hate that I can't stop staring. The white tank top he wears shows off a broad, tanned chest that tapers to narrow hips, toned arms and biceps, and I pray that I don't drool in front of him.

When he leans toward me to reach for his backpack, I take a deep intake of breath. It's that delicious smell again, and it hits me right between my thighs. *Crap, I'm in deep trouble.*

"You okay?"

I look up to see him watching me with a furrowed brow. *Why is he still leaning over me like that, one hand grabbing hold of his backpack?* I press my thighs together and exhale. "Of course, I am. Why?"

"You're, like, red all over..." he pauses before he lifts the backpack and then sits back down next to me. Then his eyes widen. "Wait, are you blushing?"

Of course, I have to blush some more. "No, I'm not! I'm... I'm probably allergic to something."

Dax turns pale. "Oh, shit, I didn't even ask you if you're allergic to pine and stuff! Are you?" He rummages through his backpack and retrieves an Epi-Pen, a device with a needle on one end that emerges only when the user jabs it into muscle, preferably the outer thigh. Dax holds it up triumphantly, his thumb on the trigger. "Tell me when!"

"No!" I exclaim, bringing my hands up in front of me. Wonderful. The last thing I need is to have some trigger-happy kid jab me with a shot of epinephrine out in the middle of nowhere. "I'm fine, Dax! Really, I am. I'm not allergic to pine or box elder, or whatever else around here." *Just you*, I almost say as a joke though I'd be lying, and he'd probably see right through it. The kid's not stupid, but he's making me laugh so hard I end up crying. "Can you put that thing down and can we just eat our lunch in peace? Please?"

He eyes me warily before putting the Epi-Pen away. "Alright, but tell me if you feel any discomfort at all, okay? Itchiness, difficulty breathing, that kind of thing. There's poison ivy around here, too," he adds, his eyes narrowing. "Do you even know what poison ivy looks like?"

"I work out in a gym, Dax, not out in the wilderness."

"So, I gather that's a no?" He sets a Tupperware bowl in front of me and removes the lid. It's one of those types of dishes I remember when I was a kid and are now considered retro.

"Basically, yes, it's a no."

"Leaves of three, let it be. But I'll show you when we come across any of them." Dax hands me a metal fork neatly wrapped in a cloth napkin. "Since we're in Frijoles Canyon, I figured a simple rice and bean salad would be perfect. Not too heavy and not too light. The dressing is red wine vinegar, and there's some green chile in there, too. And there are chips right here." He sets another Tupperware bowl between us.

"Are you always this prepared? I could have made something." Actually, I couldn't, not unless I count the days-old Greek salad in the refrigerator.

"I invited you to come along, Harlow, so you didn't have to make anything. You're my guest," Dax says as he sets two bottles of water between us. "I always pack something whenever I come here, and if I don't, Nana makes sure I do. She knows I take these day trips to rejuvenate and get away. It calms me."

"Does this count as getting away? Even with me here?" I ask, frowning.

"Yes, it does. Very much so," Dax says before his gaze drifts down to my bowl. "Now eat up, Dr. James, because I intend for you to earn your Junior Park Ranger certificate when we're done."

CHAPTER TEN

Dax

I'M afraid I killed her.

I should have warned her that we still had to hike back to the visitor center where much to her embarrassment, I persuaded the Park Rangers to give her a Junior Park Ranger certificate complete with all the fanfare of announcing it to everyone in the shop. And then after buying a few souvenirs, we had to make our way back up to the car. But Harlow is a trooper, though right now, as she sleeps in the reclined passenger seat next to me on our way back home, an exhausted one.

The hike wasn't that far, but after climbing up ladders to explore the *cavates*, and walking around the Big Kiva, Tyuonyl, Talus House, and Long House, along with the hike to view the falls, the miles added up. And for someone used to only running on a treadmill, a real hike can be killer to muscles unused to the uneven terrain. And as much as she hems and haws that she is used to it, Harlow James is not used to uneven terrain or being out in the hot sun for most of the day. If I hadn't insisted on stopping to reapply more sunscreen every two hours, she'd probably be as red as a beet by now.

She stirs the moment I slow the truck to a stop in front of a red light and sets the seat upright. "Gosh, we got back fast."

"Traffic was light, and I was starving, so that factored into just how fast I was driving—*but* I did not speed," I say as the light turns green. "Ready to get something to eat?"

"Sure, my treat this time, alright?"

I open my mouth to say, *no, I want to take you out to dinner*, but I stop myself. *Don't scare her, dude. It's not like you hadn't already fed her breakfast and lunch. Dinner would be overkill.*

"Sure."

We settle for a casual Italian restaurant in the middle of the town square that I know won't mind our dusty and tired asses walking in. The last thing I need right now is a dress code though I'm wearing my shirt over my tank top, having slipped it back on just before we got into the truck.

Harlow orders baked penne with sausage and ricotta cheese while I choose my usual, Sicilian pizza with Italian sausage, Capicola ham, and salami. I wasn't kidding when I told her I was starving.

I like that when Harlow eats, she eats, and she doesn't take pictures of her food to post on social media. I don't think I even saw her use her phone except to take pictures on our hike and nothing more. It's just us, and I like it.

"So what is a New York doctor doing in a small town

like Taos?" I ask as the waiter leaves our table after asking us if we needed anything else (we didn't).

"I wanted to explore the world outside of the hospital."

"Alone?"

"Why not?" She takes a sip of her wine. "It felt like that movie, *Thelma and Louise*, without Thelma."

"So you're the serious one? That would be Susan Sarandon's character, right?"

She laughs. "Right."

"Was there a Brad Pitt somewhere along the way?"

She giggles. "Oh, you mean that young guy who steals Thelma's heart and all their money? No, though these days, he'd have to steal what? Debit cards, PIN numbers... my phone? Times have changed. No one carries cash anymore."

I wonder if that's why she got the gun, for protection. "But you paid in cash to rent the Pearl."

Harlow shrugs. "I had just come from the bank and needed to get out some cash, and I figured, why not? Does that bother you?"

"No, it's just something Nana hasn't encountered before, but you have your receipt, and that's what matters." Hell, at five hundred a night, renting the Pearl for three weeks isn't cheap. Even though Nana gave Harlow a break in the price, it's still a lot of money.

"So, where else is Louise planning to go?"

"Maybe California, I don't know, though I need to start thinking of getting back home," she says, shrugging. "I got sidetracked in Albuquerque when I met Andrea and saw some of her patients. She runs a no-insurance clinic in the South Valley, and she needed my opinion on some tough cases."

"My friend, Gabe, is into community medicine, too, like your friend. How long did you stay down there?"

"Over a month, and I loved it. When she suggested I come up to Santa Fe to check out the outdoor market, that's when I got in my car and headed up. And from Santa Fe, someone said I should check out Taos and maybe if I had the time, Four Corners, and I thought, *why not?*"

Four Corners would be the point where the boundaries of four states meet: Colorado, Utah, Arizona and New Mexico. You could literally stand right where the four states meet. "That's an easy five-hour drive. Have you been there?"

Harlow shakes her head. "I'm still planning my route, though I may not have enough time. At first, I thought of driving up there and then down to check out the Grand Canyon, but I really am tired of all the driving, to be honest. I've been on the road roughly five months now, less one month spent in Albuquerque. That's why I thought I'd spend a few weeks doing nothing at the Pearl, figure a few things out, and then head back home." She pauses, chuckling. "But can you believe it? I'm actually working instead, finalizing research papers I brought along with me."

"Yet you're willing to have me come over and work," I say slowly. "Wouldn't that interrupt your flow?"

"No, but I thought we talked about this already, Dax. The Pearl accommodates six people. Six. It can hold meditation retreats and yoga classes. Well, *small* yoga classes," she says before adding. "Look at me. I already sound like an ad for the Pearl, and you're the owner. You can always say no."

"I didn't say I was." I eye her for a few moments. "Have you explored Taos at all since you've been here, outside of the Taos Plaza and all that?"

Harlow shakes her head. "I just got here a few days ago and have only checked out the shops at the Plaza."

"Want me to show you where the locals go?"

"Like where?"

"Local wineries, parts of the Rio Grande, even a private hot springs." Her eyes brighten, and she leans forward, resting her elbows on the table. "It's a short hike to get there, and there are even petroglyphs *if* you know where to look."

"I'm sure you'll show me where they are," she says, laughing before her brow furrows. "But I don't think I brought a swimsuit with me."

"You don't need one. A lot of people skinny dip. Honest, they do! Just wear comfortable clothes for hiking and when you're in the mood for a quick dip when we get there, I promise to turn around and look away. How about that?"

"Where are these hot springs exactly?"

"It's called Manby Hot Springs. Google it if you have to, but it's a fun place to go for us, locals. Nothing fancy. It's named after this Englishman, Arthur Manby, who bought up pieces of land around Taos including the springs. He figured he'd make money from it so he built this big bathhouse but he ended up losing the land later on when he couldn't pay his creditors. Plus, there were doubts that he even acquired the land legally, and so after he passed, the land went back to Taos and we Taoseños hang out there—for free."

"Taoseños," Harlow murmurs. "Is that what you call yourself?"

"Pretty much, just like you call yourself a New Yorker."

"To hell with New York. Right now, call me a Taoseño then, because I love this place," she says, the sound of her laughter hitting me in my solar plexus. *Shit, what the fuck's happening to me?*

"So, yes or no? We could start tomorrow and then drive a bit farther and check out Vivac Winery another day. They even make their own chocolate."

"Really?" Harlow bites her lower lip, and I have to force myself to keep my gaze on her eyes. "Lucky for you, because I'm a chocolate girl."

"Alright, chocolate girl, you game or not? We may take two days to hit the hot springs and then the drive up to the winery, but I don't know about your schedule–"

"My schedule's in your hands for the next two days, Mr. Drexel. Just make sure it's as fun as today, okay?"

I grin, my gaze moving down to her hands that lie on top of mine. When Harlow's guard is down, she's a touchy-feely type of person, and I like that. "Dax Drexel at your service, Dr. James. I promise to make it fun."

"Where does your name come from, by the way?" she asks.

I chuckle. "*The Adventurers*. Ever heard of it?"

Harlow shakes her head.

"Harold Robbins. He was an author in the late

sixties... early seventies, I think, and he was known for writing some pretty trashy novels, but Mama obviously didn't think so. She named me after the protagonist. Diogenes Alejandro Xenos, or Dax for short."

"It suits you, Dax. Danger and fun all in one."

Her phone beeps just then, and she frowns, pulling away from me and reaching for her cell from her jeans pocket. When she sees the name on the display, she frowns even more. "Sorry, but I'll need to get this," she says as she taps on the screen and excuses herself from the table.

As Harlow makes her way to the outdoor patio, I signal for the check, conveniently forgetting that she'd wanted to pay for dinner. But there's no way I'm letting someone who just paid seven grand to rent the Pearl by herself pay for dinner, too. And though I know I'm not thinking straight, how can I possibly remember such details when jealousy hits me like a freight train?

Is that her ex-boyfriend? Current boyfriend? The one she wrote the note to? Husband? Ex-husband?

When she returns, she glares at me when she sees me signing the bill. "You can take the next one," I say as I sheepishly hand the credit card slip to the waitress.

Harlow is quiet on the short drive to the Pearl, her attention clearly elsewhere as she gazes outside the window where there's only darkness. After spending the whole day with her and loving every minute of it, the last thing I want to do now is to leave her.

"Everything okay?" I ask as I turn the truck into the Greater Earthship Community, the high beam illuminating nothing but sagebrush. Even the air in the cab has become thick as if the phone call zapped all happiness from her whole being. I want to punch whoever it is who took that away from her—well, and from me.

"Everything's fine," she says, turning to look at me and smile. "Thank you so much for dinner, and for the whole day. I had a lot of fun today. Guess I'll be seeing you tomorrow."

I reach for Harlow's hand resting on the edge of her seat and squeeze it. "Yes, you will. Maybe nine. The hot springs will be perfect if you're feeling sore after today. Thank you for coming with me, Harlow. It means a lot to me," I say, pulling my hand away as I turn into her driveway and shift the truck into park.

As I walk her to her door, I wish I could hold her hand all night. Hell, I wish I could hold *her* all night and make love to her. Harlow James laughing in the sun, in her pink sleeveless top and khaki pants does things to me that I'm not too happy about. I feel like I'm in uncharted territory, my mind begging for me to stay away, but my heart says, *to hell with it, I'm jumping in anyway.*

But something is bothering her tonight, that fucking phone call acting like some midnight tolling of the bells and suddenly, everything around us that was the perfect fairy tale returns to normal. She's a woman who could be on the run from something—or someone—and here I am, just another man wanting to get into her pants.

When I get home, Nana is still up, watching one of her

favorite Mexican TV shows that she's pre-recorded. She looks up when I walk in and pauses the show.

"You don't have to do that. I was just heading straight to the shower and then to bed," I say as I give her a peck on the cheek.

"Did you have fun with Miss Harlow?" she asks, a knowing smile on her face.

"I did, and she's now a bona fide fan of Nana's special *chorizo con huevos y papas y frijoles.* That alone was a mouthful for her to say, but I think she's got it memorized now. I'm taking her to the hot springs tomorrow, and maybe even the winery." Usually, I'd sit with Nana and watch her shows, just like I did with Mama, but not tonight. I'm too jittery to sit down, and the memory of hearing Harlow saying the words as she studied the burrito this morning makes the butterflies in my belly flutter again.

There I go again. Fuck, what is happening?

"I got a call this afternoon from some lawyer," she says and I sit down across from her, frowning.

"Someone is suing me?"

"No, he wasn't calling for you, *mijo.* He was looking for Harlow. He wanted to know how to get to the Pearl. Something about papers that needed to be signed, legal stuff. He would have sent a courier, but seems like there's a rush with the documents."

So that's the courier Harlow was talking about, the one she hadn't been keen on running into when I first showed up at the Pearl.

"Did you tell him?"

Nana scoffs. "Of course not, but I think he's going to

find it, anyway. It's not like the Pearl is a big secret around town. I left her a message on her phone, and that's all I did. You know how I don't like meddling in other people's business."

I get up from the couch. "I'm sure she's checked her messages by now."

She nods, her gaze distant. "I think she needs a friend, and I'm glad you're being one to her. Being out there all by herself has got to be lonely. I know I can't do it, and I live here."

"Yeah, but it's what she wants, Nana. And if she needs a friend, we're here if she needs us."

"But you don't want her to be just a friend, *mijo*. Do you?"

I pause. I don't need to look at Nana's eyes to know that she's right. There's no way I want Harlow to be *just* a friend. I want her to be more than that, but I also don't want her to be just another fuck buddy, which is how most women in my life have ended up becoming, remembering me only for my prowess in bed but nothing else. No, Harlow's special—special in a way that I have never experienced a woman before, and it's leaving me confused.

True, that primal part of me wants to fuck her like crazy, but I also don't want to fuck her up in the process, if that even makes sense.

CHAPTER ELEVEN

Harlow

Count on Jeff to ruin what was a beautiful day. A phone call telling me—no, demanding—that I sign away my share of the Hamptons estate because I never wanted it in the first place was beyond comprehension. The nerve of the man to assume I didn't want it! But how could I want to live in a vast and empty house then, devoid of the laughter of children? Only then would it have been a home to me.

Home. The thought makes my knees grow weak as I watch Dax's truck turn left on the main highway, back to the city. Why do I feel like I'm home whenever he's near? Dax makes me think of early mornings in bed, snuggled deep under the covers, of the smell of piping hot coffee, and long, hungry kisses that last forever. He makes me yearn for things I've long forgotten before my ambition took over and now here I am, alone and thinking of a man who's way too young for me.

But then, is he really too young? Or am I just using that as an excuse to stay away from him and not get hurt?

But even if I were using his age as an excuse, then why did I just spend the last twelve hours with him, laughing and smiling more than I've ever done in years? Hearing my lawyer's message asking me to call him as soon as possible didn't even bother me the slightest.

Because you like him, Harlow James, that's why. You like him so much that even Jeff yelling on the phone like he did the last time didn't make you break into tears and crumble this time. This time, as you turned to look at the young man sneakily paying for dinner, you hung up on your ex-husband as he told you he was sending someone with the papers he expects you to sign.

I lock the doors and make my way to the master bathroom. I hate what I'm about to do, but I need it. In an area that gets only nine inches of rain a year, I shouldn't be filling my tub with enough water to provide for six people, but whatever water I use is going to end up in the grey-water system anyway, watering the plants and filling up the toilets. Besides, what's the point of the most beautiful bathtub I've ever seen? Lacquered wood that I've been dying to use since I came here?

As the tub fills with water, I undress and gaze at my reflection in the mirror. The light in the bathroom is kind, revealing my body to me with an almost dream-like quality as the steam rises from the bathtub. Even though I devoted much of my time to work, I took care of my body in a vain attempt to look as good as my achievements on paper. I worked out three times a week, enjoyed my monthly facials and body treatments, and stayed out of the sun. I took care of myself, and it shows.

But I see the imperfections, the ones brought on by time. I know there are lines on my face, especially between my eyebrows for I have this terrible habit of frowning as I work, whether I'm typing a research paper on my laptop or suturing an incision. My breasts still fill more than their share of my 36C bras though they're not as firm as they used to be. *But they're real, Harlow. And you'd be lying to yourself if you weren't aware that Dax couldn't keep his eyes off them the whole day.* My waist is narrow, my belly flat although I see the stretch marks that look like notches marking time spent carrying that one fetus to term.

Stop it, Harlow! Focus on the positive for once!

I turn around and look back at my reflection, suddenly feeling silly and realizing the tub is ready, but not before my gaze settles on my firm buttocks and I smile.

Well, whoever my birth parents were, they blessed me with a hell of a firm ass.

Three days later, I'm in bed watching the sunlight stream through the multi-colored glass bottles embedded in the dividing wall of my bedroom. I don't need to get up to know that Dax is already at the Pearl. I can almost feel his presence permeate through the space though I wish he were permeating more than just space. I laugh out loud at how horny I am, but after spending the last two days with Dax exploring Taos—and catching sight of his package as he was changing out of his swim trunks at the hot springs—I haven't been able to think of anything else. He's big.

He did get my mind out of the gutter by keeping me too preoccupied with other things, like showing me Taos only a Taoseño could. First, we stopped by the Taos Mesa Micro Brewery. Tasting various brews loosened me up and being the designated driver, Dax happily settled for apple cider before we drove to the hot springs. It was almost an hour-long hike down to the pools where I was ready to jump right in, but not before we explored the remnants of the stone bathhouse that Arthur Manby built in hopes of turning it into some world-class resort. Luckily, I did find a swimsuit in my luggage, and it was such a relief to sit in the hot springs after that hike, listening to Dax tell more stories about Manby. It was certainly no accident that our legs kept brushing against each other the whole time, something that became a game between us for the pool we had chosen was wide enough to fit five people.

We spent the second day at Arroyo Seco where we hiked to a part of the Rio Grande known as a local fishing spot before Dax took me to a winery to sample the wine and the locally made chocolate that had me moaning with bliss as the pieces melted in my mouth. We ended the day with a trip back to Nana's house to pick up my car—or at least, that was the plan. When Dyami insisted I hang out and play *Operation* with him and then *Monopoly*, I obliged and ended up drinking so much of the wine we'd bought that day that I didn't care whether I owned Park Place or ended up in jail, with no chance to pass *Go*. By eleven, long past Dyami's bedtime—and probably everyone else's—Dax drove a tipsy but happy doctor back to the Pearl. Driving over the Gorge Bridge didn't even scare me at all.

At least now, I know that we're both flirting with each other. But damn if Dax is taking his sweet time because it's driving me crazy. I've had the best time of my life since I left New York six months ago, and I can't wait to experience more of Taos. But if I were to be honest, the only thing I want to enjoy about Taos right now is in the man cave on the other side of the Pearl while I lie here in bed daydreaming of the things I want him to do to me—and me to him. The possibilities are endless.

But thanks to rational me ruining all the fun, Dax is keeping true to whatever we talked about—or rather, what *I* talked about—that he stay on his side of the Pearl, and I stay in mine... well, sort of. I hate having set boundaries because now I know that if anyone is going to break them, it'll be me.

By the time I'm in the kitchen brewing coffee, I feel it —that jittery feeling that has my heart beating so fast it's making me wonder if I might have developed some type of cardiac condition overnight. I can almost feel the blood coursing through my temples. With trembling hands, I fill two earthenware mugs with coffee and take a deep breath.

You brushed your teeth, washed your face and mussed up your hair. You'll be fine. Now bring him coffee and say hi.

I see Dax before he sees me, but I don't say anything. As far as I'm concerned, the last three days spent with him are equivalent to the sum of a lengthy foreplay and right now, I'm on fire. I'm just glad that he's too busy to notice me as I stand awkwardly by the door, acting as calmly as I can although inside, I'm bouncing all over the place.

What is wrong with me?

Dax is pulling something that looks like a wood planer though he uses it differently, pulling it toward him instead of away from him, the way I've seen carpenters do it. Instead of short slivers of wood, I see a paper-thin strip unfurl from it gracefully before Dax flicks it away and returns the planer back to the opposite end of the board. Then he does it all over again.

Through his thin white shirt, I see his muscles tighten with every movement. I could name them all if I wanted to—latissimus dorsi, triceps brachii, deltoid, infraspinatus and teres major—but I want to do more than that. I want to touch them all, run my fingers over them and feel them ripple beneath my skin. And I know I won't stop there. I want my hands to move lower down his back, feel my fingers rake against his smooth tanned skin. I want—

Suddenly Dax stops whatever he's doing, straightens his back and turns to look at me.

"Good morning, Harlow."

"Hi," I stammer, hoping my face doesn't betray my thoughts. "I... I brought you coffee."

"Thanks," he says, and that's when I see that he's brought a Thermos with him, and I feel like an idiot. Of course, the boy scout would bring his own coffee. I made the rules, didn't I? I wasn't going to entertain him, nor was he supposed to entertain me.

Oh, but do I want him to.

"I'm sorry. I didn't realize you brought your own," I turn around before he can say anything but Dax is a fast mover. Suddenly he's standing in front of me, and he takes one of the mugs from my hand.

"Thank you," he says, his gaze moving from my face down to my lips, and then the front of my robe. I didn't even bother to get dressed. And why would I? I don't want to get dressed, not with this man standing so close to me, his cologne and that man-smell of his sending my hormones into overdrive. I lick my lips.

"You're welcome."

"Did I wake you?" he asks as he sets the mug down on the table next to us.

I shake my head, keeping my eyes on his mouth. "No, I didn't even realize you were here until after I was, um, making coffee in the kitchen." *Liar. And where else would you make coffee anyway?* "So I thought, maybe..."

Dax takes the other mug from my hand and sets it down. I don't even protest. I don't know if I still have it—whatever it is that men want—but a part of me wants to find out. I want to know if it's all my imagination, the way he looks at me, and how his gaze travels from my eyes to my lips, lingering there before moving downward. I want to see that bulge in his jeans, reminding me that I'm still attractive, beautiful even.

"Harlow..." he murmurs, and I feel his fingers pushing an errant lock of hair from my face. He dips his head, and now I'm looking at his eyes. Blue and so intense. My heart beats so loud I can almost hear it echoing throughout the room.

Boom. Boom. Boom.

I stifle a moan and press my thighs together, feeling the heat rise to my chest. I bite my lower lip this time and let my gaze move down, and I exhale triumphantly. He's hard, and he's–

"There's someone at the door," he says, the words snapping me back to the present.

"What?"

Then I hear it. Someone *is* at the door.

"Oh, yes," I stammer and pulling my robe tighter around me, I turn away and rush out of the workspace. For a moment, I forget where the front door is, and when I remember, shame fills me for what I'd just done.

Have you no shame, Harlow?

No, apparently not.

The knocking comes again, along with a familiar voice. "Harlow, it's me. Open the door."

It takes me a few seconds to process seeing Frank Weston, my divorce lawyer, on the other side of the front door with its glass insert that hides nothing of my current appearance, so far from the woman he's always known. Mussed up hair, no makeup, barefoot and wearing a plush white bathrobe. I look nothing like the surgeon he knows, the woman who used to lunch with his wife a few times a week discussing who among the women at the country club had what done and whether it was done well or not.

But at least I brushed my teeth, I tell myself as I pull open the door but don't invite him in.

"Frank? What are you doing here?"

He wipes the sweat gathered on his brow and I can see his combover clearly in the light of the Taos sun.

Frank is wearing a white shirt and tailored trousers, his leather shoes already dusty from the short walk from his rental car to the front door. It's hot outside and the sun is beating down on the graveled driveway. My car is parked right in front of the garage doors, clean and shiny. I sigh. Dax didn't have to do that.

"I could have sent a courier but I figured this would be faster," he says.

"What would be faster?"

"These papers," he says, pulling a folder from his leather briefcase. "Jeff's lawyer called me two days ago and they want you to sign these."

"What is it for?"

"Your estate in the Hamptons. It's the last thing we need to settle before we can get all this over with," Frank replies, exhaling. "Look, you told me yourself, Harlow. You didn't care what happened to it, just like your Manhattan property that you signed away to Jeff. So he figures, since you always hated going to the Hamptons, he'd like for you to sign off on the property, and he'll pay you back your share of what you paid for it. That's as simple as I'm going to make it, but I'm sure you know what I mean."

"Is he out of his mind?" With the current market, the property is worth millions.

"No, but you said so yourself, Harlow. Even Belinda tells me you hate the place. You have a staff of three people taking care of it...for what? You never go there, and Jeff would gladly take it off your hands. Besides, he's getting married in less than three weeks, and he'd like to raise his family there."

Old Harlow would have burst out crying right about now and Frank would have taken me in his arms and patted me on the shoulder and say, *Now, now, dear Harlow. It's not too bad. Sign here anyway and the sooner it's done, the sooner this divorce will be over, and who knows, this depression you're experiencing will be gone, too. Some things just don't work out, no matter how hard we try.*

But Old Harlow is gone. In her place is someone new —or someone I hope is new. I look down at the folder he holds out to me, nudging it toward me.

"I've put highlight stickers on all the places you need to sign and initial–"

"Whose side are you on, Frank?"

Frank cocks his head back in surprise. "Excuse me?"

"I said, who's side are you on? I thought you were my lawyer."

"Of course, I am, and that's why I'm here, some strange house in the middle of nowhere that's good only for a fucking apocalypse," he says angrily and I see a bead of sweat roll down his temple. "You do know my trip here is on your tab, and my office will be adding this to your bill."

"Then add it," I say, hoping my voice doesn't shake for I know my insides sure are. My heart is about to burst from the shock of what I'm saying, and my knees are trembling beneath my robe. "And don't forget to add the return ticket, too. We wouldn't want you stranded here, Frank. Belinda wouldn't like it. Now get the hell out of my property."

Frank removes his sunglasses and stares at me like I

just sprouted two heads. "What the hell has gotten into you, Harlow? I thought you wanted to make this divorce go easily and that's all I'm doing here. I'm on your side, okay? Your job is to trust me, remember? Why don't you just sign the papers like a good girl and get this over with?"

"Because she's not a good girl—not to you, and not anymore," says a deep voice, and I turn my head to see Dax standing behind me, his deep blue eyes burning with anger. "She's a woman, and don't you ever forget that."

CHAPTER TWELVE

Dax

It doesn't take long for me to realize something is wrong the moment I hear the man's voice at the door. There's a whiny quality to it, and it makes my skin crawl. What the hell is a New York lawyer doing in Taos? I'm glad I made my way to the front door quietly, allowing me to hear the crap this bastard was saying to her.

Good girl, my ass. What kind of lawyer treats his client that way? Not only that, but he expects Harlow to sign away her equitable share of a house in the Hamptons? Is he out of his fucking mind?

Suddenly it hits me. *The gun, the note—and why she's so far away from home.* Those along with the sadness in her doe-eyes, it all makes sense now. If only Harlow trusts me enough to tell me herself. I just hope that suicide note wasn't to the asshole who sent her damn lawyer halfway across the country to belittle her. I stand next to Harlow, and the man named Frank stares at me, his eyes bulging out of its sockets.

"Who the fuck are you?"

"It's none of your business who I am, but if I were you, I'd get back in your car right now, and do as the lady says."

Frank turns to Harlow. "As your lawyer—and friend—I'm warning you, Harlow, this isn't the smartest move—"

"No, Frank, *this* is the smartest move I'm making in my life. As my lawyer, you had no right to come here and tell me where to sign away my claim to my property, and yet you did, just like you had no right to talk me into giving up everything I've given up so far all because you said it was for my own good," she says, her voice breaking before she takes a deep breath and continues. "But not anymore. Effective today, I am letting you go as my lawyer. Now leave, or should I call the New Mexico Bar Association to verify your license to practice law in this state?"

I pull out my phone and hand it to her. "You can use mine if you want."

"Jeff was right. You definitely lost it after Marcus," Frank scoffs as Harlow gasps, and she brings her hand to her mouth, her eyes brimming with tears. *Oh, hell no, he did not just say that.* I don't know who Marcus is, but if he was as close to Harlow as her choked gasp implies, then Frank has just crossed every fucking line imaginable. All I see is red... and Frank's face.

My fist meets his nose, and Frank howls, falling butt first to the ground. I don't know how people in Harlow's world settle things, but in mine, this usually does the trick, especially when they don't play by the rules in the first place, their carefully selected words designed to hit where it hurts the most.

"You hit me! You fucking hit me!" Frank shrieks, clutching his nose that's beginning to bleed. In a few seconds, it's going to gush, but I couldn't care less if he bled all over the place. I need the man out of my property right now.

"Get the hell out of here and don't ever bother her again," I say, flexing my fingers. Shit, I haven't hit anyone in years, not when the last time got me in trouble.

"I'm suing you!"

Like that kind of trouble. But right now, I don't care. He just insulted his own client, the woman I'm not ashamed to say I'm crazy about.

"Go right ahead. But first, what is it called when a person enters and remains on someone's private property after being told to leave?" Frank's eyes bulge even more as he pushes himself off the ground. "Oh, that's right, a misdemeanor. Right, Frank? Now, wouldn't it be interesting to see that on your license—in addition to the charge of practicing law in a state where you're not legally licensed to practice, right?"

Without another word, Frank scrambles into his car and hightails it out of there, gravel ricocheting off the back of his tires. I don't wait for him to turn onto the highway. I hurry back into the house, shut the door behind me and follow Harlow into the living room where she's pacing the floor nervously.

"Harlow, talk to me. What's going on?"

"Nothing."

"Nothing? Your divorce lawyer flies all the way here

from New York to insult your intelligence and hurt you, and that is *nothing?*" I ask as calmly as I can. Harlow continues pacing the walkway in front of the row of indoor planters, her arms crossed in front of her chest. She's so closed in and it's driving me crazy. Why can't she allow herself to talk to someone instead of hiding away in the Pearl alone—and with a fucking gun?

The thought makes me tense. Hell, the whole idea that there's a gun somewhere inside the Pearl makes me tense even as I push away the memory of seeing it on the suicide note that night. *Was it really addressed to her ex? And who's Marcus?*

"Do you still love him?"

Harlow's brown eyes flash with anger. "You mean Jeff? Are you out of your mind? Why the hell would I still love that... that asshole who sent my lawyer here to get me to sign everything away? Because Jeff sent him, no question about that. He and Frank used to play tennis at the country club, but Frank assured me they don't see each other anymore."

She wrings her hands together, and I can feel her anxiety building even more as she continues. "I should have listened to my gut and fired him a long time ago. I can't believe I let it go this far–"

I stand in front of her and envelop her hands between mine, halting her nervous habit. If she keeps doing it, even I'll be a nervous wreck just from watching her. "Harlow, stop for a second. Please."

She looks up at me, big brown eyes that have the power to undo me. But I can't let that happen—not right now.

"But you're not letting anything go now, Harlow, and that's what matters. I bet he was in collusion with Jeff's lawyer or worse, with Jeff."

She takes a deep breath and nods. "I know that now. Well, I always knew it, but I couldn't... I couldn't do anything about it because I was too..." As she pauses, I see the vulnerability on her face. "You won't understand. No one knows unless they've lost a... a child."

I'm sorry for saving others when all this time, the one thing I couldn't save was you.

The words on her suicide note return to me then, the realization hitting me like a two-by-four to the chest.

Marcus.

"Oh, Harlow, I'm so sorry." I don't stop to ask if my guess is right. I gather her in my arms, relieved that she doesn't push me away though she's still coiled as tight as a spring. Is this what she's been carrying all this time while her soon-to-be ex-husband is busy with his wedding arrangements, waiting till Harlow would finally break down and he'd have everything?

I've got many choice words just dying to get out of me, but I tell myself to calm down. If anyone should have something to say, it's Harlow. But as much as I'd want to learn more about Marcus, I also don't want her to sink back into the same world she'd been in when I first arrived at the Pearl. Marcus will have to be for another day.

"Do you have someone in mind? As far as a new lawyer?"

"Frank has partners who could easily take over my case, but I need someone new. Someone not affiliated with his firm," she says, her voice muffled against my chest. "They must have been laughing at me the whole time."

"They won't be laughing now, and that's what matters. The only reason anyone would make fun of you is because they're intimidated by you, and they know you're better than they are," I say, drawing away so I can see her face. "Look, I may have only met you, but as far as I know, you're an amazing woman and how you've managed to keep all this pain hidden is beyond me. But if there's anything I can do to help you, Harlow, please let me."

"I don't want to trouble anyone–"

"You're not troubling anyone with this. If anything, it bugs me that you refuse to let anyone help you." I tilt her chin, so she's looking up at me, my voice softening. "My company's main office and showroom are in New York, and that's also where we're incorporated. It's where my dad, who's the CFO of my company, is based out of. So if you need a name of a lawyer..."

"But I thought you're based around here."

"I stay in Flagstaff because that's where I draft and build everything, and I come here because this place is special to me. Besides, I can only handle being away from Nana and her cooking every few months. So if you need a recommendation for another lawyer who's not affiliated with that scumbag or his office, then I can ask my lawyer for one right now, but only if you'll let me. Will you let me help you?"

Harlow takes a deep breath, and I can almost feel the feeling of relief wash over her as she nods and smiles.

And if there's one thing about Harlow that I can't get enough of, it's her smile.

"If you can, I'd appreciate it," she says. "But what about Frank? What if he sues you for hitting him?"

"Then let him. That's what my lawyers are for, and he was on my private property. But don't change the subject, Harlow. I can help you—or I sure as hell am going to do whatever I can to direct you to someone better than that asshole. It'll take a few calls, but you're going to show him that you're not his good girl or anyone else's for that matter."

She chuckles dryly. "I guess I'm really more Thelma than Louise, aren't I?"

"I wouldn't say that, not after what you've been through. And you haven't given up yet, so who knows? Maybe that's why you got into your car and drove west, and why you're right here instead of back there," I say, pushing a stray lock of hair from her face. "Did you have any plans for the day?"

"No, just getting rid of Frank and keeping what's mine."

"Good. Once I get a hold of Cole, and he gets me the names of lawyers you can interview, I'll hand it over to you so you won't feel like I'm hovering while you're handling your business. Would that work for you?"

"I have all the documents stored in the bedroom, so I'm just going to go get them and get dressed," she says as she walks away from me but I take hold of her hand, and she stops, glancing up at me quizzically. "What is it?"

"You're more of a Louise than you think."

Four hours later, including a half-hour break to have lunch that I'd called to be delivered from one of my favorite restaurants, Harlow is still on the phone. I could have driven into town to get lunch but I didn't want to leave her alone, not if Frank just might decide to come back. He did leave her the documents he'd wanted her to sign, which will come in handy when it's time to sue his ass for malpractice.

But that's up to Harlow and her new lawyers, and I sure hope the court allows her the change of legal counsel. This time, I hope she gets everything from that bastard she married and for the hell that she must have gone through to want to put a bullet through her brain.

Stay calm, Dax. This isn't your fight.

But thinking of how close she'd been to losing everything still fills me with anger, especially after everything else I've overheard from my workroom. From what I've gathered, Marcus was her stillborn son, and it hasn't even been a year which means Jeff what's-his-face filed for divorce shortly after. What cold-blooded son of a bitch would do that to a grieving mother? I don't care what shit she's done, dude, but to file for divorce while she's still grieving? I don't think so.

The piece of cherry wood in front of me is receiving the brunt of my emotions, the Japanese hand planer sending long strips of paper-thin wood unfurling to the ground. The wood is useless now, actually, and if I keep on going, I'll have nothing left but the planing table in front of me.

"Hi. Is it okay if I come in?"

Harlow's voice snaps me out of my thoughts, and I turn to see her standing by the door, barefoot and wearing a blue sleeveless top and loose cotton pants. Her hair is secured in a ponytail though a few strands frame her oval face.

"You're always welcome in here."

"I just got off the phone, and I think I've got everything settled on my end. They'll call me as soon as they find out what the judge decides," Harlow continues as she stops in front of me. "So, can you show me how this works?"

"Sure," I say as I beckon for her to stand between me and the table. I smell a trace of rose oil in her hair, and it grounds me back to the warm feel of her body pressing lightly against mine, all other thoughts pushed away. As I guide her movements, one hand along the top and the side of the planer and the other hand on the opposite side, I find myself enclosing her body with my own.

Just show her how to do it. Don't think of anything else.

I rest one hand on top of her hands and the other on her far shoulder and take a deep breath. "Ready for your first lesson in hand planing, the Japanese way?"

She nods. I love the feel of her hair brushing over my arms, creating goosebumps in their wake. I force myself to focus on my hand covering hers, and slowly, I guide her hand so that she pulls the planer toward her. It takes some strength and I feel the muscles of her back tighten as she leans back into it, guiding the planer till it reaches the end of the cherry wood. Then we repeat the process again.

"American hand planes are usually pushed away from the body but Japanese ones, like this, a *hira kanna*, is pulled toward you. It allows you to use your core muscles in addition to your arms to smoothen wood like this."

I guide her body with my own, and with each motion, a thin strip of wood flutters in the air and on the third pass, she stops to catch one with one hand and studies it. "It's so thin, like paper."

"A human hair is about 100 microns across, and a droplet of water, maybe ten microns in diameter. Yet some of the best hand planers can create a wood shaving like this that's only three microns thick, even thinner than a red blood cell," I say, my gaze fixed on her profile. "The one you're holding is probably about ten or fifteen microns."

"You love what you do. You have such passion for it," she says softly. "To others, it's nothing but a piece of wood, but to you…"

"It can be a cabinet, a table, a support beam that will last for centuries," I say. "It's a combination of instrument and skill, and a passion for simplicity. None of my creations use nails or screws or glue, just joints—well, except for our bath tubs which require glue. I spend more time sharpening the blade for this *hira kanna* than actually using it, but when I do, the results are always worth the time and effort of preparing the blade."

As I speak, I'm acutely aware of how close Harlow's face is to mine, if not closer than it was earlier. I force myself to make light of things, not wanting them to go where I really want them to go, which would take us right into her bedroom. So I shrug and grin like I'm not, at that moment, fighting the urge to kiss her. "Just like your preparation to be a surgeon. So many years of training just to, I don't know, slice into a kidney or something."

Harlow chuckles and I feel the stress leave her body just then. But as she turns her head to look at me, I feel my resolve melting. Shit, this is trouble right here, and all I need to do is let go of the *hira kanna* and wrap my arms around her.

Focus, Dax. Focus. F-O-C-U-S.

But all focus disappears when Harlow slips her hands from underneath mine, and as she runs the fingers of one hand up my forearm and the other strokes my beard, all my resolve fades away. And when her lips touch mine ever so faintly, suddenly, all focus on anything else but her is gone. Completely and utterly gone.

CHAPTER THIRTEEN

Harlow

THE KISS IS soft at first, just a light brushing of our lips that sends tingles running up and down my spine. Then it deepens, the lightness of Dax's lips replaced now by an intention to drive me crazy with his tongue. Has it really been a long time since I've been kissed like this? Not just a meeting of lips before saying *goodbye, see ya tonight*, but really kissed?

And after hours of interviewing lawyers, I want this, something that will make me forget all the should-have's and could-have's that I'd set aside to pursue my career. *Should have had more fun. Should have taken more vacations. Should have said no to that transplant that I knew would change everything between Jeff and me.* Sure, it got me respect from my peers and my name on the door underneath Jeff's, but was it all worth it? Was it all worth that close call to a bullet to the brain?

I pull away from Dax, surprised to feel tears on my cheeks. *Oh, great, why the hell am I crying now? He really must think I'm crazy.*

"I'm sorry," I stammer as I raise my hands to my face, but Dax wipes the tears away first with his thumbs. "Oh, God, this is so embarrassing."

"No, it's not. I cry over beer commercials," he says, his deep blue eyes kind.

"You're just saying that to make me feel better."

"Wait till Super Bowl is here and the commercials come on, especially the ones with the horses... and puppies," Dax murmurs as he pulls me into a long embrace that for all intents and purposes should have calmed me, but instead, it does the complete opposite and soon, I'm sobbing uncontrollably. It's as if every bit of self-control I've had in keeping everything inside comes pouring out like a dam finally breaking. But Dax is there, and he holds me.

Old Harlow would have fought being in his arms, not wanting anyone to see her weakness, but the new Harlow doesn't fight it—not when it feels so good having Dax's arms around me. I haven't felt this safe in a long time.

"It's okay, Harlow. Just let it all out. Might as well now than never, right?"

I chuckle through my tears as flashes of the last few years come to me like a home movie someone is rewinding while it's still playing on the screen. Jeff and I meeting for the first time on the first day of my surgical rotation, and later, studying lab results at the doctors' lounge, or guessing mystery conditions while watching recorded episodes of the TV show, *House*. There's also the wedding that wasn't a wedding but more like a last-minute meeting to tie the knot with a few close friends at the City Hall.

I was never into those big weddings, my mind always worrying about the cost better applied to something more lasting, like a property in the Hamptons that spelled success, even if that success was never enjoyed. Then came the surgical rotations, the private practice separate from Jeff's, and everything else that only served to drive that wedge between us.

I should have known Jeff was drifting farther and farther away from me as I pursued the things I wanted—if only to prove to myself that I was better than just another foster kid no one wanted—forgetting that all Jeff wanted was for me to stay at home and have his babies. He wanted a wife and mother, not *a* surgeon, *a* wife, and *a* mother, simple articles that are anything but simple when taken into context. He'd asked me to step down and give it all up and I had said no, and oh, how I paid for it with Marcus, born with that umbilical cord wrapped tight around his neck that not even an emergency caesarean section could save. But I'd also ignored the signs that Jeff had been cheating on me, determined to be the woman who had it all and refusing to show any sign of vulnerability.

My body shakes uncontrollably as I sob, and Dax continues to hold me quietly. I'm glad he doesn't say anything, but even if he did, I'm not in any state to listen to whatever he'll say. I just want someone to hold me, and it's a realization that hits me that this is the first time I've allowed myself to let go and trust someone to see me like this. I've been running away from everyone ever since Jeff's friend served me the divorce papers and later, the day I got in the car and took off, depending only on my

GPS for the next place to drive to, and an old Thomas Guide where I'd highlighted my route so far. Hell, Dax is probably too young to know what a Thomas Guide is.

But does it even matter? He's here... with me.

I can hear Dax breathing, smell the scent of that damn cologne again mingling with that which is all his own. When I pull away, I keep my focus on his chest, where my tears have dampened the front of his shirt. If I'd been wearing make-up, I'd be seeing black smears of my mascara by now. But I haven't worn makeup for weeks, months even, settling only for the usual skin care products to keep my skin moisturized and protected from the sun. Besides, who would I wear makeup for out here in the middle of nowhere? Here, I'm not a surgeon with certificates gracing the walls of her office, one achievement piled on top of another like a deck of cards now scattered in the wind. Right now, I'm just a woman being held by a man.

When I lift my gaze up to Dax's face, I meet his dark blue eyes, and I have to catch my breath. Does Dax know just how handsome he is? Does he realize just how the chiseled lines of his jaw are even more defined by a beard that's trimmed so perfectly, making this woman's stomach tighten in knots? Is he aware just how his mouth begs to be kissed again, for me to toss every ounce of self-respect left in me out the window and just take what I can?

When I run my fingers along the furrow where his spine divides the broad musculature of his back, Dax stiffens, drawing a sudden breath. The pupils of his eyes dilate as I run my tongue along my upper lip, tasting the remnants of my tears and his kiss. He lowers his head, our lips just inches away.

"Anyone home?"

Ah, great. Someone's at the door.

Dax curses under his breath and pulls away. He leans his forehead against mine as I hear the knocking on the door, louder this time. "It's Benny. He must have just come from work to drop off my truck, which means my sister's not far behind."

I wait till Dax leaves the workroom before retreating into the bathroom so I can wash my face and hope I don't look like I've been crying. I hear Benny's voice saying that Sarah texted him about Dax needing his truck back and so here he was. I run my fingers through my hair and take one last glance at the mirror before joining Dax and Benny at the door.

"Hi, Benny. What are you guys doing out in the heat? Come on in," I say just as I see a car making its way toward the Pearl in the distance.

"I would, but Sarah will only get ticked off if I do. It's date night, and she wants no distractions," Benny says, laughing as he hands Dax the keys to his truck. "She's determined to go out to dinner and check out this movie she's been dying to see."

"Where's Dyami?" Dax asks.

"Home. Nana's with him so you're free from babysitting duties," Benny says, turning to face me. "Guess what? Dyami asked me to buy some anatomy app after that talk you guys had about kidneys and stuff. This one shows kids how the body works, like allergies and digestion and breathing. It's pretty amazing. Now he's interested in something else other than Minecraft."

"Tell him he can ask me anything anytime," I say as Sara parks the car next to Dax's truck and steps out.

"I will," Benny says, and we all watch as Sarah opens the back passenger door and takes out a cooler. "Oh, that's right; almost forgot. Nana has some stuff for you."

"Oh, no, she didn't have to," I protest as Sarah gives me a hug and hands me the cooler. It's heavy, and I set it on the bench next to the door.

"What's in it? Is it food?" Dax reaches for the cooler lid, but Sarah swats his hand away.

"It's not for you, Big D, so hands off," Sarah says, laughing as she faces me. "Nana went to the Farmer's Market today and got you some stuff she figured you'd need to try out while you're here. Locally made stuff, that kind of thing. Oh, and she made you some tamales, too."

"Tell her thank you for me. I really appreciate it."

"If my little brother starts bothering you, just kick him out," she says, laughing as Dax glowers at her. "Anyway, we gotta go, or we'll be late for dinner." They say their goodbyes, leaving us standing at the door watching the cloud of dust trailing behind their car.

"So where were we?" Dax asks as he shuts the door and turns to face me. This time, I don't hesitate.

"We were here." I kiss him then, my actions taking him by surprise. But I want Dax, and I'm tired of pretending that I don't. This time, there's an urgency to the way I kiss him back. I want him bad, and I want him now. The sooner, the better for I know that the longer I think about it, the greater the chance I'll convince myself that this is all wrong. I slide my hands under his shirt, feeling the taut muscles underneath. When I tug his shirt and pull it up along his back, Dax doesn't need any more hints about what I want. He pulls off his shirt, tossing it onto the bench by the door before pulling me toward him.

"I love where we are," Dax murmurs. His hands cradle my face as he looks at me—really looks at me—like he's drinking me in. His eyes are so blue, reminding me of the New Mexico sky. I love the way he devours me with his eyes, and when he kisses me hungrily, it's all teeth and tongue, as if the time for dancing around each other has finally run out.

I let go of all thought and let my body take over. When he palms my breast through my shirt, his thumb pressing on my nipple, I gasp. With his other hand, Dax pulls the elastic from my ponytail and weaves his fingers through my hair. His mouth leaves my lips, and I feel him blazing a trail of kisses down my neck, pulling my head back and exposing my neck to him. When he finds the sensitive spot behind my ear and sucks softly, I dig my fingers into the skin of his shoulders. My knees give way, and I cling to him just as Dax pulls away.

"What?" I ask, dazed.

"Not here," he says, taking my hand and leading me to the bedroom. Dax stops in front of the bed and faces me again, lowering his head to kiss me, this time, accompanied by a playful nibble of my lower lip. He takes his time as he undresses me, savoring every bit of skin he comes across with a nip here as he tosses my shirt to the side and a lick there when he slides my pants down my hips. Dax eyes me when I wriggle my hips before him to help the descent of my panties down to the floor, and from the way his dick is straining through his jeans, I love that my little show doesn't go unappreciated. Laughing, I push him down on the bed, my impatience getting the better of me.

I unbutton his jeans and pull them off, along with his boxer briefs, to reveal him all naked on the bed before me. For a few moments, I just stare at him, my throat suddenly dry. He's absolutely beautiful, and all I can think is how perfectly the term, *tall, dark and handsome* applies to him. As Dax props himself up on his elbows to look at me, I can name every muscle along his torso, six-pack abs begging to be touched, even licked and boy, do I plan to do just that today. I don't even know where to begin but I let my gaze drift lower, down to his muscular thighs before focusing on his penis... no, I mean, his dick. His cock. Why do I have to be so technical and call everything by their anatomical term? But holy hell, there's no need to be technical about his dick. He's big. I catch my breath, my cheeks burning. I realize then that I've only ever been with one man—until now. I pause, the thought rendering me in a panic.

"Come here," Dax murmurs, reaching for my hand and pulling me down to the bed next to him. His gaze travels down my body, and in a moment of uncertainty, I vainly cover myself with my arms.

"Harlow, we don't have to go through with it if you're not comfortable."

"But I *am* comfortable," I say almost angrily, removing my hands from my breasts before Dax kisses me again. And for the next few minutes, that's all he does —kissing me tenderly and calming the inner turmoil until it simmers down, replaced with the need to have him make love to me.

"Did you bring any, um, protection?" I ask, and Dax sits up and reaches for his jeans, pulling out a condom packet from his wallet and sets it on the bedside table.

"Of course."

The sight of a condom makes me blush even more, only because it's been a long time since I've needed to use one. Jeff and I were trying to get pregnant then, not avoid it.

"You're gonna need a few of those," I blurt out before I can stop myself and hide my face against his chest as he returns to lie on his side next to me. "Oh, God, I can't believe I just said that."

"Don't worry, because we will need a few of them before the day is over. But we don't need it just yet. I like to take my time, Harlow." Dax pushes me down on my back as he trails long, lazy kisses down my neck and breasts and my belly. Then he positions himself between my legs, parting my thighs with his hands.

Wait! He's not going down on me, is he?

I bring my hands down to cover myself. "Dax, wait..."

He looks up, his gaze questioning. "Tell me you don't want me to, Harlow, and I won't."

"It's just that... no one's ever... and I mean, no one..." I can't continue. It sounds pathetic. It's like some undiscovered country, and in many ways it is. Even I haven't discovered it yet.

Dax's brow furrows as he moves back up, so we're level on the bed again. Great. Guess I just killed the mood. "What do you mean, no one?"

I cover my face in my hands, but Dax pulls one hand away. I open one eye and see him studying my face. "But if you want to do it, then–"

"This isn't only about me or what I want, Harlow. It's about you and what you want. Would you want me to?"

His words surprise me. Not the question, but the one about this being about me and what I want. Sure, sex with Jeff had started out fun at first, but it almost felt like two nerds going at it, and before long, it became a duty because we wanted to have a baby so bad. And when IVF came along, it was almost non-existent. It didn't help that he wasn't exactly big, something I would never be caught dead mentioning to anyone, not even Jeff. Instead, I told myself for years that it was the motion of the ocean that mattered, not the size of the ship.

"Would you want me to, Harlow?" Dax asks again.

"I think so, but I have to warn you..."

His frown deepens, his expression perplexed now. "Warn me about what?"

"I'm frigid."

Dax stares at me. "You're what?"

"I'm frigid," I whisper as loud as I can as if it's a secret I don't want anyone else to know. It's also embarrassing.

"That's it? Is this from a doctor? Like a diagnosis?"

I pause. Jeff *is* a doctor. "Well, kinda, but not from a professional standpoint."

"And *he* called you frigid." Dax almost sounds

annoyed when he says it, and now I'm really uncomfortable.

"Well, yes," I stammer. "I guess I just don't... you know..."

"No, I don't know, Harlow. Tell me. I don't read minds."

"I don't... you know... climax. Orgasm... that kind of thing."

"Those are two different things, Harlow. Being frigid and not having an orgasm," he says, frowning. "Did he?"

"You mean, did he ejaculate?"

"No, I mean, come."

I feel my cheeks color. "Well, yes. Guys always do." I'm met with an arched eyebrow. "Don't they?"

This time, Dax doesn't answer right away. It's as if he's probably wondering how the hell he can get himself out of this crazy woman's bed as fast as he can and get a real woman in town instead, someone with no silly baggage like yours truly.

"God, Dax, I'm so sorry I messed this up."

"No, you didn't," he says, pushing a lock of hair behind my ear. "Look, why don't we start over?"

"Start over what? I mean, in what way?"

"Like this." Dax lowers his head and kisses me softly, his tongue brushing along my top lip. It's a kiss that sets the butterflies in my belly fluttering. "Don't think of anyone else. Right now, there's just us. You. Me. And no one else." His words alternate in between kisses, and I can't help but sigh at the sensations that engulf me. "This is all about you, Harlow."

His other hand slides down my breast, palming it. He

rubs my nipple between his thumb and index finger. Then he pinches it, and I gasp, my eyes widening. He's watching me, studying me with a gaze that's heavy with desire for me, his nostrils flaring. It's as if he's taking me in with all of his being, each glance, each kiss, every caress just for me.

"Just let go." Dax's mouth leaves my lips, his tongue tracing lazy circles on the skin of my neck down to my hollow at the base of my throat. I feel myself shiver at the many sensations that hit me, my legs instinctively parting as he settles his body between my thighs, our hips meeting and his erection pressing against my belly. "Don't worry about me or whether I come. I can take care of myself, but right now, let me take care of you."

"But..." My objection turns into a moan as his hand cups my mound, his fingers finding me soaking wet. His mouth descends on my nipple, and I grip the sheets around me.

"Just let yourself go and forget the world outside this room. This place. It's just you and me under the full moon and the stars," Dax murmurs as he slips one finger inside me and I cover my mouth with my hand as I groan. When his thumb finds my sensitive clit, I shiver with anticipation. He slips another finger inside me as he takes my other breast in his mouth, nibbling my nipple between his teeth.

"Dax..." My senses are on overdrive, the things he does to me sending me to the brink before pulling back, not letting me lose myself completely. Not yet. Dax is right; I need to shut off my brain and let my body take over. By the time he makes his way down my body, his beard tickling my belly and then my inner thighs, I offer no resistance. He flattens his tongue against my slick folds, and I lean back into the pillows, the feel of his tongue warm and heavenly.

He grips the sides of my thighs, keeping me in place as I lose myself in the many sensations that hit me. I feel my body tighten, an orgasm building as Dax alternates between sucking my sensitive clit and fucking me with his tongue and his fingers. I must have screamed with that first orgasm, and then the next one after that. And when I completely let go, finally let go, I swear I see stars.

CHAPTER FOURTEEN

Dax

WHEN HARLOW TOLD me no one had ever gone down on her before, to say I went to town would have been an understatement. What did she mean, no one had ever gone down on her before? She tastes fucking amazing, and I could have gone longer than the hour I did, hearing her—feeling her—come for me four times, her cries echoing throughout the room as her body shuddered with each orgasm. Lil D begged for release but he'd have to wait, not when I was on a damn mission to prove to Harlow just what she'd been missing all this time.

Is her ex-husband blind? Harlow is the most beautiful woman I've ever met. Naked and vulnerable, she's perfection. A woman with brains and a body made for sin, her skin smelling of vanilla and lavender with the perfect curves that make me rock hard at the mere sight of her. Her breasts, her slim waist, her broad hips—even the horizontal scar just below her belly—all uniquely her. And her taste—I can't get enough of it, and to think no one had never tasted her essence before tonight was a rush like nothing I'd ever felt before. I felt like fucking Columbus sighting the Americas for the first time. Sure, it's a bit of an overkill saying that but I'm a fucking dude, and knowing I'm her first in something like this is a huge turn-on. With Harlow, it definitely is for me, and I want this to be all about her.

For the next few minutes, I watch Harlow sleep. There's no trace of tension on her face now; she's glowing like a cat, fully sated and there's a faint smile on her lips. It's no myth when they say sex can get rid of pent-up frustrations. It does, and it doesn't even have to be fucking, but a sexual release that allows the body to let go. And man, did Harlow let go.

I gently move my arm from under her head and quietly slide out of bed. I hate to leave her, but I need to make a few calls. I should have done it the moment I got home to Nana's house the night Harlow had her gun out, but I'd also been in the midst of getting some business stuff squared away with the main office. I also didn't want to pry. It's not my style to pry.

But things have changed. I like Harlow—a lot—and that can be a dangerous thing, just like Nana told me the night after I took her with me to Bandolier National Park.

You love too much, mijo. Just be careful, okay? She's going to break your heart just like—

I'll be fine, Nana, I had assured her, not wanting to hear her say their names. They were ex-girlfriends for a reason. *I'm cool.*

But after today, I'm not so sure just how cool I can be around Harlow. I just punched her lawyer, for crying out loud. And even if the asshole deserved it, that's still assault and battery.

I go back to my workroom to retrieve my phone. Standing by the window, the moon is hidden by thick clouds tonight. Solar lights I'd set up along the perimeter of the Pearl and even its circular roofs make it look like a beacon in the darkness, complete with lights bordering the gravel driveway. It's a beautiful place to find peace, though right now, peace is the farthest thing from my mind.

I want answers.

Why would her lawyer fly all the way here to deliver those documents? How much is this Hamptons property? Must be a lot for him to haul his ass all the way here.

I dial my friend, Cole Chambers, a lawyer at Chambers, Maynard, & Lipman. He's not yet a senior partner, but his father, Lionel Chambers, heads the firm that represents corporations like my own. Lionel and my dad are friends from way back, and when I started making a name for myself in the custom furniture business, it made sense to have them represent my company. And though no one has sued me over a broken handle or accused me of faulty design, there are people out there quick to claim that they invented it first even though it doesn't do them any good to sue me. But if it gets their name in the headlines, sometimes the risk is worth it.

"Hey, dude, what's up?" Cole answers on the third ring as I head to the far end of the Earthship. I don't want Harlow to hear what I'm about to say. "I hear Phoebe Taylor is representing your lady friend as soon as the judge approves the change."

"I guess that will take time, right?"

"Maybe, but Phoebe specializes in that kind of thing, and that's why I referred her," Cole says. "So, my man, what's up?"

"What do you know about this Jeff guy? Her ex-husband?"

"Manhattan may be small, Dax, but it's not *that* small," Cole says, laughing. "He's a regular at the club, that I can tell you."

"Where Dad goes?"

Cole laughs. "Yeah, where your dad raves to everyone about your latest accomplishments and your designs."

"Oh, great. He's still doing that?"

"Damn straight. How do you think you're getting all those orders pouring in with barely any advertising? Your dad's proud of you, man. Hey, I know you're in your man-cave right now, but is your old man still in Flagstaff?"

"Yes, and probably hating every minute of it," I reply, chuckling. Dad actually doesn't hate the place. He just hates being there alone because it makes him sad. It's where Mama retreated after her cancer diagnosis, falling in love with Flagstaff while visiting an old high school friend who'd settled there. It's also where she requested to have some of her ashes scattered, and right now, there's a River Birch tree growing right where she used to sit next to a stream behind the house. And I bet, right now, Dad's there talking to her. We both do.

"So why are you asking about this Jeff guy? He's some big-shot surgeon, from what I've heard, but then, so is his wife. She's one of the top transplant surgeons in the country. Or she was, if the talk is to be believed," Cole says.

"What talk?"

"My cousin, Jen, works at Miller Gen, and she told me that Dr. James had to leave the hospital six months ago. One day she was doing her usual rounds, and the next day, she was gone," Cole replies.

"No malpractice?"

"Not that I know of, but Jen told me that Jeff threatened the Board he was going to some other hospital if they didn't let her go. I mean, he's Director of Transplant Surgery, so I'm sure the Board had to work around that situation very carefully so she wouldn't sue them. But guess what? Jen says Dr. James does have reason to sue them. The nurses think it's harassment, and that her record is impeccable. No reason for them at all to let her go the way they did. I don't care if it's bad practice to have two doctors in the midst of an acrimonious divorce treating patients in the same hospital, but there are ways to go around that legally." Cole exhales before continuing. "Jen did say that Dr. James had a nervous breakdown after her baby was born. They couldn't save the kid, and after that, nothing could save the marriage. They'd been trying to get pregnant for five years."

"Jen sure knows a lot," I mutter, my muscles tightening at the thought of Harlow and her baby.

"She works in the OR, so she was right there when everything was going down. She says he'd been having an affair with his office assistant all through his wife's pregnancy. Everyone knew but his wife. She was too busy juggling her surgery schedule and dealing with her pregnancy. Why she didn't just take an early maternity leave I have no idea."

If I already hated the guy, I hate him even more. "Did anything else happen?"

"Nah, just the usual divorce shit you wouldn't wish on anyone," Cole replies. "And with two highly successful people like Jeff Gardner and Harlow James, it all boils down to money. Who gets what, how much, depreciation, appreciation, everything. Too bad she delayed the divorce because his big wedding in the Hamptons sure ain't happening now."

"Can you blame her? And so soon after their kid dying? It hasn't even been a year then," I say, seething.

"No, it hasn't."

"Can you believe that her lawyer flew all the way here to get her to sign off her share of their property in the Hamptons? He said, and I quote, 'be a good girl and sign it,' before she told him to fuck off."

"That was unprofessional of him. And to fly all the way to New Mexico to advise his client is not very smart," Cole says, his voice serious now.

"I punched him."

"That wasn't very smart of you either. I sure hope he was on your property when you did it. Still, that's something I'll deal with when he decides to sue."

"*When* he decides to sue?"

Cole chuckles. "What can I say? He's a lawyer, and so am I. It takes one to know one. But you do have one of the best firms in the country representing you so even if he does, you're in good hands."

"Thanks for the support," I say wryly. "I'll remember that when Millie emails me the dimensions of that custom tub she wants for your wedding present."

"Hey! Now don't get me in trouble with my girl," Cole protests before he lapses into silence for a few moments. "Say it ain't so, Dax, my man. You really like this one."

The memory of Harlow making the first move comes back to me and my stomach tightens. That kiss had come as a surprise though one that was certainly far from unwelcome.

I look at the direction of the master bedroom where the woman I can't stop thinking about lies sleeping. "Even if I do, don't be spreading it around, alright?"

Harlow wakes up an hour later although she doesn't say anything as she gazes at the ceiling.

I've been watching her all this time, memorizing the contours of her cheekbones and the slope of the bridge of her nose, even the exact placement of what looks like a chicken pox scar on her left temple. I had decided the moment I got back into bed that I was going to gaze at the most beautiful woman I've ever met—a transplant surgeon and a professor, no less. I don't even care that she's still, technically, married to an asshole.

There's vulnerability to Harlow as she sleeps, in the way she tucks her face against my chest when I gather her in my arms. There's no trace of the transplant surgeon who knows way more stuff than I do, only the woman I'm falling too hard and fast for.

"Penny for your thoughts," I murmur as she turns her head to face me.

"Thank you for staying," Harlow says, her voice hoarse.

"I wouldn't want to overstay my welcome, not when you've already paid for your stay."

"It's only money, Dax. You can't take it with you."

"You're right," I say, regretting my words. I don't even give a shit about the money. The only reason I rent out the Pearl is so that it's not empty most of the year. I also like the idea of my mother's namesake being a sanctuary for people from all over the world.

"What if Frank comes back?" Harlow asks as she turns to face me.

The concern is a valid one, and I see the worry in her eyes. "He won't, not if he knows what's good for him. Do you think he'll come back after what happened?"

"No, but I just realized how isolated this place is."

I chuckle. "You did? Just now?"

"No, it was when you were, um," she casts her gaze downward, to the space between our hips hidden underneath the sheets, "down there getting busy, and you made me come so hard I could have sworn I screamed."

"You did. But I'm not complaining."

"It made me realize that while I probably won't need to worry about neighbors complaining, it's probably not good if I'm in trouble. Like in an emergency."

She does have a point, but I've stayed here by myself countless times. But then, I don't have lawyers flying halfway across the country demanding I sign documents, and there are the Villier brothers, one of them an ex-Marine. "Would you like me to stay?"

"Just for tonight, if you don't have any other plans."

I shake my head. "Well, now that you mentioned it. I need to cancel my date with this hot chick—"

"You wouldn't dare, Dax Drexel!" She fake punches my chest, and I pull her to me, inhaling the scent of her hair. Great, there goes my dick snapping to attention at just the scent of vanilla and lavender. Harlow looks up at me. "You never got to, you know—"

"No, I don't know. Tell me," I reply, my eyes narrowing as her gaze lowers and her cheeks redden. Am I mistaken, or is Harlow embarrassed to say the words? Surely she can't be...I can't even think of the word, but just like no one's ever gone down on her, has her sex life been pretty much, well, *boring*?

But before I can conclude that her sex life was that boring until I came along, Harlow slips her hand under the sheets and traces a straight line from my sternum down to my belly button. Her hand moves lower, finding me already hard and throbbing. When she glides her palm along the underside of my dick to cup my balls and give them a gentle squeeze, I just about lose it. Her sex life before me may have been boring, but Harlow is full of surprises.

"I sure hope you're not just teasing me, Harlow," I say, figuring that if she doesn't say it, I have no complaints about hands-on demonstrations. "If you play, you gotta pay."

She leans closer and kisses me softly on the lips. "Is this kiss payment enough?"

"Nope."

"What about this one?" She plants a kiss on my chest,

her tongue circling my left nipple as she wraps her hand around my length and squeezes again.

"A little, but you're still running a deficit, Dr. James. May I suggest going a little lower?"

"Really?"

"Really."

Harlow slides her body lower on the bed, her tongue tracing an imaginary line down my torso. By the time she positions herself between my legs, I allow her to push me flat on my back as I tuck a pillow under my head so I can watch her.

"Is this low enough?" she asks, and this time, I have no words left as Harlow first runs her tongue along the underside of my dick, taking her time as she goes from base to tip. Then she covers the head with her mouth, sucks and then releases it with a gentle smacking sound before repeating the move again, and a few other moves that leave me gripping the sheets and moaning.

Her technique is flawless, her hands also keeping busy and sending tingles up and down my spine all the way to the tips of my toes. Fuck! It's all I can do to finally let go and come and I sure can if I wanted to, but I don't want to. I want to be inside her. Now.

"Damn, Harlow! Did you write the manual?" I pull Harlow toward me, so her face is level with mine. Any more of her mouth on my dick and it will all be over.

She runs her tongue along her lips playfully. "Well, thanks to your free Wi-Fi, not all my online research has been about transplant medicine."

How a woman can inflame me like she does, making me want to risk everything, I have no idea. All I know is that I want Harlow James—if that is even her name—though I'm beyond caring. She could be Thelma and Louise all rolled into one, on the run with a gun and a damn good story that I'm falling hard for.

But right now, I don't care about the details. The only details that matter are the feel of her body against mine, the taste of her mouth on my tongue and the feeling of being inside her. I push her onto her back and kiss her neck, running my tongue along the skin between her neck and shoulders. She digs her fingers into the skin of my back as I keep going, kissing her breasts and sucking on her nipple, one and then the other. I move lower, raking my fingers along the skin of her back as I kiss her belly, running my tongue along the horizontal scar just above her mound.

I reach for the condom packet from the bedside table, ripping it open with my teeth. Harlow sits up just as I start rolling it on my cock and brings her hands over mine.

"May I? It's part of my research, too."

I gently pull my hands away, allowing her to take over as she does the honors with surgical precision as my cock throbs in front of her. Fuck, but she's going to be the death of me.

"You did have more than one of these, right? Because you're going to need more than one," she teases as I push her down on the bed and position my cock at her entrance. I can feel her so wet, the feel of her so exquisite.

"I have more than one, alright," I chuckle. "I've got a whole box."

Capturing her lips in a deep kiss, I bury myself inside her, feeling her nails raking my back. I feel her walls squeeze around me, adjusting to me. The sensations that hit me send me gasping for breath.

Her moans fill the room, her head arched back as she cries out my name. I move my hips, feeling her walls wrap around my cock, and I know I can't speak anymore. I let my actions tell her what I want her to know, that she's beautiful and amazing, and that she's perfect just the way she is no matter what the ghosts inside her head tell her.

There's nothing else in this world I want to do but make her happy and if it's another box of condoms and a whole lot of chafing in the morning, then so be it. But I also know that this is not just about the sex. There's something else, but I'm not about to say it out loud. Not yet.

But as I look into Harlow's brown eyes, there's one thing I can no longer deny. I'm more lost than I've ever been before. It's a feeling that's calmed only by the touch of her fingers on my face as we both come together, and the taste of her lips on mine when she breathes my name.

CHAPTER FIFTEEN

There, I've done it. Technically, I've just had my first extramarital affair! I am still married, after all, although, at this moment, I don't care. If I were honest, what I really want to say is, *I don't give a flying fuck if I had an affair or not.*

I liked it. Who am I kidding? I loved it.

And when Dax made love to me the second and third times last night, I loved it even more. I think I'm addicted to it. To dick. Dax's dick. Oh, great. I'm even saying it—dick.

My mind is racing. My body is numb. Or maybe not so numb. Sore. Especially down there. Chafed is probably a better word. But who wouldn't get chafed if you've been going at it all night and after a break to have an early morning dinner that was really breakfast, you were at it again? Do women have this problem? Maybe they do; it's not like my research extends to what other women feel, although I did research positions and blowjobs, specifically, how to give the best, mind-blowing blowjob. *Thank you, Cosmo.*

Even my lips are numb as are my forearms. Who knew my forearms would need work? Maybe it's technique? Or maybe it's because, before Dax, I've never given anyone a blowjob before? Jeff surely didn't want one, not from me—something about him not wanting to see me doing "such a thing" because I was better than that, whatever *that* meant. Of course, I bought it then and thought myself pretty damn special, so special that he couldn't see me going down on him, which gave him the perfect excuse not to go down on me at all. But that was before I overheard the nurses talk about how Leilani gave him blowjobs that she'd boasted about it at a party one of the nurse practitioners attended. That's how their affair had started, her giving him blowjobs in his office when he'd stay late, supposedly writing his patient notes. Sure.

My mind is a jumble of thoughts and questions that it feels like a full-blown conference in there. All the observations are about my body and how I'm feeling. It's as if I'm back in my body again after being out of it for so long, always in my head analyzing everything until there's nothing left to analyze.

But I'm back, even though I don't recall a time when I was ever in my body, to begin with. I'd always been the foster kid who moved from school to school, burying her nose in books in the hopes that one day, she wouldn't need anyone to want her and eventually adopt her. She wouldn't end up in households that didn't deserve having a single kid under its roof. She'd be an island, doing well if not better, all by herself.

Well, you did become an island, Harlow. You alienated everyone with your damn brilliance, and here you are, all alone.

I force myself back to the present, back in the bed that I'm sharing with Dax. He's still asleep and totally worn out, poor kid. I hate calling him a kid but that's what he is. I don't even know how old he is, but I'm pretty sure he hasn't seen thirty, which means he's more than ten years my junior. He must think me starved for sex, like a cougar on the hunt for her next victim.

But Dax would be right to think it. I haven't had sex since before I got pregnant with Marcus, which means I'm pushing almost two years. Jeff and I had stopped having sex because of the stress from the fertility treatments, and probably because IVF made it easy for us not to bother trying. He ejaculated into a cup while my eggs matured in a lab and from there, some equipment did the rest. Coupled with my current schedule then—surgeries and conferences—it proved the perfect combination to kill anyone's sex drive including mine. I still remember the exact time it happened, too, although this one had nothing to do with stress, and I told myself I'd never ask for it again.

That night, I was standing by the door of his office in our Upper East Side apartment, dressed in a sexy get-up supposedly guaranteed to turn on any man—or woman, for that matter. But apparently, no one had told Jeff. He'd been working on something on his laptop, his headphones on when he finally looked up after I stood there for almost two minutes, feeling more uncomfortable with each passing second.

Frisky, eh? He'd asked, raising his eyebrows and laughing, amused.

The words stung, but I persevered. I was so horny that I didn't care if his little dick was going to please me even though what I had wanted most of all was to feel sexy again. To feel like a woman. I wanted him to want me, not because we needed to get pregnant, but just for me, as a woman.

I was just thinking, maybe you and me—

Come on, Harlow. You're better than that. You're my wife, not some two-bit whore. Now take that thing off and let's pretend this fucking thing didn't happen. If you want us to do it, pick a better time. And then Jeff chuckled, shaking his head before returning to whatever it was he was watching on his laptop.

Up until then, I'd thought he was working on a new research paper, but he wasn't. The reflection on his reading glasses of some woman in the middle of a three-way told me exactly what was more important to him that night, and every night after that. But I wasn't about to stoop to his level and address that then, not after I'd just been rebuffed like, well, some two-bit whore whose time had long been up.

Two years later that laugh still taunts me whenever I feel ugly. But at the same time, I should have known how much he hated me then, and how, after getting used to hearing me described as *Dr. Gardner's wife*, he suddenly found himself answering to *Dr. James's husband.*

I want a wife and mother to my kids, Harlow, he told me after one more person described him as Dr. James' husband at a conference where we were both speakers, *not someone who's going to be in competition for every damn achievement.*

I should have stayed home like Jeff wanted. I should have cut back on my hours and taken better care of myself, getting my body ready to carry another fetus to term instead of always thinking I could do it all—a wife, a mother, and a surgeon.

But what good would all that wishing do me now? I don't want to be Jeff's wife. Sure, the day someone served me my divorce papers in front of my patients ranks up there as one of the most humiliating days of my life, but so did the night Jeff laughed at me. After that night, I didn't want to be his wife or his partner, someone he apparently detested but stayed with because it would have looked bad on his reputation. *Our reputation.* We had been a team, and that's why I had stayed, too—until suddenly we weren't a team at all. Holding little Marcus in my arms alone in that hospital suite months later finally hammered that message through my stubborn head. Jeff couldn't even hold his stillborn son.

I get up from the bed and slip on a robe. Why can't the memories leave me alone? I want this moment to be about Dax, damn it, not Jeff. I walk out to the living room, remnants of our meal still on the table from the food Anita had packed in the cooler. Tamales for him and some locally made Greek salad for me. I'd been too nervous to eat a full meal, not when all I wanted to do was jump him on any surface that could hold us. We even watched the sunrise from the patio before hurrying back inside the master bedroom and making love again till he complained that Little D—who in reality is not little at all—needed a break. He also needed sleep.

I can't help but smile. Everything about Dax represents youth and happiness, something I desperately need right now. Ever since staying at the Pearl, today was the first time I watched the sunrise with a real smile on my face. It felt as if the sun was cleansing me of every regret I'd long held close to me like armor.

So, right now, I'll take what I can get. In two weeks, my life will be back to normal. Even with the divorce settlement delayed, Jeff will probably still have some ceremony in our Hamptons home because he can, permission I had granted through Frank over a bad connection while stopping in Houston to get my first taste of crawfish. I didn't care then if he got married on our lawn, but I sure as heck care now.

Being with Dax has awoken something inside me, and at times, it's scary. It has me feeling like a brand new person, someone I barely know yet *want* to know. After being emotionally numb for so long, I feel more alive than I've ever felt before, and now I can't help feeling selfish. I want everything that had once belonged to me returned to me.

Except for Jeff. Leilani can keep him.

I spot the messages on my phone a few minutes later. Two are from Kathy letting me know that she needs me to review a few patient files on the secure server. She also adds that I need to RSVP to Penny's party and that I should check my emails since the invitation had yet to be opened. The other two are from Penny's father, Senator Leon Kingston, asking me to call him back as soon as I get his messages. He answers on the second ring.

"Hello, Senator, it's me, Dr. James."

"What's this I hear about you being out of town? Kathy told me you're in, what, Taos? In New Mexico?"

"Yes, it is, and it's beautiful out here."

Senator Kingston chuckles. "I don't mean to pry, but after Kathy told me where you were, it made my little girl nervous. She's afraid you're not coming back to New York at all. She had to look up where Taos was."

"And I hope she found it. Many people think the state is still part of Mexico."

He laughs. "No, she knows her geography quite well. She's kept all the postcards you've sent her, although she told me the last one she got was from Albuquerque a month ago."

I sigh. Has it really been more than a month since I first stayed in Albuquerque and saw Andrea's patients at no cost? It had felt so good to return to my roots, consulting with patients who needed me the most but who wouldn't have been able to afford my rates. There's a reason why I'm Penny Kingston's doctor and why her father has the direct line to my cell phone. I've also become a boutique surgeon of sorts, hand-picked by the rich and famous to perform the required surgeries or consultations whenever I'm in the Hamptons with no worries about insurance co-payments and deductions. Seeing patients at Andrea's community clinic almost seemed like a penance, and maybe that's why she finally suggested I needed to see the rest of the state and find my joy.

You can't see patients for free forever, Harlow. Just because you're doing good here doesn't change the fact that you're still running away from something—and I'm afraid it's from yourself.

"Please tell her not to worry. I'll be there." But even as I say the words, I know that if I were to drive back, I need to start getting ready to leave. Instead, what am I doing but thinking of the young man asleep on the bed behind me and wondering when I can be with him again.

"I can send a plane for you if you want. I think there's a municipal airport in Taos, and if not there, definitely Santa Fe. We fly there a few times a year," he says before pausing. "But that's not the only reason I needed to talk to you. I also have an offer for you."

"An offer?"

"I know you never talk about what happened at Miller General, and it's something I commend you for, but one of my buddies mentioned a position that could be perfect for you. In fact, when they heard your name, they were very excited."

"What position is that?"

"Director of the Pediatric Transplant Surgery in New Haven Hospital," he replies. "Apparently, they're looking for someone to succeed the current Director, and while talking about Penny's condition, of course, your name came up."

"Wow," is all I can say for a few seconds. "But I haven't applied for anything."

"Well, now you have a reason to," the senator says.

"It's yours if you want it, and I know first-hand just how qualified you are for the position, and the people at New Haven do, too. They just need you to let them know that you're interested, and the position is yours, but you only have about two weeks to let them know and after that, it will take about six months to get you settled."

That would mean I'd need to move to Connecticut, which isn't such a bad thing. It's not that far from New York at all. I can even start over. I swallow, my throat suddenly dry. *Then why am I not saying anything yet? Why haven't I asked him the contact information?*

"I know it's a shock, but think about it. I'll have my assistant send you the details," he adds. "New Haven's not far at all, and you'll still be Penny's personal *doctor-surgeon*, as she calls you."

"Thank you, Senator," I manage to say, my voice emerging as a croak. "You don't have to do this."

"Oh, but I want to. You gave my daughter a new lease on life. Soon, she'll be running outside with her friends, and her life will be back to normal again. You have no idea just how much you've made her and us so happy. In fact, my daughter misses you more than you know."

"I miss her, too, but you have to remember that I'm only her transplant surgeon. Dr. Rowe is her transplant physician."

I hear Senator Kingston exhale on the other line. "Yes, but you were the first person she saw after her surgery. You stayed with her all night when I thought my wife was at the hospital all that time, but she'd gone home. Remember that? You have no idea how much that means to me."

Of course, I remember. I couldn't come home to our empty East Side apartment then knowing there was still a nursery that needed to be emptied. Our housekeeper didn't want to accept anything I wanted to give away, telling me that anything I had purchased for Marcus was jinxed. She was superstitious and morbid. I chose to sleep by Penny's bedside for reasons that were more for my own than for Penny. She gave me a reason not to come home, not when it was no longer a home, just another expensive space enclosed by four walls with a view of Central Park.

"I just did what any other doctor would have done, Senator," I murmur, hearing movement in the bedroom. "Sorry, but I have to go. I'll call you in a few days and touch base about Penny's birthday party. I wouldn't miss it for the world. Please give her a hug for me."

I hang up just as Dax walks out of the bedroom, already dressed in his jeans and the shirt he wore yesterday. He's even wearing his boots. "Wow, you're up and dressed. And here I was thinking we'd do another round."

"Maybe later," he says, chuckling. "You tired me out, you wild woman, you."

"So, is that why you're itching to get away from me before I get my claws on you again?"

Dax comes up to me and kisses the tip of my nose. "No, but Nana is worried about me. I didn't come home last night, you see, and neither did I let her know that I was staying over." He pauses as I make a worried face before continuing. "Benny texted me and said he and

Sarah kept her company in the living room watching some Mexican soap opera till four in the morning. She said she couldn't sleep because she'd drank coffee too late, but they suspect she was waiting up for me. Benny says he now has a greater appreciation for Mexican telenovelas."

"I had no idea you had a curfew, Dax."

"I didn't either. But it's my fault. I didn't let her know that I was staying over. As far as she knows, I'm only supposed to stay here during the day."

"So what are you going to tell her?"

He shrugs. "The truth."

"That you're sleeping with your guest?"

"That I'm staying over," he replies matter-of-factly. "You said so yourself. The Pearl has six rooms, three bathrooms, and..."

"Alright, alright, you made your point," I say, laughing as Dax continues enumerating the features of the Pearl playfully, his voice lowering as he nuzzles his face against mine. "Funny that even with all those features, you still ended up in the one room that happened to be occupied."

"That's because that room is the best one. It's like Goldilocks and the three bears. She picked the best room in the house."

"Really?" I eye him playfully. "So does that mean you're Goldilocks?"

"Shut up." Dax grins, his arms circling my waist. "No, I'm the little bear, and right now, you're sleeping in little bear's bed. But he has been taught to share, and that's what he's doing."

"But you're not as little as you think, not-so-little bear. You're larger than you think, larger than that...oh."

I pause as Dax's face clouds, and I can guess what he's thinking. While trying different positions last night, his condom broke, and it scared him. *Harlow,* he had said as he pulled away, *I don't want to get you—*

I didn't let him finish, pressing my finger to his lips. *I won't get pregnant, if that's what you're worried about, Dax.* And then I lied. *I'm on the Pill.* I really shouldn't have done it, but the last thing I wanted him to worry about was getting me pregnant, not when the only times I'd gotten pregnant was with IVF.

Dax smiles, resting his forehead against mine. "Should I call myself Big Bear then? Would that make Goldilocks happy?"

Dax doesn't wait for an answer as kisses me, his tongue slipping between my teeth, and I feel my knees giving way, the butterflies in my belly fluttering wildly. My hands move down his shirt, from his broad chest to his tight abs, to the front of his jeans where, already, he's hard. I rub my palm against his erection through his jeans, my imagination running wild at all the things I want to do with him under the sun-shaped skylight.

"You're ready to go again," he murmurs.

I pout. "I am, but unfortunately, you're heading home ."

"I have to," he says, exhaling as I remove my hand from the front of his jeans and give him a break. "I need to reassure Nana I'm okay."

"Are you coming back?"

"Would you like me to?" Dax asks.

"Yes. I'll even promise not to touch you."

I catch a trace of a blush on his cheeks as he looks down at his boots. "I don't know about that promise, but I'll be back tonight. Maybe we can do something fun... dinner or something."

"That would be great."

"If Frank comes back, don't let him in. Call me, okay? I'll have the brothers keep an eye out for him."

"The brothers?"

Dax cocks his head to the window and points to the nearest Earthship a quarter of a mile away. It's much smaller than the Pearl and I see two trucks parked outside, their glass windows reflecting in the sun. "Todd and Sawyer Villier live over there. They helped me build the Pearl and sometimes they keep an eye out for me when the place is unoccupied."

"Oh."

"They're good people." Dax gives me one last kiss before I walk him to the door, and I force myself to turn away the moment he drives off. I don't want to watch him leave, not when the Pearl already feels so empty without him. But maybe it's only because Dax is so damn good in bed that I'm feeling this way, and soon, I'll forget all about him.

This is all temporary, I tell myself as I force all thoughts of Dax out of my mind, power up my laptop, and get to work.

CHAPTER SIXTEEN

Dax

I'M *twenty-seven years old and last I looked, I didn't have a fucking curfew.*

That's what I tell myself again and again as I drive back to Nana's house. The thought smarts, but then why the hell does it? Is it because I actually feel terrible for purposely not telling Nana that I was staying over, knowing she'd assume I'd sleep with Harlow?

Nana already knows I'm smitten, fawning over Harlow like a lap dog. I hang on to her every word, even though she barely says anything about her life. What little I know about her seems like it's been regulated by a damn PR company.

She doesn't trust anyone, mijo. She's been hurt, and I'm afraid she's going to hurt you.

Who knows? Maybe Nana is right. But I can't deny what my heart is telling me—hell, what my whole body has been screaming at me since I first crashed into her. It vibrates around Harlow, making me feel so alive. All I can think of are the many things I want to make with her in mind. Exquisite boxes, cabinets, doorways with the moon and the stars, just the way I see her lighting up my night sky. I want to create a lotus-shaped tub in her name, maybe in some exotic wood I've yet to find. Damn! Cole is right. I like Harlow. No, I don't just like her. I'm falling for her. Hard.

Just before the intersection leading to Nana's house, I make a U-turn back into town. I need to do something first, even if it means I'm assuming too much. Would it even matter to her that I'm about to do something I haven't done this fast before? Whatever. Right now, it matters to me. I'll make my way to Nana's house after I'm done.

I glance at the rearview mirror, glad that I don't bear signs of what happened in the last few hours. There are no visible hickeys and that's a good thing. I already look like a lovesick puppy as it is. The last thing I need is for people to see Harlow's marks on me because, damn, but that woman bites!

Ten minutes later, I enter the Vasquez Family Practice office and walk up to the front desk where Claudia Romero eyes me suspiciously. She's a striking woman, with hazel eyes that she emphasizes with way too much eyeliner and thin lips that she fills in with stark red lipstick. She's really a naturally beautiful girl underneath all that makeup, but it's also her business card. When she's not harassing patients like me from behind the counter, she's applying makeup to teens for quinciñera and wedding parties. She's clearly not happy to see me but I'm here as a patient, not as her childhood friend and former boyfriend.

"What do you want, Dax?" Her voice is clipped, matching her angry expression and I give her a quizzical look. *What the fuck did I do now?*

"I need to see the doctor."

"Do you have an appointment?"

I look around me where all the seats are empty, magazines in disarray. "No, Claudia, but there's no one else here, so guess that means he should be ready to see me now."

"There's no one here because we're on lunch and I was just getting ready to lock the door. You'll need to come back when we reopen at three." She jabs her index finger to the clock behind her, telling me it's just after one in the afternoon.

"I need to see him now, Claudia—if he's available. I know he's here because his car's right outside." I prop my elbows on the counter and engage her in a glaring contest. Gabriel "Gabe" Vasquez is one of my best friends who busted his ass to be the first doctor in his family. He could be working full-time at some big hospital in the big city, but he opted to open a small clinic closer to home instead. To help pay for his student loans, he drives down to Albuquerque every other weekend to work two shifts as an ER doctor at some big private hospital.

"No," Claudia says, scowling. "He's busy."

"Did I just hear Big D out there?" shouts a voice from the hallway and Claudia rolls her eyes as she mouths the words, *lucky bastard*, and pushes herself away from the counter. I wrinkle my nose at her, and she scowls even more.

To say Claudia and I didn't have a clean break-up is an understatement, considering she's still clearly pissed off at me. Gabe, Claudia, and I grew up together and I've dated her on and off since high school. I've only had two serious relationships in my life so far, her and Madison. But somehow Claudia thinks I left her for Madison even though she was the one who cheated on me first with some guy she met at a bar in Albuquerque, not realizing that I was in town that same weekend—and at the same club hoping to surprise her. The guy told me so himself when I was in the men's bathroom taking a leak.

You need to pay more attention to your girl, dude. I just fucked her, and she liked it.

He was so drunk when he said it, barely able to keep himself upright, but like I cared. In less than a minute, he was a drunk missing a few teeth and clinging to the urinal till he slipped and ended up with his face full of piss. He was my first battery charge, and until I punched Harlow's lawyer, he would have been my last. My parents and Nana grounding me for the whole summer drilled my need for anger management even though Mama later admitted that she would have done the same thing if she were a man.

What would you have done then, I remember asking her, *you know, you being a woman?*

I'd have punched her lights out, just the same.

Claudia later told me that she did it to make me jealous, hoping I'd spend more time with her than with my mentor, Takeshi-san, learning Japanese carpentry. Five years later, and she still looks at me like I'm the most despicable man to walk the earth for choosing to focus on my craft. I wouldn't have traded that experience for anything, not when a year later, Takeshi-san would be gone.

Gabe emerges from one of the treatment rooms and buzzes me in. I push the door open, ignoring Claudia as she brushes past me in a huff. If she weren't Gabe's cousin, her ass would have been fired by now but she knows she can get away with it. And of course, I let her. Taos is a small town and the three of us grew up together. Claudia and I were each other's firsts—first love, first time, first breakup, although that last one would be repeated quite a few times. Maybe one day we'd look back and laugh about it all, but today isn't the day.

"Told ya she still likes you," Gabe says, chuckling under his breath. "You're still single, right?"

"Shut up, man."

Gabe laughs as he gives me a quick hug. He probably would have hated me for breaking his cousin's heart if he hadn't been inside that bathroom with me and heard what the guy said. "I thought you weren't going to be in town for two more weeks."

"I'm not, but I got my days all wrong," I reply. "No wonder Dad was, like, *what do you mean I need to fly up there and take over?* But he knows better than to complain. He's just as in tune to my need to recharge like Nana is."

Gabe eyes me curiously. "Well, you got to do what you got to do, man. You're winning awards, sure, but sometimes, you just gotta take time off for yourself." He pauses and takes a deep breath. "So I hear you're here as a patient; that's a first. Got the clap or something?"

I glare at him.

"Looks like you lost your sense of humor somewhere along the way from Flagstaff to Taos."

"I need you to test me," I say, shifting my weight from foot to foot. "You know, one of those things that show if I've got some STD or something. Or AIDS. Whatever guys get to prove to people they're clean, that kind of thing."

"You're really serious, aren't you?"

"What do you think?"

"You'll have to pee in a cup."

"I'll do it."

"I'll swab the inside of your cheek like they do on *CSI*."

I shrug. "I brushed my teeth so my breath won't kill you."

"I'll have to draw blood."

I grit my teeth. "Bring it on, man."

Gabe takes a deep breath and slaps my shoulder. "Okay then, let's get you started."

With one of his phlebotomists still in the office labeling a few vials, it's my lucky day. After she swabs the inside of my cheek and has me pee in a cup, she orders me to sit down on a seat in front of her and make a fist while tying a piece of rubber tubing around my bicep. I can't even look at her name tag to make casual conversation, not when my heart is beating so fast the moment I feel the needle pierce my skin. A few minutes later she's done, and I blow out a long deep breath as she tells me to place my finger on a piece of gauze and she slaps on a strip of tape on it. For someone who hates needles and the sight of blood, I can't believe I'm doing this.

"Double-check your name on the stickers, please," she says before pointing to a few lines on a medical form and handing me a pen. "Sign here and print your name."

As soon as I finish signing the patient form, I hurry out of the room and meet Gabe in the hallway.

"So who is she?" he asks, beckoning me to step into his office and sit down. "You've never asked me to do this before. But don't worry. I won't tell anyone. Your information is confidential."

"And Claudia?"

"If she doesn't want our office to get in trouble with HIPAA, then she won't say anything. But I can drop off the paperwork at the Pearl the moment I get it, so no one else can see it. Want me to do that?"

"That would be great. Call me first in case I may not be at the Pearl."

Gabe frowns. "You staying with Nana then? How come?"

"Because someone's renting my place," I wonder how much I should tell him but decide today's not the day for that. "Actually, it's complicated."

"How so?" Gabe eyes me curiously. "You're not worried you got something, are you?"

I shake my head. "Hell, no. I may be a man-whore, man, but it's safe sex all the way."

"But...?"

I exhale. No, I'm not ready to tell anyone just yet. "You know the drill, man."

"She asked you to get one?"

I start to get up from the chair. "Nope. This is all me. Anyway, call me as soon as you have the results, okay? I don't want to intrude on your lunch."

"Is this the woman you had dinner with the other day? Everyone's talking about it."

I sit back down, frowning. I know Taos is a small town, but it's not *that* small. "What's everyone talking about?"

"Dyami told his classmates all about the woman doctor Tito Dax had over for dinner at the house," Gabe says, grinning. "He said she told him about how pee-pees work."

"Oh, great, and I'm sure a lot of what she said is now lost in the telling." I make a mental note to tell Dyami to stop blabbing about my love life, or I'll tell Santa not to get him an X-box for Christmas.

"Now you know why Claudia's ticked off with you—again."

"She can't keep hoping she and I will get togeth-er," I say. "Isn't she seeing Tony what's-his-name?"

"Tony? Nah, not anymore. He's working on some TV series in Vancouver but she didn't want to move there. Can you imagine Claudia out there? She's such a South-west chick it's not funny."

We both shake our heads, chuckling because we both know we're no different. Even I can't imagine myself out there. I love the sun too much. While I don't mind skiing, what with Taos Ski Valley just an hour away, I hate the snow—specifically, Eastern seaboard snow which turns gray and wet as it melts, just like Mama hated it while living in Manhattan. She'd met Dad as a student at Hunter college while hanging out with her friends at some Midtown bar. He courted her the old-fashioned way with flowers, dinners, and picnics at the park—even love letters whenever she returned to Taos for the holidays—which essentially won even Nana's heart.

She tried to live in Manhattan after they got married and had Sarah. Dad's brokerage company was based right in the Financial District, but eventually, she couldn't stand the sound of one more blast of a car horn or the shout of an irate New Yorker. By the time she was pregnant with me, she decided to move back in with Nana, and Dad had to commute. Heck, he still does, though this time, it's so he can oversee my company's books in Flagstaff and pop in to say hello to Sarah and Nana.

"Why don't you two come over the house tomorrow? We're having a barbecue," Gabe says. "You got me curious about this woman now, especially one who can impress Dyami like that, or have you come in here and allow someone to jab you with a needle without you knocking their lights out first."

"She just might be busy, but I'll ask her."

"She's on vacation, right?" Gabe says. "Come on over at two or three. Heck, anytime, for that matter. I'll be grilling some steaks, man."

"Let's play it by ear."

"We're making *barbacoa*," he adds in a sing-song voice.

I stare at him for a few moments, my mouth watering

at the thought of slow-roasted meat smothered with adobo sauce and accompanied with lime rice and bottles of chilled beer. "You better be making *barbacoa*, man. Don't torture me like that."

Gabe chuckles, studying me. "You must really like her, Dax. You're never like this."

"Shut up," I say as Gabe's office phone rings, but he waits till it goes to voicemail. I get up from my chair. Any more talk about Harlow and I'll be spilling my guts out about liking her too much too fast. This is not like me at all.

Gabe gets up from his chair. "Well, if you can make it, great. If not, I'll catch you next time. The folks would love to see you, though. But I'll see if I can drop this off as soon as I get the results."

"Just don't tell anyone."

"Of course, I won't. I'm a fucking doctor, man. We don't say nothing to no one."

I have to laugh out loud. Sounds just like a doctor I know, though with Gabe, I don't see him sitting around with a gun lying in front of him and a note asking for forgiveness.

When I arrive at Nana's, she's outside weeding her vegetable garden. She plants kale, lettuce, onions, eggplants, tomatoes, and cucumbers as well as herbs like cilantro, dill, and basil. I love rubbing my fingers between the leaves of the lemon verbena bush right by the driveway and smell its aroma on my skin. Sometimes she allows the older kids from the preschool next door to come over and help her harvest, teaching them how to spot an eggplant that's ready or a cucumber that's best used for its seeds instead.

She grows peppers, too. If I had my way, I'd have green chile on everything, even my fried eggs. Dad used to roll his eyes whenever I'd return from Nana's house with bags of red and green New Mexican chile packed in the cab of my truck, but I've also seen him sneak a bag or two in his luggage back to New York.

"Want to help me with these, *mijo?*" she asks as I sit on my haunches next to her and begin pulling some weeds. She doesn't need to tell me what to do for it was always my chore since I was a kid to do the weeding though I have been slacking off since I arrived.

We don't speak for a few minutes, and I shift my position so I'm kneeling on a foam pad she hands me from her gardening basket and dive into my new task. I don't care that my hands get dirty or that I'm not wearing gloves. Nana doesn't wear them either unless she's weeding. She likes talking to her plants, gently encouraging them to grow.

As she brushes against me to hand me a worn basket to toss the weeds in, I'm glad I took a quick shower in one of the smaller bathrooms while Harlow was on the phone because anyone would have smelled sex on me from the get-go. I can almost hear my heart beating against my ears, and I can't help feeling like I'm a teen again, sent home early after another fight at school because some kid called me stupid.

When Nana finally speaks, it's in Spanish, and I

know better than to answer her in English. *Do you like her, mijo?*

"Si." I don't even hesitate. With Nana, I have nothing to hide though we don't look at each as we speak. Suddenly, I'm running out of weeds to pull and I remind myself to slow down, knowing my actions are merely matching the beating of my heart. Panic mode.

Does it bother you that she's still married?

She's getting a divorce. It's complicated. They have property. And from what I hear, it's pretty expensive, probably in the millions.

I sound defensive, and I am. I hate that Harlow's husband took advantage of her grief and filed for divorce. I hate that he continues to harass her even when she clearly bailed out of the state to get away from him and everything else. I don't want to be her knight in shining armor, but I also don't want to stand on the sidelines and watch her fall apart over her vengeful husband's latest antics. Why can't he leave her alone? She also has a gun which scares the crap out of me, but at the moment, I don't know how to bring it up without giving away the fact that I was there the night she almost killed herself. I'm almost positive that had been her intention though I'd be more than happy to be proven wrong.

I can tell from the way Harlow carries herself that she's someone important. Being a pediatric transplant surgeon can't be small potatoes. She must have worked her ass off to get to that point in her career, and maybe that's where she turned to when her marriage fell apart— her work—until she had no more work to turn to, and she got in her car and drove west, ending up, of all places, at the Pearl. I really don't know. I'm just guessing because Harlow trusts no one.

Just be careful, mijo, Nana says as she starts to get up and I quickly stand up and help her to her feet. *Remember, she's only here for two weeks, and I don't want your heart broken.*

It won't.

Her eyes narrow as she studies me and I don't have to guess that she doesn't believe me. I'm in full denial, that's for sure, but I've just spent the night with the hottest, smartest woman I know and right now, I'm fried. Nana's gaze moves from the top of my mussed up hair to the tips of my boots. I wonder if there's a hickey I missed spotting in the rear-view mirror and I absently scratch my neck.

"I called Father McGuire and dedicated Sunday Mass to your Mama," she says.

"This Sunday? But her anniversary isn't until three weeks."

"*Si,* but I doubt you'll be staying here that long, *mijo.* Not to mention, your Dad is going to go crazy up in Flagstaff by himself."

I nod. She's definitely right about that.

"You're here early so we might as well celebrate Mass early, too, in case you have to go back to work sooner," she continues.

"Okay," I reply.

"Are you hungry? I made your favorite for lunch. It's on the table."

With Nana, everything she makes is my favorite, but I'll take a guess. I'm also starving I can smell it. "Adobada?"

Nana's lined face breaks into a broad grin as she cocks her head toward the house. "With *sopapillas*. Now go inside and eat up."

I stifle a yawn, nodding. "Thank you, Nana. You know I love you more than anything, right?"

"Shut up and go inside, Dax," she says, laughing when I kiss her on the cheek before she nudges me into the house. "And get some sleep. You look like something the cat dragged in."

Harlow

Dax doesn't return until it's almost nine, showered and dressed in a tight t-shirt and running pants that emphasize a very defined ass. Even though he has a key to the place, he knocks on the door, apologizing profusely for being late. He also brings me a dozen flowers. Long-stemmed red roses that remind me it's been too long since someone gave me any flowers.

"I fell asleep and just woke up." He hands me the bouquet, and for a few seconds, we do the awkward should-I-kiss-you-on-the-cheek-or-on-the-lips routine that probably plagues new lovers until he settles it with a kiss on the lips. It's a welcome treat after an afternoon that would have been overtaken by work, worry over the Senator's recommendation, and going through legal paperwork had I not left the Pearl to do some shopping.

I can't believe that in just a few hours, I've already missed the taste of Dax's lips on mine, the feel of his arms wrapped around me coupled with the smell of clean soap and that unique scent that's guaranteed to melt me into a puddle right there and then. It's based on more than 900,000 variations of the estimated 400 gene coding for the receptors in our noses. But right now, I'll settle for *man-smell*.

Dax sets his duffel bag on the couch and unzips it. "I know it's late, but I thought that maybe we could do movie night. Wi-Fi isn't the best out here and so…"

"That's an excellent idea."

He pulls out a stack of DVD's that range from total guy flicks like *Reservoir Dogs, Transformers, Tombstone,* and then a few chick flicks that he probably snagged from his sister's DVD collection. *Bridget Jones's Diary, While You Were Sleeping, Say Anything, Some Kind of Wonderful,* and *Steel Magnolias.*

"I should have called to ask if you've had anything to eat yet," he says as he follows me to the kitchen.

"I haven't, but I went to town to get some groceries and got a few other things." I pull out two bottles from a reusable grocery bag. A Pinot Noir '12 and Cabernet Sauvignon '11. I'm acutely aware that the wine cellar in the Pearl is Dax's and wonder if he's noticed that an expensive bottle—of all the wines I had to open on what would have been my last night on earth—is missing. So I'm making up for it, or I'm trying to.

"Oh, good! You found the Black Mesa Winery. They have amazing local wines," he says, grinning. "So which one would you like to try tonight?"

"Take your pick." I set two wine glasses on the kitchen counter and a wine opener.

"I like the Cabernet, but it's best with something from the grill, so maybe we can save that for later?" He picks up the Pinot Noir and peels the foil wrapper. "This one's from 100 percent New Mexico grapes, similar to the one we went to the other day. Why don't we try this one?"

"Sure." I stand in front of the open refrigerator to see what will best go with the wine—or I try to—for I have no idea what foods go with Cabernet. Anna Maria took care of things like these when Jeff and I were still together.

I hate that I feel so out of my element, and it's over something so simple, like deciding what dish to make that will go with a Cabernet. Deciding which suture to use during transplant surgery surely is a lot easier than this.

"You okay?" Dax asks as the cork pops and he deftly pours two glasses of wine, sets the bottle on the counter and stands behind me.

"I'm fine. Why do you ask?"

He wraps his arms around my waist and nuzzles his face into my neck, his beard tickling my skin. "Because you're looking too serious right now. Flustered, too."

My stomach does its usual flip-flops, and my knees just about turn to jelly as Dax squeezes me against him and breathes in my hair. I feel myself clench, memories of our night together rushing forth and I know if he keeps at this, I'll be begging him to fuck me on the dining table. *But no*, I tell myself. It's movie night.

For some weird reason, I'm curious to see how we fare without sex. I'm also sore all over, in places I didn't expect to be sore. My hips, my thighs, and... well, *down there*. I can't even say it, as if saying the alternative words for vagina is so wrong though I loved hearing them when he said them last night, of how good it felt, and how tight.

Oh, God, there I go again, my thoughts drifting, but they drift anyway.

I also hate condoms. I wish I could go, how do they call it, bareback. I know I'm free of any sexually transmitted diseases, considering I've gone through two annual gynecological exams before last night, almost two years since I've had sex. I should pull out the latest medical results from my folder, the one that I had Andrea do when I first volunteered to help out at her clinic. But then, that would be too presumptuous of me that he'd want to have sex with me without any protection. Besides, what about him? For someone as hot as Dax Drexel, just how many women has he slept with? Come to think of it, we've never talked about those things. What do people talk about on one-night stands, anyway? Surely nothing that has to do with the rates of transmission of sexually transmitted diseases and fungal infections that plague short-term relationships.

"You really are thinking quite hard about something." Dax gives me one more squeeze, a gentle graze of his lips along my neck and lets me go. "Why don't we see what you picked up from the store?"

One more second of him holding me like that and feeling his hard-on along my back and I'd have turned around and gone down on him. *No sex, Harlow. No. Sex.*

We end up preparing gourmet pizza. One is a blend of Thai chicken pizza with pre-cooked chicken pieces, with peanut sauce that Dax mixes with lemon and other spices, sprinkled with crushed peanuts on a piece of flatbread, and the second is a classic cheese pizza topped with whatever else we find on the refrigerator shelves.

Dax pulls out two thick comforters from one of the bedrooms and sets it on the couch in front of the flat screen TV. By the time we're settled with our second glasses of wine and the fully cooked pizzas in front of us, the first movie starts to play. It's *Tombstone*, and he knows the dialogue by heart. He makes me laugh with his love for Doc Holiday, and I find myself wondering what I did right in my life to deserve a moment like this. There's no pressure, and no worries of the past and the future. There's just us snuggled on the couch enjoying our wine and homemade pizzas with the new moon a sliver in the sky, and above the greenhouse before us, the sun-shaped skylight reveals a tapestry of stars.

I find myself daydreaming about us in New York doing the same thing, snuggled on the couch. Some nights we'd probably see a play or a musical, and during the summers, check out Shakespeare in the Park or stay at the Hamptons. *Can we really go beyond this moment and take it all the way out into the real world? My world? Would we make it? But is that what I really want to return to when this, right here, is perfect just the way it is?*

"The TV is over there," Dax murmurs, and I realize I'm staring at him instead of the screen.

"It is?" My hand drifts lower, slipping inside the elastic of his running pants but Dax catches hold of my wrist and rests it over the comforters where he can see it.

"It's movie night, remember?"

"Oh, that's right." I bury my face in his chest. God, he smells amazing it's driving me crazy. "So no making out?"

Dax shakes his head, grinning. "Nope, just like your rule of no wild parties."

I pout. I knew my decision was going to haunt me.

After we clean up and put everything away, we pick our next movie, *Some Kind of Wonderful*, and this time, we decide to play the DVD in the bedroom. There's no drama to our movements; nothing is forced at all. Even standing side by side in front of the bathroom mirror as we brush our teeth feels so right it scares me. There's a lot of flirting and gentle bumping of body parts going on. Dax is playful, and I love it. He seems to pull out that silly part of me I never knew I had.

By the time Mary Stuart-Masterson opens the movie with her character, a tomboy named Watts, beating on the drums, Dax and I are snuggled in bed, propped up with pillows we've kidnapped from the other rooms.

I can feel the beating of his heart as he wraps one arm around me and I drape my arms around his waist. We don't talk as if talking would ruin the lighthearted mood we're in. I'm also pretty much buzzed from the wine, and at the moment I don't want sex and neither, it seems, does Dax. He just holds me next to him, intently watching a movie that came out a year before he was born.

I hear a gentle knocking on the door the next morning as I step out of the bathroom and find a young man standing outside. I panic at the sight of him, thinking him to be a courier with some paperwork from Jeff. Still, I force myself to go to the door, though I don't open it.

He's young, about Dax's age, and clean-cut, with thick dark hair, and green eyes, and he's wearing a checkered button-down shirt and jeans. I open the door halfway.

"Sorry to bother you, miss, but is Dax here, by any chance? I'm Gabe... well, Dr. Gabriel Vasquez. Family Practice over in town. Dax wanted me to drop something off for him, and his grandmother said I'd find him here. I've been trying to call and text him, but his phone must be turned off."

"He's still asleep. I can wake him up."

"No! No!" His voice hushed as he hands me an envelope. "Can you just give it to him when he wakes up, please? I know it's early, and I'm sorry if I scared you."

I take it and turn it over. It has *Vasquez Family Practice* with an address in Taos. Then, remembering my manners and glad that I had just brushed my teeth with the intention of waking Dax with some morning sex, I open the door wider and hold out my hand.

"I'm Harlow, by the way. Harlow James." I hold out my hand, and he grasps it firmly.

"Dr. James! You're the doctor Dyami talked about. Very pleased to meet you." His voice still hushed as if the Pearl is a tiny house and his voice carries. "I hope you both can make the barbecue over at our house this afternoon. Dyami will be there with Sarah and Benny."

"I'll tell Dax."

His phone beeps then and he glances at it. "Oops! I gotta go. I'm in the office half-day today, but I hope to see you this afternoon, Dr. James."

"Call me Harlow."

"Call me Gabe. See you then? It starts at three."

"I'll ask Dax, but that'd be great."

As I watch Gabe drive away, I can't help but smile. The man's enthusiasm is infectious, and I wonder if Dax told him about me, and if he did, what did he say? As for this barbecue, Dax never mentioned it. But we also didn't get to talk much about anything but the two movies we saw last night, from what Doc Holiday died from (tuberculosis), and what Wyatt Earp's wife was addicted to (laudanum), to the fate of the earrings at the end of *Some Kind of Wonderful* which bothered Dax more than anything else.

He'll just be fixing cars again, he had protested, indignant as he fluffed up his pillows and lay back down. *That was his college education! How can he throw away his future like that for a pair of earrings?*

I'd like to think she did the practical thing and returned it in the morning, Dax.

He had chuckled then, kissing my forehead. *You think so?*

Yes, like right now, the most practical thing is to go to bed. Mr. Drexel, instead of worrying about a movie.

But we are in bed.

Smart ass. I had to giggle, but Dax was serious, his brow still furrowed as if still mulling the movie's ending. *I meant, go to bed.*

Are those doctors' orders?

Yup.

And what happens in the morning, Doctor James?

I had to think of the perfect answer. *I was thinking of being your huckleberry.*

He grinned. *That sounds like a good idea.*

It is, I had said, rolling away from him and feeling

him spoon his body behind me. *Now go to sleep or you won't have anything to look forward to in the morning.*

A few minutes later, I felt him stir as his arm drew me tighter. *And how can a simple pair of earrings cost the equivalent of a college education? Where'd he buy them in that little town? Harry Winston?*

Apparently, it still bothered him.

But right now, the only thing that bothers me is what's in the envelope that a doctor deemed necessary enough to hand-deliver so early in the morning?

"Morning."

Dax's voice startles me, and I turn around to see him walking toward me, though he stops when he spots Gabe's car driving away.

"Oh, shit, he must have been trying to text me, but I turned off my phone," he mutters as I hand him the envelope. He opens the flap and then pauses to glance at me before shrugging and pulling out a piece of folded paper.

"Is everything okay?" My curiosity is hitting the roof as I watch him. If it's from a doctor, what could it be?

Dax scans the paper for a few moments before he hands it to me. "It's just a bunch of numbers and figures that tell me what I already know, but it's really for you. I know it's presumptive of me, but..."

I recognize the test results right away, my face reddening. When I look up at Dax, he's running his fingers through his hair, looking sheepish. "When that condom broke the other night, I...I didn't want you to worry that I, you know, have, like the clap or anything."

"It's okay, Dax. I'm on the Pill, remember?" I lie, hating that I feel like I have to, but then, I can't have children, so why worry about it? Like Dax just said, there's still the issue of disease and infection. "But while we're on the subject of medical tests, I... I have the same thing for you." I walk to the dining table and pull out an envelope from my leather briefcase sitting on one of the chairs. It's the test I took a month ago at Andrea's clinic, just before I started seeing patients. I hand it to him. "I had her throw in the usual tests for STD. Just in case."

We stand in front of each other for a few moments as if not knowing how to proceed from here. Learning that Dax had gone to have himself tested yesterday makes the butterflies in my belly flutter, and then there's that area between my legs. God, why can't I even say it?

"So, how's the chafing?" I ask before I can stop myself. *Great!* Of all things, it's what comes out of my mouth, like I'm back to doctor mode again. Of course, there's no chafing. It's almost become a running joke between us although we did have many sessions that first night and I had to pick up some water-based lube while I was in town this afternoon. Just in case.

"It feels fine," Dax replies. "But it's probably better if I have a professional examine it, don't you think?"

I nod. "I highly recommend it. Care to step into my office and lie down?"

He stands closer. "How much is it going to cost me?"

"For you, I think I'll knock down the price. Maybe a kiss to start. You know, installments."

"I see. Are there any specifics about this kiss? Duration and location, maybe?"

I think for a few seconds. "Why don't you just show me? Usually, that's more accurate."

"You're right." Dax cups my face in his hands. "Like this?"

The kiss starts as a feathering of our lips. He tastes of peppermint, his lips soft and warm. My hands automatically land on his hips, my fingers resting on his firm ass. Dax groans, his tongue slipping between my teeth, his erection rubbing against me. My mind is filled with so many possibilities. *What position are we trying this time?*

Part of my online research yesterday had to do with new positions or the names of the ones we tried the day before. Reverse cowgirl, shoulder holder, crisscross. I feel like a student trying to make up for lost time. And boy, what a lot of time I'd lost!

When Dax lifts me off my feet, I wrap my legs around his hips as he carries me to the bedroom. I can't believe how we seem to fit so well, our bodies molding so easily with each other. We tumble onto the bed, the momentary separation of our bodies leading to clothes flying in all directions. In our jammies, it's pretty easy— one tug of my bottoms, and they're off, and another tug of my top over my head and I'm unabashedly naked in front of him. When he pulls off his shirt, I've sat up, and my lips graze the skin of his taut belly, his six-pack abs tensing.

Together we take turns exploring each other with our hands, our mouths, our bodies. He licks and sucks his way down my body, his hands palming my breasts before he takes a nipple in his mouth, his tongue swirling lazy circles that send me gasping. Then he makes his way lower down my torso and I feel his beard grazing the top of my pubis, his tongue tracing the sensitive scar just above it.

"You're so beautiful, Harlow. Everything about you is fucking amazing."

I look down, swallowing nervously when he traces the scar of my C-section with his tongue. "Even my scar?"

"Especially your scar. It's what makes you even more beautiful."

He dips his finger inside me. I close my eyes, letting the sensations wash over me. He inserts two fingers, letting it go deeper as I open my eyes and see him watching me. "Fuck, you're so wet."

He brings his fingers to my lips, and I taste myself. I hear him groan as he watches me before bringing his hand back down. When Dax slides his tongue along my clit, I shudder with expectation and soon, I'm moaning his name as his finger hits my G-spot and his mouth and tongue work their wonders, sending me through the roof with multiple orgasms I've lost count. *Wait! Why the hell am I counting them anyway?*

By the time Dax moves up on top of me and kisses me, letting me taste myself on his tongue, I'm so far gone. When he enters me, the sensation is exquisite. Lights flash behind my eyelids as I muffle my cries with my hand. His strokes are deep and slow, rhythmic, his gaze never leaving my face. Each thrust sends me moaning and I realize I feel no shame at all in what we're doing. When Dax orders me to touch my breasts and play with myself, I don't even think twice. I do what he says, squeezing my breasts and pinching my nipples as he rubs his thumb over my sensitive nub. I feel like I'm in unexplored territory, discovering parts of me I'd never allowed myself to discover. My nipples, my clit, my... my pussy. There, I said it.

New Harlow is in the house.

Dax lets go of my knees, and I wrap my legs around his waist as he kisses me again, soft, gentle kisses on my lips, my cheeks, my eyelids. I love the way his cock fills me with each thrust, and oh, how I hate it when he pulls back. My moans fill the room as I feel my orgasm building up again, stronger this time. I'm so close now, and Dax knows it, his strokes deepening, speeding up. When his mouth finds the sensitive spot behind my ear, I shatter, crying out his name as my body shudders beneath him. My fingers rake the skin on his back, leaving new marks over old ones. I feel Dax swell inside me, before he buries his face in my neck, allowing his release to claim him as he utters my name.

Today, I'm not a surgeon whose only care in the world is her reputation. I'm just a woman in the arms of a man. And I don't even care that when this is all over, Dax and I will go our separate ways and life will go back to normal. But until then, I'll take whatever I can get.

CHAPTER EIGHTEEN

Dax

By the time my alarm chirps to remind me of Gabe's barbecue at three, it's one in the afternoon. Harlow and I are lying on our sides, her back nestled in front of me as I spoon her. Since we returned to bed this morning, all we've done is fuck and fuck some more, with Harlow showing me more than her adventurous side. She's funny and curious, wanting to try out different positions beyond the ones I already know that she somehow has given names to. The one she named criss-cross was interesting, although I'm sure we're going to need a bigger bed if we keep at this. I'm all for new positions, sure, but some of them could fracture a dick or worse, break it. I also might need to look into yoga.

I love to hear Harlow laugh. It's a throaty laugh that's so fucking sexy it sends tingles up and down my spine. Shit, so much about her does exactly that. I love how she's so enthusiastic about just about everything we do in bed as if she's never done them before.

Hard to believe, but she's never gone down on a man,

and I believe her. She's too formal sometimes it takes her a few tries to let herself go, but when she does, man, but it's a damn beautiful sight. It suits her more than the armor she carries around with her even if it's because she's lost so much. She did tell me that she did try going down on someone, but then, I don't know what that means. *She tried, and he said no?* Was he out of his fucking mind? Oh, well, his loss, not mine.

Harlow can get all nerdy in bed, too, naming the parts of my dick while running her tongue over them, like she's giving a demonstration. Name the part, then lick. Name what it does, and then lick and suck some more. I did have to put a stop to having her tell me how erections work because I sure as hell know how, at least as a man and not a doctor. I don't need to know what seminal vesicles are. What matters to me is that my junk works just fine, if they're not being overworked as it is. But I'm not complaining. When she takes my cock in her mouth, there's nothing like seeing her look up at me, watching my reaction to everything she does.

I'm stupid for not wearing protection, but just as Harlow believes I'm clean (hell, even Gabe can attest to that), I believe her, too. We even have the damn paperwork to prove it, like two candidates applying for the same job and showing off their achievements. But instead of saying how long we've been at some previous position and with whom, what really matters are names like Hepatitis and HIV, and the accompanying words, NON-REACTIVE. It's crazy, but I don't care. Hell, I'll believe everything she says at this point, though right now if she wants another round, I'm going to beg off. I'm too exhausted even to think of sex, and Lil D is beat. I'm also starving, and somewhere in Taos is a *barbacoa* with my name on it.

But first, I need Harlow to talk and maybe even trust me a little. I pull her closer to me, and she moans, reaching behind her to squeeze my ass. "Tell me about New York. About the Harlow James who lives there."

She doesn't answer right away, but I wait.

"There's not much to say. She was, by all accounts, uptight. She was interesting when it came to her work and boring when it came to everything else. She didn't cheat on her husband, or take vacations. She just worked like it was the only thing that mattered to her, saving lives and," she pauses, chuckling dryly, "trying her darnedest to get pregnant. She hoped that maybe a baby would make her whole and even save her marriage so she'd have a semblance of a family. But when that didn't happen... well, you roll with the punches and move on."

Her openness breaks my heart. I'm too young to think of kids, but I've changed enough of Dyami's diapers and babysat him to say I wouldn't mind a couple of my own. "I'm sorry, Harlow."

"It's okay. Things are looking much better. Well, out here instead of back there."

I pull her closer, inhaling the sweet scent of her hair as I decide to ask the question that's been bugging me since I first returned to the Pearl that night. "Has it ever gotten so bad for you that you thought of, you know, ending it all?"

I feel her body stiffen for a few seconds, and she turns

to look at me, frowning before she rests her head back on the pillow. "Don't we all?"

Not really. Some of us drink or work it off, I almost tell her but keep my mouth shut.

"Maybe. But I'm still here, aren't I? With you," she says, shrugging. "And that's about it to Harlow James, the uptight pediatric kidney transplant surgeon, assistant professor, imperfect woman, and incompetent wife."

"No one's perfect, Harlow, even transplant surgeons and master craftsmen. But just because you're going through a divorce doesn't make you an incompetent wife either. Some marriages just don't work out."

"That's easy for you to say. You've never been married, have you?"

I shrug. "No, but it doesn't mean I'm clueless about it. My parents had a happy marriage, even if Dad had to travel."

She sighs. "I'm sorry. You're right."

"You're one amazing woman, with or without your degrees. And if you weren't aware of that before today, then I hope you are from here on. You're fucking amazing, Harlow James. Really. And I'm not just saying that because we're sleeping together. I really mean it."

"Thanks," she says, giggling. "Can you head my fan club?"

"Anytime." Suddenly I don't want to talk about this New York version of Harlow James, the one with no friends to go back to. I like the New Mexico Harlow so much better, the one I went on hikes with just days earlier, climbing up cavates and searching for petroglyphs with a constant smile on her face.

"Tell me what makes you smile," I ask her as she rolls onto her back to face me.

"You," she replies, smiling as she strokes my bearded jaw and I can't stop grinning like a schoolboy, all thoughts of New York Harlow forgotten.

"What else?"

"Your smile," she replies, tracing my bottom lip with her index finger before moving down my neck and my chest. "Your pecs, and your abs. Your ass, and your…"

I grab her wandering hand and bring it to my lips. "What else—one that's not on this bed, for starters."

She giggles. "Oh, *that's* what you meant."

"Yes, Harlow, that's what I meant."

She turns serious. "This place. Even the name—Pearl—is so peaceful and so perfect. And this state. It truly is the Land of Enchantment as the brochures say. Your family and your friends make it even more special."

"By friends, you must mean Gabe, because as far as I know, he's the only one you've met." *So far.* I just hope she's ready because I have a ton of them.

She nods. "Yes, and I forgot to tell you, but he hopes to see us at the barbecue this afternoon."

Thank God for friends like Gabe. "And would you like to come with me? Nana and Sarah are going to be there. Dyami, too, and Benny, of course. I just hope my family won't be too overwhelming."

"They're not overwhelming at all, Dax," Harlow murmurs, her expression turning distant. "You're a lucky man. You have family and friends who love you. Really love you."

"I'm sure you do, too. They're just back in New York."

"No, they're not," she replies, sighing. "I paid more attention to my career than I did in my personal life to keep friends."

"What about family? Your parents? Brothers and sisters?"

She sighs. "I'm a foster kid, Dax. I went from family to family, counting the days until someone would adopt me but no one ever did. It wasn't their fault; I was a sickly kid, always having these crazy asthma attacks at the mere sight of a dust mite, or an A-minus on my paper. I'm sure that didn't help make me good enough to adopt."

"Dyami sometimes gets asthma attacks when the winds kick up, but I've seen nothing like it with you, not when we went to Bandolier."

"It disappeared when I was eighteen after I graduated from high school. But by then, I'd aged out of the system," she replies, shrugging. "Someone said it was all psychosomatic, that I was so stressed out over my changing surroundings that it must have manifested in my lungs, and maybe they're right. But by then, I'd won a scholarship to a college, and I kept on going until I got my MD. And even when I should have stopped because I'd achieved everything I thought I wanted with my career, I still kept on going. It wasn't unusual for me to put in seventeen-hour days, Dax, and looking back now, that's just not normal, not for a married woman who wants to be a mother, too."

"Something's gotta give, Harlow. Seventeen hours is crazy."

"I know." She pauses, her gaze distant. "No wonder I always miscarried. And even when I was pregnant with Marcus, I kept on going, thinking I could be a transplant surgeon, and still be wife and mother, too. Ambitious, isn't it?"

"It still doesn't change the fact that you changed children's lives, Harlow, and their families, too. You didn't just change their lives; you saved them. Never forget that."

She weaves her fingers with mine and kisses the back of my hand. "How do they say it online? *TL;DR. Too Long; Did Not Read.* I took everything for granted."

"And now?"

"I honestly can't afford to anymore," she replies. "Anyway, I may take a position in New Haven or I may not. But right now, I have no idea."

"But is that what you really want, more of the same thing?"

"If I take it, it's only because I don't know how to do anything else. I thought I wanted to be a mother but that never happened. Being a doctor is all I've ever been, and so I go back to what's familiar."

"Don't you want to do anything different? Try living in a different place, maybe?"

She shrugs. "I really have no idea, Dax. But what I do know is that I've never felt as happy as I do now, right here with you. But then, it could be because I've got vacation on the brain and when this is all over, my life goes back to normal again."

I don't like her version of normal at all, not when

what we are right now is perfect for me. It's my new normal and I like it. I want more of it.

"I don't know about you, Harlow, but I like this kind of normal." I kiss her and for a few moments, that's all we do, kiss and explore each other like we haven't already been doing that all morning. But I also need a reprieve from everything she's told me so far if only to process the life she's had which is so opposite to mine. How would she react when she sees just how extended my family can get, that it goes beyond Nana, Sarah, and Dyami? It's such a different world from the one she knew with her asshole soon-to-be ex-husband.

At the thought of her ex-husband, I pull away from her. "What about Jeff?"

She looks at me, surprised. "What about him?"

"What if he wants you back?"

"Why would he want me back? He hasn't wanted me in two years."

"But what if he does now? What if he has a change of heart?"

"He won't, and even if he did, I can't go back to anyone who's hurt me as much as he has," Harlow says. "Can you?"

I think of Claudia and the night she cheated on me. I've forgiven her, but I can't forget the humiliation and anger I felt in that men's bathroom, first when the idiot told me he had fucked her, and later, when she admitted it was true.

"No," I reply. "Forget it. That was a stupid question anyway."

"No, it wasn't, but you got your answer, Mr. Drexel. TL;DR. No, I'm not going back to Jeff."

"You and your internet lingo," I say just as my phone chirps to remind me about Gabe's barbecue again. "We better start getting ready. We need to hop in the shower."

"Oh, that's right. The moment they take one whiff of us they'll know what we've been up to, that's for sure," Harlow says as she rolls out of bed, smacks my ass and then runs to the bathroom shrieking with laughter when I follow right behind her. I catch up with her in front of the mirror and whip her around to face me.

"And what exactly have we been up to, Dr. James? Because I just want more of it."

Harlow's eyes grow wide in shock as my erection presses against her belly, ready for another round just when I thought I couldn't go again. She bites her lower lip playfully before I kiss her and feel her body mold into mine like she was made for me.

TL;DR, Harlow James, I think I'm in love with you.

Harlow is a hit at the barbecue, especially among the women who can't stop asking her health-related questions like, *so what do you think of this blood pressure reading?* But she handles it like a champ although she lights up the most when she's with children like Dyami who can't stop telling everyone that he met her first. The kids love her, and she loves them right back. Her face just lights up at the sight of them, especially babies.

I should have warned her that Gabe has a big extended family that pops out kids like it's going out of style. Luckily, they're all so tight-knit they could form their own daycare if they wanted to, and everyone would still get a few days off. Already, Gabe's got ten nephews and nieces, four of them from one cousin, Letty, who just had quadruplets three months ago. If I had thought Sarah having Dyami was a full-time job, I can only imagine having four of them all at once. But all I need to do is look at Alex, Letty's husband, and I get it. Sure, he looks just as exhausted as Letty, but nothing can beat the glow on his face when he's with his family. It's the same glow that fills Harlow's face right now: pure bliss.

Before long, my friends drag me away from Harlow, eager to catch up with the latest news about my life, my work, and of course, my date. They all want to know who she is, how and where we met, and most of all, when. That's the big question—*when*—since they know I just got in a few days ago, alone. But the fact that she's a pediatric transplant surgeon is enough to shut them up before we go for the tried and true: shooting the breeze as we attack the food.

I'm just glad that Claudia isn't here. Gabe told me she suddenly had other plans as soon as she learned I was bringing Harlow, and secretly, I'm glad she didn't make it. She'd have busted a gasket if she'd seen Harlow. I know Claudia wishes I'd forgive her—and I have—but I've also moved on. Besides, Tony, her boyfriend who's now working on a TV set in Vancouver, was the guy in that damn bathroom that night, and I have a misdemeanor on my record, thanks to him.

An hour later, while Harlow is outside talking to

Nana and Sarah, I run into Gabe reading something on his phone as I emerge out of the bathroom. When he looks up and sees me, he nods his head as he puts his phone away. "Hope you don't mind, but I just looked Harlow up, and wow, I can only dream of doing what she does."

"Transplant surgery?"

"Do you have any idea how long it takes to be one, man? I can only dream of doing that. Assistant Director of Transplant Surgery at Miller General! She even helped set it up!"

I can't help but feel a surge of pride at Gabe's enthusiasm as I do my best to walk casually to the refrigerator and take out a bottle of water. Gotta stay cool like I'm not already freaking out over how to persuade Harlow to stay longer than she'd planned. Maybe we could get to know each other better with no departure date looming over our heads. I lean on the kitchen sink and face him, twist open the lid and take a sip of water. "Thanks for dropping off the test results, man. Sorry, I missed your texts. I had turned off my phone."

"I promised you I'd drop it off, and that's exactly what I did. And I'm not talking as a doctor here, but it's because of her, right? The test?"

I shrug. "Maybe. Or it could be, you know, I was curious."

"Whatever your reason, man, it's always good to know that stuff anyway," Gabe continues, before his brow furrows and his voice lowers. "Look, don't take this wrong, alright, but some of the aunts are freaking out. Isn't she, like, older than you?"

My guard goes up. *What the hell?* "And your point?"

"It doesn't bother you?" Gabe peers at me curiously before turning to look outside the glass doors where we see Harlow talking to Nana, Letty, and Alex. Sarah and Benny are there, too, and they're all laughing at something Letty is saying. One of the quadruplets with a pink headband is cradled in Harlow's arms, and my chest tightens. Harlow is glowing, cooing to the three-month-old who's looking up at her and reaching a pudgy hand to touch Harlow's face.

"Should it?" I ask, irritated. My patience meter has suddenly run out of tokens. "Is that why you invited her, so you could point that out to me, like I had no clue? What am I? Stupid?"

Gabe brings his hands up in mock surrender. "Whoa! Dax, chill, alright? I'm just asking; that's all. I don't mean anything by it, honest to God, man."

"Then why are you asking? It's none of your business, *Doctor*." I twist the cap back on the bottle of water and walk away, but Gabe stops me with a hand on my arm.

"Look, Dax, I'm just worried about you, alright? She's still married, for crying out loud—to the fucking Director of Transplant Surgery, of all people."

"She's getting a divorce," I say through gritted teeth. "It's not final yet, but she's working on it. That good enough for you?"

Gabe exhales. "Alright, sorry, I'm butting in where I shouldn't. Guess there's nothing to worry about then."

"There isn't. Since when is it your business to worry about me?"

"Since you lost it when Claudia cheated on you. You

could have killed Tony in that bathroom, did you know that? What if I hadn't been there?" Gabe says, his voice calm. "Look, I don't want to see you hurt, alright? I mean, you *really* like Harlow, and I don't blame you."

"And your point?"

"Nothing; you just like her, and honestly, I couldn't be happier for you," Gabe says. "You know I'll do anything for you. You're my brother from another mother, remember?"

His hand on my shoulder snaps me out of my irritation, and I take a deep breath and exhale. "Come on, let's go outside before someone asks her to tell them what the color of their piss means."

But as Gabe and I make our way back outside, there are two facts about Harlow that I can no longer deny, no matter how hard I choose to ignore them. Harlow is way older than me, and she's still, technically, married.

Two hours later, with Gabe's cousins and friends forming an impromptu mariachi band howling away in the backyard, I finally find Harlow alone in the kitchen discarding paper plates into the trash bin. Without a word, I take her hand and lead her into the laundry room, the only empty room in the Vasquez household. I don't care that the dryer's going and the washer's thumping against the wall as it goes through its spin cycle. I cradle Harlow's face in my hands and kiss her long and hard, trapping her between me and the wall. I've never wanted any woman as much as I want her, and it's not that *I want to fuck you right now* kind of way, but the, *you're the one that I want to wake up to forever* way. It's scary as hell, but something shifted when I saw her with Letty's baby.

One day, she'll be holding ours.

But even as that thought comes to me, another one hits me right in the solar plexus, sucking the breath out of me.

Just how bad did Harlow want to have a baby? Does she still want to get pregnant now, enough to lie to me about being on the Pill?

The thought jars me for a few moments, and I pull away from her, frowning.

"Are you okay?"

"Yeah, I'm fine. I just missed you," I say as I rest my forehead against hers. I'm not lying. I have missed her, even if right now, I feel myself panicking, my decision to fuck her without protection coming back to haunt me. But surely it can't happen, can it? Not after a few rounds in the last few hours, or when the condom broke last night? *But what if it does?*

"I missed you, too, Mr. Drexel," she murmurs.

"Everyone loves you, Harlow."

"They love *you*. They can't stop telling me all about you and you and Gabe's antics growing up," she says, laughing. "And they're so proud of you, too."

"This is my second home, so they know all my secrets. Unfortunately." I roll my eyes as Harlow giggles and nods in agreement. Her smile pushes all doubts out of my head. I don't even hear the washer thumping against the wall, not even thinking that all I need to do is open the lid and adjust the damn load to make it stop. But no, I'm smitten, and it's bad.

Her expression turns serious. "But something's bothering you, Dax. Is anything wrong?"

"Just tell me when you're ready to leave," I mutter.

"Are *you* ready to go?"

I gaze into her eyes, drinking her in. "I am, though given that we're at a Vasquez barbecue, it's gonna take us, at the very least, an hour to say our goodbyes. They'll do their darnedest to get us to stay."

"Is that the way it usually goes?"

"Pretty much. Never a dull moment around here."

"So I guess we better get started saying goodbye then," Harlow says, glancing at the door as we hear the sound of voices outside. "We're also not alone. People must think we're bumping uglies in here. Either that or the spin cycle's giving me too many ideas."

But the spin cycle's the least of our problems, for as Harlow pulls open the door, Dyami and Gabe's nieces and nephews on the other side scatter back, staring at us with wide eyes and open mouths.

"How long have you guys been eavesdropping out here?" I demand as the washer thumps rhythmically against the wall behind us. *Thump-thump-thump.*

"So was the doctor giving you an ex-uh-mi-nay-shon in there?" asks one of the younger kids as I grab Harlow's hand and storm out. Forget the lengthy goodbyes. I just want to be alone with Harlow even if I end up offending half of Taos to do it.

CHAPTER NINETEEN

Harlow

WHY DO I feel like the honeymoon is over?

To say that the barbecue was a disaster would have been an understatement, even though on the outside we're all smiles as we say our goodbyes. Somehow, somewhere, someone said something and everything simply unraveled. Now Dax is clearly upset, and it's not even about the children eavesdropping on us. But even if he doesn't tell me, I know what it is. After working in hospitals for so long and my month-long stint at Andrea's South Valley clinic in Albuquerque, I know enough Spanish to understand most of what everyone is saying when they think I'm not paying attention.

She's so much older than him. Did you know she's still married?

I know people can't help themselves, especially when they're right. I am older than Dax, and I'm also still married even if I'm in the process of getting a divorce. And Dax isn't an idiot. I'm sure someone said something to him along those lines, wiping that familiar grin that I love off his handsome face for the rest of the afternoon. He's introspective now, and as we drive back to the Pearl with music streaming from the speakers, I can see the whites of his knuckles as he grips the steering wheel.

"They're right, you know," I say, breaking the long silence between us that not even Paul Simon singing about loving someone like a rock of ages can ease.

"What?"

"Whatever they were saying about me. That I'm much older than you, and that I'm technically still married."

"You and I both know you're getting a divorce, and as far as I'm concerned, that means you're not married," he mutters. "Did they say that to your face, or behind your back?"

I shrug. Everyone was too polite and in awe of me being a transplant surgeon to say anything to my face. "Does it matter? It's true anyway. Until my divorce is final, I'm still married in their eyes, and it doesn't take a rocket scientist to figure out that we're sleeping together."

"So? Is there a law against that?"

"I'm also so much older than you."

"So what? Does it bother me? No. Did it bother me before we got together? No." Dax exhales before continuing. "I see men walking around with women half their age, and I don't see anyone complaining. But turn the tables around, and suddenly, everyone's got their panties in a twist. What is so wrong about you being older than me?"

"I don't know, Dax. It just is... to a lot of people."

Dax eases the truck to a stop, parking next to a row of

cars along the side of the road just before the Rio Grande Gorge Bridge, though he doesn't shut off the engine.

"Is it a big deal to you?"

My hesitation gives him the answer he's waiting for, and before I can say anything else, Dax shuts off the engine, opens the door and gets out. For a few moments, he paces the ground before he walks around the truck to open my door. "Why don't we take a walk before I drop you off?"

"On the bridge?"

"Why not?" Dax's eyes narrow as he studies my face. "Are you afraid of heights?"

"A bit," I reply, swallowing for my throat suddenly feels dry. "Alright, I am. It goes pretty far down, doesn't it?"

"We are about 565 feet from the bottom, yes, so you could say it goes pretty far down." Dax looks out toward the bridge, and I follow his gaze. There are a few tourists on it, standing against the railing and taking selfies. Some take pictures of the view with their phones. Two cars away, a van parks and a family of three hops out, including a young child, eager to see the gorge below.

"Why don't I drop you off and give you some time alone?" Dax says, pushing my door shut but I stop him. If all those people can do it, why the heck can't I? I need to stop being afraid.

"No, not yet. I'll walk with you on the bridge first, and then you can drop me off. I've always wanted to check out the view, just not by myself," I say, forcing a smile.

"What if you freak out?"

"I won't. Besides, I've got you with me," I say, hoping to get a smile from him but I don't. I hate the chasm that's springing between us as we stand in front of each other. I hold out my hand hopefully, and Dax takes it. "Promise to hold my hand all the way to the end and back?"

He nods. "I promise."

It's a miracle that I manage to walk to one end of the bridge and back without hyperventilating, even though I have to let go of Dax's hand when the family of three passes us and I grab hold onto the railing. But with Dax by my side, it doesn't feel as scary as I thought. Sure, the bridge shakes when cars drive through it, but it's sturdy just like the man standing next to me, looking up at the sky, big puffy clouds covering the mountain ridges straight ahead. Too young for me or not, Dax is far from the boy I keep telling myself he is.

"Mama used to take us on hikes along the Rio Grande. Not right below us, but a bit farther up," he says as we lean against the railing. Wind whips at my hair and face and I love the feel of it against my skin. "When Dad would fly into town, we'd all go to Arroyo Seco and go fishing for wild trout. It's a short drive from here, along the 150 toward Taos Ski Valley. My mom taught me how to flyfish. Even Dad."

"I wish I could have met her," I say as Dax brings his arm over my shoulders and I wrap my arms around his torso.

"I do, too. It's been five years since she died."

"I'm sorry," I murmur as I look down the eastern side of the gorge and see a battered car halfway down the ridge. I look away, not wanting to know how it got there. "What was she like?"

"She was amazing," Dax begins, his voice deep and low against my ear. "She moved out here when she was pregnant because she couldn't stand another day living in New York and trying to be a Manhattan socialite. She was a proud New Mexican, and she was determined to raise her second child here. Sarah wasn't thrilled, of course. She was eight by the time I was born, and she was not a happy camper moving out here."

"Yet here she is."

"She moved to New York for college but came back after she experienced her first blizzard and said, fuck that. When she returned, she met Benny, and they had Dyami, and they've been on and off ever since. But that's only because my sister's a firecracker," Dax says, chuckling before he turns serious again. "Mama flew out here, had me, and then Dad had no choice after that but to commute between New York and Taos. She wanted me to have a normal life out here around family. Lots of family."

"Did he mind it? Having to travel just to see his kids?"

"Maybe at first, but I would have been too young to notice. By the time I was the little terror about town, he looked forward to staying for weeks at a time. He had to drive down to Santa Fe to work remotely, but it beat having him in New York. He owns a brokerage firm in the Financial District although he's cut down his hours at the office so he can oversee my company's finances. So for weeks at a time, it was just Mama and Nana raising me, two strong women who took no prisoners. But they gave me the idyllic childhood people write about in books. I was happy as a clam, and nothing, not even vacations in Paris or Rome could take me away from here. Sarah says I'm just like Mama, rooted to the earth, the sky, the wind, and the Rio Grande. And she's right."

"What happened to her?"

"Ovarian cancer. She didn't catch it till it was Stage 4 when she suddenly looked like she was eight months pregnant and at that time, we were all on vacation in Tuscany. I think they called it ascites, or something like that. But until then, she never told anyone that she'd been in so much pain. All that time, she thought she just had a bad back, along with some major bloating that she self-medicated with whatever she could find. After we got back, Dad took a leave of absence from his company and stayed here the entire time—two full years. I wanted to take care of her, but I was only twenty, trying to be the big man when I was so far from one. But I did what I could."

"Did she receive any chemo? Radiation?"

He nods. "She went through surgery first to remove all the cancerous parts before any of the radiation treatments could be done. Later on, she signed up for trials, but even she knew that none of them would help. By the time one of the medications seeped out of the skin of her palms and her feet, she knew she was close." Dax pauses then smiles wistfully. "But until then, looking at her, you wouldn't know she had cancer, Harlow. She had such light inside her. She still volunteered and helped out any way she could. She learned how to draw, make pottery, and even learned a new language, Italian. She had to keep busy, she said, because she knew it would be all over if she stopped."

"You're so much like her. You've got so much light inside you," I say, pulling him closer. I bury my face against his chest and inhale his scent. I don't even break it down this time. To hell with pheromones. He smells like a man.

"That's when I drew all my designs, the ones that won awards years later," Dax continues. "They were all done while we were in Flagstaff during her final weeks. Most of them looked impossible, even on paper, like cherry wood molded to appear like organic waves on staircases, designs people swore wouldn't work but they did, just as Mama said they would. There's this creek behind the house we have in Flagstaff, and she loved to sit by the water listening to the birds and the rustling of the leaves in the trees. Nana, Sarah, and Dyami came out there, too, during those last weeks. Benny, too. None of us wanted to leave her alone."

"Dax, I'm so sorry. I really am."

"She died in the hospital. A blood clot made it to her lungs," he says, his gaze straight ahead, where both sides of the Rio Grande appear to meet in the distance. "That's when Dad announced that Mama's wish was not to have a memorial. No gathering, no nothing. It devastated so many people not to be able to come and pay their respects, but Dad wanted to honor her final wishes. She wanted people to think of her like she never left, and she's right. When you don't get to say goodbye, somehow, the ones you love are always still around. That's when I decided to buy property away from everything else and build the Pearl. That's her name, by the way, Pearl Anaya Drexel."

"She raised an amazing son," I say as I fight back the tears of shame. *What if I'd ended my life that night in the very place he'd built to honor his mother's memory?* I look up at Dax and study the contours of his face, the gentle slope of his Roman nose and the way his thick dark lashes curl naturally, brightening his blue eyes. His beard reveals a strong jaw and the hint of a cleft chin. I bring one hand to his face and stroke his beard, letting my fingers slide toward his ear to feel the short hairs at the back of his neck.

"What are you looking at?" Dax murmurs as he tears his gaze from the horizon and looks at me. In an hour, it will be dark.

"You. I'm looking at you."

"And what do you see?"

I weave my fingers between his and bring his hand to my lips. Fuck everyone, and whatever they think about him being too young for me. "I see a man, Dax. I see you."

"Thank you." Dax smiles and kisses the back of my hand before bringing me into his arms in an embrace. We don't talk for a few moments. We simply soak up the view before us and even though a few cars rumble through the bridge, the structure vibrating beneath our feet, I don't feel afraid. I feel safe.

Then he takes a deep breath and blows it out through his lips. "How bad do you want to get pregnant, Harlow?"

I stiffen, although Dax only holds me tighter. I could

lie, just like I lied twice to him about being on the Pill when I'm not, or I could just tell him the truth. Don't I owe him that? If I lose him now because of my lies, then it just might be better this way. The sooner we cut the ties that have bound us to this vacation fling, the better it will be for everyone.

"You could say it was all I ever wanted back then," I say softly.

"Back then? What about now? Do you still want it bad enough to lie to me about being on the Pill?" he asks, his voice eerily calm. "I might be wrong about all this–"

"You're not," I say, pulling away so I can look up at him. "You're right; I'm not on the Pill and I'm sorry I lied to you. I shouldn't have, but..."

"But what?" His dark blue eyes seem more intense in the approaching darkness.

"I haven't been on the Pill for a long time, and I can't get pregnant on my own, not without any help."

"You could have told me that then instead of lying to me. What if you get pregnant?"

I shake my head. "I can't, and God knows I tried. The doctors didn't know why although a few of them suggested that I could also be undergoing early menopause. Premature ovarian failure was how they called it. Just my luck that I put everything else ahead of having children that by the time I wanted one, it was too late."

"Has it ever occurred to you that Jeff could be the problem?"

"He's going to be a father to his secretary's baby, Dax. How can he be the problem?" I snap, pulling away from

Dax completely and grip the railing with both hands as I stare at the lone truck halfway down the ridge. I force myself to focus on it, no matter how morbid it seems, the metal now gray from being out in the elements for, who knows, how long. "I'm sorry I lied to you. I really am. But the only reason I ever got pregnant was because of IVF. Four times. Three of those ending in miscarriages, and the fourth...well, Marcus was stillborn. I know it sounds selfish but I only wanted to... I don't know... feel you. All of you."

My cheeks color as I say that last part, although it's true. I wanted all of Dax, everything he could give me. I wanted everything I could take, even for just those few moments we were together before everything came crashing down, like that car on the side of the gorge. It's selfish, but it's done. And honestly, what are the chances?

I can feel Dax studying my face, but I can't look at him, not when I sound like a woman so desperate to have children she'll say anything—do anything—to have one. And I just did. I have no excuse for what I've done, and my silence probably tells Dax just as much.

He rests his hand over mine as I continue to grip the railing. "Why don't we get you back to the Pearl before it gets too dark?"

CHAPTER TWENTY

Dax

It takes a few moments for Harlow's words to sink in, and by the time we're halfway to the Pearl, I'm so angry I can barely see the road in front of me. Just because she could only get pregnant with the help of IVF, she didn't feel it was important enough to tell me the truth—that she wasn't on the Pill?

Instead, Harlow stood right in front of me in the living room just after I handed her that damn paper saying I was clean, and lied to me. And because I let my dick call the shots instead of my fucking brain, I fell for it. Not only that, but I fell too hard and too fast for her, and that's why I'm feeling this way. But is it because of the gun and that note? No, it can't be because if it were, I wouldn't be feeling this way. I don't pity Harlow at all. On the contrary, I admire her for being smart—too smart sometimes—and for her resilience. And as much as I hate how closed in she is, it's served her well. Yet I can't deny that she's also letting me see more of her than she's probably allowed anyone else to see.

She's also a terrible liar.

At that last thought, I feel my temper rise again, and I take a deep breath, hoping I can rein it in. But as I park the truck in front of the Pearl, I know I can't. God help me, but I can't. I hate feeling like I've just been taken for a fool, and it's only because I like her too fucking much for my own good.

You love too much, mijo.

I switch off the engine, and for a few moments, we sit in silence. She's been watching me the whole time, not speaking, and I'm glad she hasn't said a word or I'd have blown up inside the damn cab. It's been awhile since I've felt this way, not when the last time I let my anger get the best of me, I almost killed a man. I sure as heck am not about to kill anyone, but I'm too close to the situation to be rational right now. Everything about me is all emotion. I've been on such a high the past few days that I can't think straight.

I need to walk away the same way I've done the last two times someone I cared so much for lied to me. I need to disengage. I get out and walk to her side to open the door. I can't look Harlow in the face. Not when I'll lose myself in her eyes, and so I let my gaze drift lower.

She's just Goldilocks with great tits, man, and a tight pussy to boot, I tell myself. *You'll get over her in a heartbeat, just like you got over Claudia.*

We walk to the Pearl in silence, the space between us growing even wider with each step I take. If she can lie as easily as she did about being on the Pill, what about everything else? Her husband? Their marriage? Everything?

Just end it now and be done with it, dude. Ask her.

Harlow unlocks the front door and steps inside before turning to face me as she holds the door open. "Would you like to come in for a while?"

"Not really."

"Oh, okay." She swallows, glancing down at the floor before looking back at me. "Thank you for taking me to the barbecue, Dax. It was really nice to meet Gabe–"

"When were you going to tell me about the night you planned to kill yourself in my house?"

All color fades from Harlow's face. I hate that I've just implicated myself for being on the property that night, but I'm too angry to think straight. Talking about my mother brought everything back; the joy of the life she devoted to her children, followed by the pain of watching her die in front of my eyes that the only way I could deal with the loss was to build the Pearl with my bare hands. How dare some big shot New York doctor come in here then, and taint my labor of love with her petty problems? Who does Harlow James think she is?

Harlow doesn't answer my question, not when she's staring at me with her big doe eyes in shock, her mouth hanging open. I feel a hole tear open inside my chest, like some damn alien burrowing its way inside me before it snakes its way right in the solar plexus. I hate myself for feeling this way, but I focus, telling myself that she fucking lied to me. She used me.

"What if you did kill yourself that night, Harlow? Were you expecting Nana to find your body and clean up after you? Me? Because in case you haven't noticed, I don't hire a cleaning crew to take care of this place. It's all family. *My family.*"

"No! I... I was going to do it outside—" Suddenly, she gasps and covers her mouth with her hand, the realization of what she just said probably hitting her then.

I stare at her, speechless. If knowing she'd lied to me about being on the Pill was bad enough, this was worse.

"Dax, I'm so sorry–"

"You bet your ass you're sorry," I say, knowing I'm about to lose it any second. As much as I hate knowing that it's true—Harlow did plan on killing herself that night—I never wanted to hear her actually say it. It's wishful thinking. It's why I never asked her about the gun in the first place. I wanted to keep that perfect image of Harlow James sacred inside my head—the surgeon who operated on kids, the woman who made me melt inside with a glance, the very same woman who told me she'd only been with one other man before me, and I believed her. But she's also the same woman who is slowly killing me with her lies. "Whether you did it here or outside doesn't change the fact that you thought of killing yourself on my property. If you really wanted to spite your fucking husband, then do whatever you need to do in the Hamptons, not here. I'm sure he can easily hire a crew to clean up after your mess and still have his damn wedding."

"Dax!" Harlow's eyes brim with tears, but I force my gaze lower. *Her tits. Look at her fucking tits.*

"What about me? Did it even occur to you to ask me what I thought about the possibility of being a father? Am I just another sperm donor to you, at your service, anytime you want? Is that why it bothers you that I'm much younger than you because you don't believe I can think for myself? That I have a fucking brain?"

"That's not true! I care about you, Dax. I've–"

"You care about me? You care enough about me to fuck me but not trust me with the truth? Is that it? Because that's the way it looks like right now."

"I didn't say that–"

"You're right; you didn't say it. But the things you don't say speak louder than the things you do, Goldie, and right now, I've heard enough," I say, knowing I need to step away before I punch the glass door and cut my fucking hand.

"Dax, please, let's talk."

"No, we've got nothing to talk about, but you do. Just not with me," I say, turning to face her one last time. "Get help, Harlow. Whatever you do, just get help. Please."

I don't look back, not even when I feel Harlow's hand grasp mine. I shake it off angrily, and I'm grateful she doesn't push her luck. Thank God, Goldilocks knows when she's no longer wanted, and right now, I want nothing to do with her.

But as I drive away from her and the Pearl, not caring if I'm spraying rocks far and wide behind me, I wonder why there's a pain gnawing deep inside my chest. Why does it feel like I've turned my back on a lifetime that could have been?

I don't go straight home. The lights are on at the Villier brothers' Earthship, and that's where I go instead. I could call Gabe but I don't want any conversation to veer to Harlow or hints of her. Right now, I want to start letting go, and if it means hanging out with the Villier brothers talking shit about video games or their latest adventures in beer-making, then that's fine with me.

As I drive up, Todd comes out to meet me, holding an opened can of beer. Through the windows, I see his brother, Sawyer, sitting in front of the TV playing a video game, a thick beard covering the lower half of his face. Though the brothers are pretty popular around town with the ladies, Todd is the outgoing one while Sawyer is the brooding one. Sawyer gives the impression of someone who doesn't give a shit about anything, but after Mama died, I got to see firsthand just how much the guy does care, and I owe the guy my life.

"Hey, hey, hey, Big D, how ya doing?" Todd exclaims, grasping my hand tightly through the open window. "You been MIA, my man!"

"What are you bitching about? I'm here," I reply, forcing a grin as I get out of the truck. "You still have that thing I had you keep for me?"

Todd's face darkens, but he nods and beckons for me to follow him inside. It's something I dropped off after I arrived back in Taos, just after I first saw Harlow asleep on my bed. I hate just how quickly I excused everything —most of all that damn gun—hoping she'd finally say something about it until I couldn't stand it anymore.

As Todd and I stride through the living room, Sawyer looks up from his game to nod at me before killing off some bad guys with a big-ass gun on the flat screen TV. The brothers share a three-bedroom Earthship that's just like the Pearl, only more organic-looking, with its use of sloping lines and sculptural accents. Like the Pearl, it comes with a water reservoir, control room for all the solar panels and water filtration unit, and an indoor garden. My garden looks like a damn forest compared to theirs, but they make the best of what they have, with vegetables they rotate each year and fruit trees, avocado and lime. There's even a banana tree and a macadamia nut bush somewhere, the seeds smuggled from Hawaii and carefully nurtured for the past five years, maybe longer.

"See anything good lately?" I ask, cocking my head toward the telescope by the window as Todd and I stand in front of one of his bookshelves. He runs his index finger along their spines until he stops in front of one that says *Dracula* and pulls it out. It's a hardbound book that he's converted into one of those hideaway safes to hide keys and other valuables by hollowing out the pages. He generally hides his medicinal pot in there, but not this time.

"Nah, it's just some woman... and some guy who can't keep his hands off her. Oh wait, that's you."

I glare at him. "Shut up and stop being such peeping Toms, you two."

"Hey! Who you calling a peeping Tom?" Sawyer grumbles, his attention still on the TV screen as I dip my hands into the niche inside the book. "You know I look at the stars, Dax. It's Todd you need to worry about."

"So you want them back?" Todd asks as I hold a

bullet still in its casing between my thumb and index finger. "Because we sure could use them for shooting practice. Still want these babies back?"

"No, but if you want them, great. If not, I'll let Neil have them." Neil is the cop friend from Albuquerque. Of course, if I handed these to him, he's bound to ask me more questions like, *where's the fucking gun, man?*

"One bullet is all it takes, you know," Todd says, taking the bullet from my fingers. "A .22 just rattles inside your skull and turns your brain into mush. But no, this one just blows everything up inside–"

"That's not funny, man," Sawyer says angrily, his focus still on the game although it's obvious he's also listening in on my conversation with his brother.

Sawyer served in Afghanistan and after being one of two members of his squad to survive an IED blast, he decided to live out here, away from everyone. Nana found him digging in the trash behind the house one day, and she asked him inside for a meal. That's how I first got to know Sawyer, sitting at my table looking like a mountain man and enjoying Nana's cooking. Sawyer joined the team at the Earthship community shortly after, helping build the structures by hand while learning all he could by taking every class they offered. Todd left his job as a TV writer in Hollywood to live out here with his brother. He still writes and even self-publishes his books, but he lives out here to make sure Sawyer doesn't do anything stupid. Not that Sawyer would. He actually works for a private security firm, and some weeks he's out of town protecting some rock star or rich kid though he never talks about it.

Todd shrugs, returning the bullet into the niche and closing the book. "Hey, you're the one who brought them in, alright? And I trust you when you say you haven't shot anything—or anyone with whatever gun this came from. Besides, you're more a lover than a fighter, my man."

"Shut up."

"So where'd you get them?"

I don't have an answer to his question, not right away. I didn't just trespass private property the night I walked in on Harlow as she lay passed out on my bed, hours after she considered ending her life. I committed theft, too. But there was no way I was leaving a loaded gun inside the Pearl with a suicidal woman, not after I read that damn note. The fact that she hasn't said anything tells me she either doesn't know that her gun is empty, or she doesn't remember removing the bullets herself; I have no idea. I just hope she doesn't have extra bullets hanging around somewhere.

"Does it matter where I got them?" I mutter.

Todd thinks about it for a few seconds before shaking his head. "Nah, it doesn't matter one bit. As a matter of fact, I don't want to know what gun it came from, and from whom, man."

"No, you don't."

"I figured." He slips the hollowed-out book back into the shelf and cocks his head toward the living room. "So, you want a beer? I got a few macadamia nuts, too, and they come straight from the plant itself. Turns out, they fall to the ground, and that's how you harvest them."

"Only took forever," Sawyer mutters as I sit next to him and pop open a beer that Todd tosses to me.

Through the windows, I can see the solar lights of the Pearl shining like a beacon in the night, only this time, it doesn't give me any peace knowing how I'd left it and the person staying there. I take a long sip and settle back into the couch, watching Todd take a hammer to one of the tough macadamia nuts still in its shell and smash it down against the coffee table. It rolls away from him, but he grabs it and positions it on a crack in the wood. Thank goodness their table's something they picked up during one of their dumpster-diving runs around Santa Fe. If it had been any of my custom tables, I'd have punched Todd's lights out for daring to ruin the wood.

The macadamia nut cracks, sending pieces of its tough shell flying at us like shrapnel. As Sawyer protests, reminding Todd to check online for a macadamia nut cracker, I feel my anger dissipating. There's no drama with the Villier brothers. What you see is what you get. They're funny, uncomplicated, and just what I need to forget Goldilocks for the night, if not forever.

By the time I make it back to Nana's house, it's almost one in the morning. Everyone's asleep, and I'm glad. Even though the Villier brothers' crazy antics made me forget all about Harlow, I miss her more than ever, the memories of the last two nights hitting me as soon as I shut my bedroom door.

It took every ounce of my willpower not to turn that truck back to the Pearl as I left the brothers' Earthship. The lights were still on in the living room, and though I couldn't see her clearly, I saw movement through the windows, just beyond the kumquat tree. I wondered what she was thinking, what she was doing. I wondered if

I did the right thing to walk away from her, vowing never to look back. I wish I could rewind everything and take back the things I said.

Still, Harlow lied to my face—twice.

As I step in the shower, the thought of being a father hits me like a punch to the chest with another one right in the gut. Sure, the chances are slim. Like, really slim, but what if she does get pregnant?

Will Harlow even tell me?

CHAPTER TWENTY-ONE

Harlow

It takes me a few hours to recover from Dax's anger. I can easily tell myself that he overreacted, but at the same time, I'd opened a raw wound when I asked about his mother and then admitted that I'd almost killed myself in the place he'd built to honor her. Not only that, but I lied to him about being on the Pill.

As I watch the sky fill with stars, I know he has every right to be angry at me. It didn't even hit me until after he said it, but it's true. *What about him? Did I even bother to ask Dax what he thought about being a father? Did I even consider his feelings? What if I do get pregnant? What then?*

But, of course, I didn't even factor him in, not when I was too blinded by my bitterness to see beyond my own needs. And he's right, too. *I am selfish.* Somehow, I had it inside my head that just because I'd lost so much—the miscarriages, Marcus, the end of my marriage and even having to walk away from the career I'd devoted most of my life to—I believed that the world owed me something.

Just because I saved so many children's lives, I bought the arrogant belief that I'm somehow entitled to something more than the fees I received for my services. And who the hell am I to search for payback out here, from people who had nothing to do with my shortcomings back in New York.

Anita, Sarah, Dyami, Benny... even Dax.

I should be ashamed of myself—and I am. Thank God I'm not drowning my shame with wine like I did eleven nights ago.

I chuckle in the darkness. Difficult to believe, but it's been eleven days since I almost pulled that trigger and ended it all. *And for what?* A man whom I allowed to obliterate my sense of self-worth all because he needed someone to belittle? Little Dick Jeff. I laugh again. Up until this moment, I'd barely even given him any thought, too busy living life to the fullest with Dax and learning so much about myself—the things I have, the things I want, and the woman that I am underneath all the professional titles I hold. Maybe I should celebrate this new development with a glass of wine after all.

And it's not the only thing I need to be proud of. Haven't I come far from that woman who walked out that door with the gun in her hand? The same woman who was determined to blow her brains out if not for that rational part of her succeeding in talking her off that ledge? I could even say that I barely recognize that desperate woman now. And maybe that's why I was meant to be here at the Pearl, so I could let that part of me die in some way without having pulled a real trigger. But I also know that I'm in this place now because of

Dax, who tried so hard to be a man for me even though, in the end, he failed, saying I should have killed myself in the Hamptons.

Harsh, I know. But he's also right, at least, about one thing. Jeff wouldn't bat an eye at the mess I'd leave behind. He'd simply move his wedding elsewhere. He'd also get everything he'd wanted from me—my half of the Hamptons property and everything else. He's still, legally, my husband in an equitable division state and God knows I've put more than my share into the properties he so wants all to himself.

I begin to pack my things, glad that I didn't bring too much on this trip. If I stay any longer, I'm afraid I'll seek Dax out and ask for his forgiveness again. But I can't allow myself to do that, not when he walked away the way he did. And he had every right to. I wanted to be pregnant so bad that I lied about being on the Pill to the first perfect sperm donor I slept with.

Sperm donor.

It's cruel to call him that because Dax is so much more than just a man with a big dick, but it's the only way I can justify letting him go.

I know I'm running, just like I did after Jeff filed for divorce, the same day after Oscar Peletierre, Chairman of Miller General, confided to me that the Board was getting ready to let me go because they feared for my mental health after Marcus. It didn't even matter that they had no burden of proof to their claim, that I had become mentally unbalanced and therefore a threat to my patients. Up until then, I had performed all my duties as a transplant surgeon without any problems. But

Jeff had threatened to go to another hospital if I wasn't let go.

Oscar had said that last part to me as a friend. After all, we were all members of the same club, and I had lunched with his wife, Dianne. But I knew better. He said it to me as *Jeff's friend*. He wasn't even going to go to bat for me by defending my performance record or bringing up how Senator Kingston had chosen me to do Penny's transplant over Jeff. Like all our mutual friends and acquaintances, he'd chosen which side he was on the moment Jeff filed for divorce. Not that I made the decision difficult; Jeff is personable while I'm distant, choosing to show the world how aloof I am because inside, I'm still that awkward foster kid who didn't feel like she fit in anywhere without her laurels.

But I know now that I don't have to fit in anywhere to feel whole. I'm heading home, even though I don't exactly know where home is anymore, not after finding it here at the Pearl... and in Dax's arms.

But that's only my foolish heart talking and not my brain, the one that knows I have a divorce to take care of, a career to fight for, and a promise to keep to a little girl who's going to see her tenth birthday in less than two weeks.

By five in the morning, the car's packed and I'm ready to go. I've spent the last hour cleaning up the place, emptying the refrigerator of any food I'd bought during my stay. I'm determined to return the Pearl the way I found it, for Anita's sake. It gave me more time to think things through.

Realizing now that Dax was inside the Pearl the night I almost killed myself angers me. He'd seen me at my most vulnerable and yet he never said anything. He knew. All this time, he knew. When I retrieve my gun hidden in my luggage, I discover it's not loaded. I must have been too hung over to notice how much lighter the gun felt when I put it away.

It only means one thing. Dax had seen the gun and removed all the bullets, just to make sure I wouldn't hurt myself. Now it makes sense why he came that day with the so-called amended rental agreement, saying something about extenuating circumstances. It had been an act all along. He came only because he wanted to make sure I wouldn't hurt myself on his property. Worse, it means that he read my note. *My damn suicide note.*

Dax knew.

The realization that dawns on me next strips me of every warm thought I'd felt for him. Was his choice to be with me done all out of pity then? The trips to Bandolier, the hot springs, even being with me? Sure, I'd given him many good reasons to feel sorry for me—my thoughts of suicide, my divorce, and my inability to have children— but did he have to keep it going for as long as he did, making me believe that he really cared for me? Did his whole family know?

Does it matter now, Harlow? You're leaving.

Thank God for rational Harlow or I'll never stop asking the questions. As I set the keys to the Pearl on the dining room table, I hear my phone ringing from somewhere inside my purse. I'm not answering any calls right now, not when I'm feeling too vulnerable. But I pull out my phone anyway, wondering if it's Dax calling to apologize, because if it is, I'm definitely not answering.

It isn't Dax but I don't answer it either.

I switch off my phone and return it into my purse, slinging it over my shoulder as I take one last look at my home away from home. I'm going to miss this place, no matter how quirky it is with its sun-shaped skylight, the indoor garden, and the colorful bottle wall that filters the emerging dawn. And no matter how angry I am at Dax right now, how can I forget the hours we spent making love on that king-sized bed, doing it in positions I never thought possible, and laughing more than I've ever laughed in a long time. Yes, I'm going to miss everything about this place, and as much as I loathe the thought right now, especially Dax Drexel.

I make my way to the front door, hating each step that takes me away from the one place that gave me so much happiness when I needed it the most. Maybe Pearl Anaya Drexel's ghost was looking out for me somehow, keeping me from pulling the trigger that night. I don't believe in ghosts, but I do believe in intention, and maybe that's it. Everything that she represents to her son permeates through the whole place—peace, love, and healing— even if it's out here in the middle of nowhere.

A beacon in the darkness.

"Thank you," I whisper to no one in particular before I flip the interior lock on the doorknob and step outside. Then I close the door behind me, and make my way to my car, getting behind the wheel and starting the engine.

As the night's condensation against the glass slowly evaporates, I watch my last Taos sunrise unfold before me, ignoring the tears that stream down my face until I can't stand it anymore. Then I wipe away my tears with the back of my hand, shift the car into gear, and make my long way home.

CHAPTER TWENTY-TWO

Dax

Harlow's car isn't at the Pearl when I drive up after attending church services with Nana, Sarah, and Dyami. I've had to beg off going with them to brunch, and already, I know Nana could tell something was wrong. I probably drove everyone sitting in our pew crazy from my nervous foot tapping all throughout the hour-long service. But with the service dedicated to Mama, there was no way I would have missed it for the world, even though a part of me wanted only to hurry back to Harlow as soon as I spied the sunrise through my window.

I'm not a religious man, but I'm spiritual enough. I commune through my hands, creating things of beauty with domestic and exotic hardwoods, and depending on what I'm building, blending them with forged steel, copper, and bronze. I'm there when a mighty three-hundred-year-old elm tree needs to be taken down because of Dutch elm disease, only to be given new life with my hands and my tools. The process can take years, with the piece needing to go through a drying process, but clients wait the same way they waited for Master Takeshi-san to create their custom furniture.

Some people have said that just like my mentor, I'm respectful of nature and what it gifts me—and I am—although there's nothing respectful with the way I treated Harlow last night, and it's something I'm going to make up for, no matter what I need to do. And so I say goodbye to Nana and everyone else, apologizing for not making it to the brunch with them, and hurry to my truck. Sarah can drive Nana home.

I need to check up on Harlow. I need to know she's okay after I royally fucked up and went all drama queen on her. Nana will probably kick me upside the head if she knew of the things I'd said, and she's not even violent in any way. But she'll be angry as hell either way.

Nana didn't raise me to talk to any woman the way I did with Harlow, no matter what she's done. I'm no Prince Charming and I don't pretend to be, though I've been called a few other things. Stuck-up asshole, because when I am in work mode, I *am* in work mode, and nothing can rip my attention away from what I need to do —definitely not when customers pay thousands of dollars for a simple dining table, a custom-built door, a bath tub, or heaven forbid, an intricate staircase that requires perfect measurements to match where it's supposed to be installed the first and only time. Prick, because that's what I am when I'm in man-whore mode when all I want is a one-night stand and not some damn commitment. Cold-hearted bastard, because when Madison almost bled out from an abortion she never bothered to tell me she had, I was there for her the whole time she was recovering in the hospital until she got better, before going back to work a week later as if nothing happened—*as if it wasn't my kid she just got rid of*. That's when I dumped her, and she called me a cold-hearted bastard, among other names like slow-witted and illiterate. After all, I'm still dyslexic; you don't outgrow that shit.

But if there's one thing I should have outgrown, it's my anger. I should have reined that shit in. I should have taken a deep breath, counted to ten, or twenty, or a hundred. I should have turned around and talked to her like the mature adult I tell myself I am. But no, I had to be an asshole, and here I am staring at the space where Harlow's car is usually parked and finding it empty.

Maybe she's in town getting breakfast or shopping. Maybe she finally decided to use the garage and park her car in there. I know she's still got a week before she has to return to New York, a week for me to apologize to her and convince her that what we have together, even if we'd only just met, can work.

But first, I need to apologize.

I sit inside the cab of my truck for a few minutes, watching the sun beat down on the landscape in front of me. In the distance, I see the Villier brothers' Earthship and know that they're probably still asleep. I get out of my truck and hurry to the front door. I knock, but there's no answer. I walk to the front of the Pearl, peer through the tempered windows and find the place empty. I return to the front door and this time, I fish out my keys. To hell with knocking. I don't care if I'm trespassing, but I'm going in.

My hand trembles as I slide the key into the lock and

turn it. How many times in the last week have I stepped through that door feeling like I was walking on cloud nine because I knew Harlow was on the other side?

But the moment I take a step inside the Pearl, my heart sinks. Harlow's gone. I can feel it in the air. The place feels empty and desolate though I still go through the motions of walking straight into the bedroom even though I already know what I'm going to see. Her luggage is gone, and so are the little items she'd arranged on the table by the TV, like little rocks and twigs she'd gathered along her walks around the Pearl and during our trips to Bandolier and the hot springs. And then there's the pile of medical journals she had a terrible habit of reading while in bed when she should have been relaxing, marking passages with a highlighter.

I gaze at the bed absently, perfectly made with not a wrinkle in sight. But I barely notice the details, not when all I can see inside my mind is us together in that very bed, the covers bunched down at our feet as we laughed, talked, made love and sometimes, just gazed at each other. How I loved it when Harlow studied me, her fingers making their way down my torso as she named each muscle and function, giggling triumphantly when she'd hit a ticklish spot, and I'd trap her hand between my own to stop her from tormenting me any further. And those moments when I'd taste every inch of her, smelling the scent that's like ambrosia, some chemical makeup that was created just for me. And oh, God, her laughter, her smile, her eyes. I miss her.

As I turn back toward the door, a piece of paper on

top of the pillow catches my eye. With a pounding heart, I pick it up.

Dearest Dax,

I'm sorry for leaving without notice, but I think it's best for both of us that we end whatever we have here before things go from bad to worse between us. Please know that I've never been as happy as I was here with you no matter how brief that time was, and I'm sorry for lying to you about being on the Pill, though I don't believe I owe you an explanation about owning a gun. Whatever I do with it is my choice to make, but even if I did plan on ending my life that night, I didn't, and that's what matters. I did not end my life. Instead, I chose to live, and I met you, and maybe that's how Fate works. But our time is over, and we both always knew this was going to end. You have your life, and I have mine, and now I have to return to my life and live it. If I should get pregnant, though I know I won't, I promise to inform you, and from there, we can determine terms of custody and what's best for the child. If I'm not, then you will not hear from me. I think it's for the best. You're young and you've got your whole life ahead of you, Dax. Live it to the fullest. Don't let me hold you back.

Love, Harlow

Anger fills me as I read the last lines again, my vision clouding. *Custody?* Is she already considering custody? I pull out my phone, wanting nothing more than to call her and tell her exactly what I think about this crap she's just pulled. And what does she mean, *I think it's for the best?* What about me? Just because I'm 27, I don't have a fucking brain? Sure, I fucked up yesterday when I lost my temper but still...

My call immediately goes into voicemail which tells me her phone is turned off. I listen to Harlow's voice instructing me to leave a message.

Please leave a message after the tone and I'll return your call as soon as I can. Cold and impersonal, just like its speaker.

"Harlow, I just read your note–"

Outside the bedroom, the front door slams shut. "Harlow, you here, baby?"

Great. Now, who the fuck is that?

I'm so angry that I can barely see straight—or continue speaking—and if I force myself to say something right now, I know I'll regret it. I fold up her note and hang up, slipping the phone back into my jeans pocket as I step out of the bedroom.

A man of medium height stands in the middle of the living room looking around, his expression bordering between amused and perplexed. When he removes his sunglasses, squinting as he looks at me, I see that he has light blue eyes. His blonde hair bears traces of gray that give him an authoritarian look. His jaw reveals day-old stubble, and he wears a blue button-down shirt under a light jacket and tan slacks, revealing a lean body that tells me he takes care of himself. I'm terrible with people's ages, but he seems to be in his late forties or early fifties, and right now, he looks like he's lost.

"Can I help you?"

"I'm looking for Dr. Harlow James."

I feel my jaw clench, my hands forming into fists. If this is another lawyer her husband sent over to have her sign those damn documents, then he's about to get chased out of here. "Was she expecting you?"

"Probably not. I'm not even supposed to be here." The man takes a deep breath and exhales. "But what can you do when you've made the biggest mistake of your life, and you have to do everything in your power to get back the one woman you love?"

I stare at him in disbelief. *Jeff-Fucking-Gardner? No way!* I fight back the anger roiling inside me and count to ten. *Keep your cool, man. Whatever you fucking do, keep your cool.* "I'm Dax, and I own the place." I hold out my hand, and he shakes it, his eyes narrowing.

"Do you know where I can find her? I was told she's renting this place."

"She left this morning. I'm here to get the keys she left behind and wait for the cleaning people," I lie as Jeff pulls out a handkerchief from his pants pocket and wipes his hands as if he'd just touched cooties.

"I'm Dr. Jeff Gardner, Harlow's husband. Do you know where she went?"

I shake my head. "I'm afraid not."

As if Jeff doesn't hear me, he continues, slipping his hands into his pants pockets as he gazes at the view outside the windows. "Sorry if I'm rambling but I've just spent the last few hours sitting on a plane and then driving up here from Santa Fe only to get lost. I didn't realize just how off-grid this place is. So not like her to stay so far away from the city, you know. Coffee, the gym, that sort of thing. She couldn't be without any of those nearby."

"She didn't seem to mind renting this place."

Jeff turns to face me. "She must have needed time to think. And it's all my fault. I drove her away." He pauses and shakes his head. "After we lost our son, everything just fell apart. All we wanted was to have kids, you know?"

No, I don't want to know so stop talking to me, I almost yell at him, but I stay silent, keeping my clenched fists along my side. *Count to twenty, Dax. Whatever you do, don't lose it. Hell, count backward.* "I'm sorry, man."

"I should have been there for her, but I wasn't. And now I realize what an asshole I've been when I should have been there for her." Jeff takes a step toward me. *Why he's telling me all this when he doesn't know who I am... or does he?* "Man to man, I'm sure you get what I'm trying to say, right? I need to tell her that I love her. She needs to know that she's the only woman I've ever truly loved. She's the only woman who understands me, my motivations, my ambitions. She's the only one who knows the real me, just like I'm the only one who knows the real her. We shared so much through the years, you see. But I—"

"Cheated on her?" The words come out before I can stop them, and I almost curse under my breath at my stupidity. But Jeff only pauses, nodding his head slowly in reply.

"Yeah, as a matter of fact, I did. And it's the biggest mistake of my life. Now I'm going to do anything to get her back. Anything."

I almost remind him that they're in the middle of a divorce, but what's the point? He knows that already. Instead, I focus on pretending I don't care, pulling out my phone to see that I just received an incoming text message from Gabe though I don't open it. I just need to focus my attention on something else so I don't give in to the desire to beat up the asshole standing in front of me. Besides, Jeff-Fucking-Gardner is not worth it. I put my phone away. I'll deal with Gabe later. "So what happened to the other girl? Was she worth it?"

"Oh, her." Jeff shrugs. "She was a no good, lying bitch. Why do women do that, huh? Lie through their teeth as they look you in the eye?"

"Probably the same reason we do the same thing. So you think she's going to forgive you? Harlow? I mean, Miss James?"

"I know she will. Because I know she still loves me. She always has. What we had was nothing but growing pains in a marriage. In fact, I've asked my lawyer to hold off the divorce so I could talk to her, discuss things like we used to. We used to be able to talk things out, weigh the pros and cons of the things--"

"Marriage isn't about weighing the pros and cons, man. It's about working together as a couple."

He studies me for a few seconds. "You ever been married?"

I shake my head.

"One day you'll understand." Jeff eyes me curiously, his blue eyes crinkling. "But look at you. You must not have any problems nailing chicks, looking the way you do. You look like you take care of yourself. They must be falling all over themselves to get you in the sack. What I wouldn't give to be as young as you again—"

"We need to get going," I blurt out, cocking my head toward the door. "The cleaning people will be here in a few minutes, and they can cause quite a racket."

Jeff walks toward the door, and I follow behind him. "My wife is the best thing that's ever happened to me, and I'll do anything in my power to get her back—and I know I will get her back. She still loves me." We reach the door, and he steps outside. "What possessed me to let her go like that, all because of some cheap—"

"Look, man. I'm sorry you guys were having marital issues, but really it's none of my business. I just rent this place out." I shut the door behind me harder than I planned.

"You're right. Sorry, I unloaded all that on you. Hey, did I tell you we're both surgeons? We work together— have worked together for years—and we've always been the perfect team. We even built an excellent department together—one of the best in the world. But sometimes people just make mistakes. No one is perfect."

Take a deep breath, Dax. You're almost there. He'll be gone soon. You can punch that bag at the gym. "Hope you get back to New York safely."

Jeff's brow furrows. "How'd you know I'm from New York? Harlow tell you that?"

"It's in her rental agreement. She had to sign one before she could rent this place."

"Ah, that's right. Anyway... Dex, right? Thanks so much for listening to me ramble like this. I appreciate it." Jeff sticks out his hand, but I pretend not to see it and turn away, walking toward my truck.

Fuck this. I'm tired of counting to ten, twenty, or thirty just to keep my temper in check, but I also know I can't go around punching people's lights out just because they can't help being assholes. But why do I have a feeling Jeff knows who I am? Frank must have told him about me. But in the end, it doesn't matter if anyone told Jeff. He's here, announcing that he's getting Harlow back, like some alpha marking his territory. I get into my truck and sit behind the wheel, watching Jeff enter into his rented SUV and drive away.

Damn it, Harlow. Please don't tell me he's right—that you'll just go back to him, that you'll forgive him. Please don't tell me that you still love that jerk.

I lean my forehead against the steering wheel, visions of Harlow and me now replaced with something else, and I don't like it one bit. Her with Jeff Gardner, the perfect team with their medical certificates probably fighting for space on their office walls. Successful Harlow James with equally successful Jeff Gardner.

And what have you got, Dax? You never even went to college. You only have a high school diploma and some mentorship with some Japanese craftsman... maybe even a year spent in Japan. But still... What's she going to tell her friends back home? That she only has you around for your big dick? Will she even tell anyone back home about you?

You're nothing but a distraction to her. And what's going to happen now that her husband wants her back? Come on, get real. She almost ended her fucking life for that man, and now he wants her back. He'll do anything to get her back.

Fuck this.

I put on my sunglasses and start the truck, knowing that I'm only going to work myself up over something I have no control over. But even though I may not be a fucking surgeon, I'm a master craftsman just the same. I just work with wood while Harlow and her husband work on bodies. And whether I have a college degree or not, I'm just as good as they are.

CHAPTER TWENTY-THREE

Harlow

WHAT A SURPRISE TO run into Gabe at a gas station when I arrive in Albuquerque four hours later. I would have made it down sooner, but I had to stop for breakfast in Santa Fe first. It wasn't like I was in such a hurry. But whether my world has suddenly become smaller, or it's simply fate, I spot Gabe topping off his gas tank on the other side of the platform like they tell you not to. He jiggles the lever, milking that pump of every last drop. He spots me the moment I get out of my car, his face breaking into a broad grin.

"Harlow, what are you doing down here?"

Clearly, Dax hadn't yet spoken to him about the latest developments between us. "I'm heading home."

He stares at me, surprised, as he returns the pump into its holder. "But Dax told me that you're staying for two more weeks." Then his expression turns stricken. "I'm sorry about my aunts at the barbecue yesterday. I overheard them talking about you, and I–"

"There's nothing to be sorry about. It's not like they

were talking about something I didn't already know. I am older than Dax, and I'm technically still married." I swipe my card through the reader and punch in my zip code. I try to be cheerful as if saying those two things don't create this stabbing feeling deep inside my chest.

"I still want to apologize for what they said, because true or not, it was still rude. And between you and me, they still hope that he ends up with my cousin, but even I know that's never gonna happen again. Honestly, I've never seen Dax this happy in a long time." He pauses and crosses the platform that separates us. "Want some help with that?"

"No, thanks. I'm alright." As I start to gas up my car, Gabe studies me, and I need desperately to change the subject before my face betrays how I'm really feeling. My eyes are still puffy from crying, and I'm glad my sunglasses keep that detail from him. "So what about you? What are you doing down here?"

"I've got a shift starting at noon at the ER," he says. "I do this every other weekend and then head back."

"Wow, Gabe, that's a long drive."

"It's only about two hours each way, and it's not bad. I listen to audiobooks on the way, so it makes the time go by fast." He shrugs, crossing his arms in front of his chest. "Pays good, too—for this area. I'm sure it's a lot more in New York."

"It depends. You're doing Family medicine, right?"

"Yeah, I am, and I have a Master's in Public Health, which is where I want to focus my private practice up in Taos. I want to improve primary care delivery and chronic disease care in low-resource settings."

"The world needs more people like you," I say, though I wonder how long his idealism will last before one more unpaid bill comes back to his office. "Just like Andrea Martin, down in the South Valley. She runs this for-profit, non-profit type of clinic, and they win grants for their equipment and work with UNM residents."

"You know Andrea?" Gabe's face lights up. "What a small world! We both did our residencies at UNM. So how do you know her?"

"I heard about her when she won that grant last year, and so I decided to stop by and check her clinic out. I volunteered my services for a full month." I finish pumping gas, and this time, I let Gabe take the hose and fit it back into its holder. I twist the cap to the gas tank and flip the lid closed.

"Not at all," he says, his brow furrowing. "But I don't get it. I thought you and Dax–"

"You and I know that wasn't going to last forever, Gabe."

He frowns. "But–"

"Dax and I are over, Gabe, and I'm going home."

His face turns pale. "I hope it has nothing to do with my aunts at the barbecue. I'm sorry–"

"No, it's got nothing to do with your relatives or anyone else, for that matter." I can see a bit of myself in Gabe from so many years ago before ambition overtook everything I believed in. Sure, I transplant kidneys and transform lives, but beyond the pre-op and post-op meetings with the patients, I normally don't have much interaction with them. I come in for the evaluation, what little I know about my patients gleaned from fellow doctors' crazy scribblings on medical charts and transcribed notes more than from my brief meetings with them. Penny was the only patient I allowed myself to get close to because I didn't want her to wake up alone after her surgery, and afterward, I didn't want to disappoint her by leaving too soon.

"But you don't have to leave so quickly," Gabe protests.

"I need to start driving back, so it's not like I have a choice." I pull open my car door. Behind Gabe's car, a driver honks his horn. "Gabe, can I tell you something?"

He glowers at the driver before turning back to look at me. "Sure."

"Never forget why you went into medicine. Don't let the bright and shiny things distract you from what's important—the happiness you get from doing what you love. Sometimes it's easy to lose sight of that, and then you end up losing sight of who you are."

"Is that what happened with you?"

"What do you think?" I sigh, feeling foolish for dispensing unsolicited wisdom. "Anyway, I gotta go."

Ignoring the driver in the car behind him, Gabe takes a step toward me. "Are you happy, Harlow? I mean, *really* happy?"

I think for a few moments. "What if I told you that I don't know?"

"Then I'll tell you right back that *I don't know* isn't good enough." Gabe takes another step closer as I push my sunglasses higher up my nose. "Did being with Dax make you happy? I hate to pry, and I know you two just met, but you both looked really great together."

I fight back the tears as I swallow, my throat suddenly dry. "Yes, Dax made me happy, Gabe, but now I have things to do in New York." I get in behind the wheel and close the door. "I didn't exactly come here without baggage."

"I understand." He nods, sadness filling his features. "But it doesn't mean you can't share the weight if he's willing."

The driver behind him honks his horn again, and I start the car, reaching out of the car window to grasp Gabe's hand. "Take care, Gabe. It's really nice running into you."

"Drive safe, Harlow." I hear him say as I ease my car out of the gas station. The streets in Albuquerque look deserted, and if this were Manhattan, I'd worry if an epidemic hit the city. But maybe like Dax and Nana, everyone's at church or enjoying brunch, or like Gabe, headed for work. Or maybe they're like me, just another tourist making her long way home, her itinerary all written down and scheduled down to her time of arrival at every stop, with her office manager in New York keeping tabs this time and new lawyer doing her darnedest to get the court to approve the change in counsel so this time, she can face things head-on instead of running away. The only thing Kathy or Phoebe won't know is that I need to return the gun I'd bought in Texas, ridding myself of the reminder that once upon a time, I bought it for a reason other than protection.

My phone rings as I cross the state line into Texas hours later. The moment I see that it's Kathy, I answer the call, putting it on speaker.

"Are you at the hotel yet?"

"No, Kathy. Probably in another hour, and then I'll need to walk all this sitting out on the treadmill. I'll call you the moment I check in."

"You promise? You won't be going under the radar on me again like you did the last five months? I don't think I can handle receiving just your emails this time."

I can tell the concern in Kathy's voice, and I can't blame her. I barely answered her calls when I left even though I responded to her emails because they were related to work. But I didn't want her to hear the despair in my voice, afraid I'd burst out crying the moment I'd speak to someone who knew of my pain firsthand.

Kathy had been there when I was first pregnant, just as she'd been there when it ended in a miscarriage right before the end of the first trimester. By the time I made the announcement for the third pregnancy only to see it end up in a D&C, I kept the fourth one to myself, only telling Jeff I'd lost the baby again and vowed to try one last time before giving up. Marcus was the result of that last final attempt, and this time, I waited till after I cleared the first trimester before making the announcement. If I had my way, I would have waited until the second trimester, but people noticed the difference right away. Apparently, I had a pregnancy glow, probably much like most pregnant women do. But like the others, Marcus was not to be, and this time, the attending doctors and nurses saw the anguish on my face when I held him, my beautiful son forever asleep.

"I promise, Kathy. Things will be different this time."

"How different?"

"For one, I have a new lawyer, Phoebe Taylor, and once the court allows the change in legal representation, I'll be doing everything right this time. I'm not giving anything away that is rightfully mine."

There is silence on the line, and I hear Kathy exhale. "That is the best thing I've ever heard coming from you since all this craziness began with the hospital and Jeff. Will you need a place to stay? With your ex living in the apartment with his fiancée, I wouldn't think the Hamptons would be ideal, not unless you plan to do everything from there."

"No, I'm not. Do you think you can find me an apartment? It doesn't have to be big. It can even be a sublet. It's temporary. A studio will do."

"Are you sure? You know how small studios are here in Manhattan. It'll be the size of a closet compared to what you're used to–"

"Yes, I'm sure. As soon as the divorce is final, Jeff and I will have split the properties equitably, and that's all I want. I can decide on buying my place then, but only then. Right now, I have some funds available, but I don't need a huge place."

"There's a studio that's opening up in a week or so on my floor."

Kathy lives in a two-bedroom apartment in the Upper East Side, a few blocks from where Jeff and I lived. All I remember is that she lives in an old building, one that is well-maintained. I can't be choosy right now, not when my priorities lie in focusing all my energies on my divorce and the hospital.

"If she doesn't mind such short notice, I'd love to take it. Do you know the owner?"

"Oh, yes. Riley's my next-door neighbor. Sweet, sweet girl. She just moved in with her boyfriend, some big-shot Hollywood actor who lives in the West Village," Kathy continues. "She was just telling me how she'd like to rent it out, but she didn't want to take out an ad. She doesn't want to do those short-term rental things. She'd get in trouble with the co-op board if she did."

"Are they okay with a sublet?" I can feel my heart race as I think of the possibilities that await me at home. Whether it's the size of a closet or not, it's a new beginning which is exactly what I need right now.

"They are, and you'd probably just need to sign some temporary lease, but you won't need to get approved by the board or anything. I'll ask her for you, and if she says no, I'll keep looking. She's a very sweet girl, really quiet and all that," Kathy pauses, before chuckling as she continues, "until she started seeing this actor."

I chuckle. Dax and I engaged in a lot of it, and fortunately, we were too far away from civilization to get any complaints. "Noisy sex?"

She snorts. "You got that right. Right through the walls, and to think that half of the floor is deaf because we're all too damn old as it is, but their sexy times go beyond just noise. I swear the walls rattle."

"You're exaggerating, Kathy." I can't help laughing, the memories of the many positions I tried out with Dax coming back to me. *This isn't going to be easy. I miss him.*

"Not when you live next to her, I'm not. But thankfully, it's been quiet since she moved in with her boyfriend. But don't get me wrong. I love that girl to bits."

"So can you ask her as soon as you can? I'll take care of the bank stuff the moment you let me know if she says yes." I switch on my headlights. Behind me, I can see the sunset from my rear-view mirror, glorious hues of red, orange and yellow. I already miss the lazy afternoons I sat behind the glass windows of the Pearl to watch the sunset free from the insects buzzing around me outside. How quickly everything would turn dark and then, the stars would come out, filling the night sky.

"I will," Kathy says before pausing for a few moments. "I'm glad you're coming back to fight him, Dr. James. And the hospital, too..."

"Thank you."

"What Peletierre did was still wrong, and if what you told me in your email is true—that you're coming back to fight the hospital, too—then good for you. If anyone should go down in all this, it's not you. It's Dr. Gardner and his poker buddy, Peletierre."

And his country club buddy, Frank.

I sigh. I don't really want to get worked up while I'm driving, and not when I need to get off the road soon. "Thank you, Kathy. I'll call you when I check in, alright?"

As I hang up, I can't help but feel sad again, the idea of another night without Dax next to me killing whatever happiness I'd felt just minutes earlier. But I know I'll get used to it. I'd told myself when this all began that Dax was just a distraction, and I was right. And as much as it hurt to hear him say the words he said to me, I'm secretly glad he did. Dax made it much easier for me to leave him.

Self-preservation at its finest.

CHAPTER TWENTY-FOUR

Dax

I KNOW Dad is in the workshop long before he makes his presence known by clearing his throat. He's a big man, imposing in every way, only to surprise people who assume he must be some retired football star when they find out that he's a stockbroker. But he did play football in his college years, earned a scholarship, and played his cards right till he graduated top of his class. He owned a brokerage company with offices close to the Twin Towers, and after they fell, he vowed to stay close to his family in Taos, even if it meant commuting as often as he could from New York to Santa Fe, chartering flights if he had to. It takes a real man to commit to his family like that, and I appreciate that. I always wondered why he didn't just sell the company after 9/11, but Mama told me she made him promise her that he wouldn't. Without his business, we wouldn't have been able to afford the luxuries we grew up with.

It's been two days since Harlow left, and I'm now back in Flagstaff. I waited till everyone got back from brunch that day before telling them I was heading back home. I didn't give them time to talk me out of it. I was packed and ready to go, and without any explanation, I left. They didn't need one. The news that Gabe had run into Harlow in Albuquerque traveled fast. As fast as the news spread around Taos that I was seeing an older married woman, the gossip that she had left the following day traveled just as quickly.

I can never forget the disappointment on Dyami and Nana's faces but a man's gotta do what a man's gotta do, and the last thing I wanted them to see was a lovesick Dax who fucked up big time and lost the woman he fell in love with. I needed to regroup, but I couldn't do it at the Pearl, not when everything reminded me of Harlow.

"Nana called." Dad's voice is a deep baritone, one of the traits I inherited from the man, along with his height, although my coloring is more like Mama's, New Mexican all the way. "She's worried about you, Dax. So is everyone else, even the guys here."

I continue planing the top edges of the wooden box I made that afternoon. I created the lid last, and now, it just needs to lay flat on its base which isn't as even as I'd like. I feel my muscles tense, not from what I'm doing but from what my father just said. From the corner of my eye, I see him pull up a chair and sit down.

"Why? Are they worried I'm going to hurt myself?"

"Should they be?"

That's Daniel Drexel for you, a man of a few words. He's been here since the day before I drove to Taos, thinking I had the Pearl all to myself only to find a passed out woman in my bed.

"Shouldn't you be back in New York, Dad? I've been back two days, and you're usually gone by now." I'm being rude, but I can't help it. There's a reason why I'm working late at the workshop long after everyone has gone home. Right now, I just want to be alone with my thoughts and complete my little project. It takes my mind off Harlow even though I haven't thought of anything else but her since she left.

"I get it, son. She hurt you."

I set the *hira kanna* next to me on the floor. It's where I've been sitting all afternoon, surrounded by wood shavings and the rest of my tools, a wooden mallet, and a chisel that took me longer to sharpen than use. It's how my mentor, Takeshi-san, worked, on the floor so he could use his feet and legs if he had to for leverage. He'd hold down a piece of wood with his foot as he chiseled, measured and put together the joinery, and it's just how he taught me, too. Just as it seems to root him to the earth, it grounds me, too, putting me in the zone of creativity, even if I'm only building a simple box without a single nail, screw or even glue. I don't do this for all projects, not when my company employs fifteen other woodworkers adept with modern machinery and the latest 3D technology. I only go back to the basics when I need to think—or create something personal, like the box in front of me.

"I'm alright, Dad. Really, I am. You know I get over these things fast." Yup, like a trip to the bar and then fucking some girl for the night without knowing her name. I don't want to do that now, though, not even when my phone has been buzzing with messages from women who just found out that I'm back in town.

Dad is quiet as he watches me pick up the lid sitting next to me and place it over the box to check for fit. It slides into the hand-chiseled grooves perfectly. By the time this rectangular box is done, it will have something hand-carved on top of it, one that hopefully represents its receiver, and then stained with a finish meant only to preserve the exotic wood I've chosen.

"Did he bring her flowers?"

I look up from my work, surprised. "Who?"

"Dr. Gardner. Did he bring his wife flowers when he showed up at the Pearl?"

"How'd you know that he was there? I didn't tell anyone."

"He ended up at the Villiers' place first, thinking it was the Pearl. Just walked in like he owned the place, and Sawyer almost shot his head off."

"Shit." Just like he walked into the Pearl like he fucking owned it, too, calling Harlow *baby*. "Is Sawyer okay?"

"He's fine. It's Jeff Gardner's head everyone should be worried about, but at least, the brothers had a good laugh. Todd ran into Sarah at the supermarket and told her," Dad says. "But you didn't answer my question, Dax. Flowers? Chocolates? Did Dr. Gardner bring any with him when he went into the Pearl looking for his wife?"

I hate how Dad enunciates the word, *wife*. "They're getting a divorce, you know."

"I know that, but until that divorce is final, she's still his wife." Dad enunciates the word again, and it hits me right in the solar plexus, made even more painful with the word that precedes it. *His.* But I force myself back to

Dad's question, and I wonder if Todd was watching the exchange between Jeff and me the entire time. Maybe that damn telescope is good for something after all.

"No, he didn't bring anything..." My voice fades as I realize the real purpose of Dad's question. It's not out of curiosity. He knows the answer already.

"If Dr. James left you, it's for a reason that has nothing to do with you."

And there you have it, the real reason he's here to talk to me, even if they have it all wrong. I fucked up first, and she left. Her divorce had always been there, sure, but I still screwed up. It's also a harsh reminder that nothing is ever a secret around Taos, and Dad knows that Harlow wasn't just a tenant to me. "What else did Nana tell you?"

"Nothing I wouldn't have heard from everyone else... that you're seeing some surgeon from New York. It didn't take me long to connect the dots, certainly not after Sarah told me who showed up at the Pearl while you were there." He pauses, takes a deep breath and exhales. "Nana also said that there are certain things best discussed between two grown men."

I set the box aside and get up from the floor, dusting the sawdust from my shirt and jeans. "So what are these 'certain things' that we need to discuss, Dad? Are you going to tell me that they're right? That she's still married to that jerk, so I should stay away?"

"Exactly."

I roll my eyes. "Oh, great. You, too. Why won't any of you give me a fucking break?"

Dad gets up from his chair. While I stand a good inch

over six feet, he's five inches taller than me and burly, a trait Sarah inherited while I got Mama's leaner build. "Because you can't afford this fucking break, or whatever you think this is, Dax. I don't know what happened between you two, or how she ended up at the Pearl, of all places. But what I do know is that you can't afford to get caught up in the middle of their divorce, not when it's already as fucked up as it is. She also needs to take care of things on her end first before she thinks she can run out here and have fun with my son and drag him into her mess."

"That's not what happened–"

"Why do you think Jeff Gardner showed up at the Pearl? Do you really believe he's there to get back together with her? Without a single bouquet or chocolates, or whatever it is we men would give some girl we want back so badly? Wouldn't we give her the moon if we could? I know I would if it means I can have your Mama back."

"He was hoping to catch us together," I murmur. "Just like her lawyer found us together at the Pearl. He must have been the one who told Jeff where she was."

"I don't know why he was there, son, but whatever it was, it was important enough for him to fly out to New Mexico."

"He wants her to give up her share of their Hamptons property like she gave up her share of their Manhattan–"

"It's not your business, Dax, or anyone else's," Dad says, his hand on my shoulder. "That's between them and their lawyers."

I exhale. Of course, Dad is right, like he always is whenever I end up too adrift in my emotions. Harlow's divorce is none of my business, and it's not like I didn't know it then before she and I ended up sleeping together. It's why I stayed away after I called Cole to see if he could help her with recommendations finding a new lawyer. Yet here I am, getting caught up in her business like it's my own.

"I'm not saying she's a bad person, Dax," he continues. "I don't know her, but I know her reputation precedes her. She's a good surgeon with better bedside manners than most, definitely more than her husband. But she's also in the middle of a divorce that she needs to take care on her own. The last thing she needs–"

"But what if she's pregnant with my kid, Dad? I was stupid. I..."

Dad pauses, and I see his jaw clench. Along with Nana, he was there to pick up the pieces after I found out what Madison did. Sure, I was too young, and she thought me incapable to be a father to our child, but it still hurt knowing I had no choice in the matter. "Then she's pregnant. But until then, you stay away and let her do what she needs to do. I know that box you just made is for her, and if you think you can send it to her now, please don't. Start over, son. Start clean with Dr. James when she's ready. If it's meant to be, then it will happen. And if she's pregnant, I know you'll know what to do. Your Mama and I wouldn't expect anything less."

Before I can say anything, Dad pulls me in a quick embrace and with a grin and a pat on the back, adds,

"Since you're so eager to get me out of here, my flight leaves in the morning. Can you drive me to the airport?"

***

Dad and I don't speak about Harlow at all when I take him to the airport. For the first time since I got back, we talk business like we always do when we're not reminiscing about Mama or talking about family, like Dyami's latest shenanigans. Dad is pleased with the new designs I've come up with, the orders we've recently completed and shipped, and my upcoming visit to New York in a few weeks.

For the last two years, a marketing firm has handled my visits to New York four times a year. I call them appearances, but Dad just calls it work. After all, I can't hide in my workshop forever. With articles written about me every time my designs win an award, he wants everyone to know who I am. The fact that at twenty-seven, I'm considered a master woodworker is a huge deal for him. To him, men like me are a dying breed. It's an accomplishment that wouldn't have been possible if I'd attended college instead of mentoring under a master woodworker like Takeshi-san. So for one week four times a year, I meet with clients from nine in the morning till seven at night. They fight over schedule availability even when they know that their orders may not be completed for another year or two—even longer for freshly acquired woods that need to be aged first. Some wait, some don't, but my production schedule is guaranteed for the next two years.

After my appointments, Dad used to take me to the private club as his guest, where he has his own bottle of cognac on the wall next to everyone else's, their names spelling out the Who's Who of Manhattan. He earned his place through hard work, handling investments of some of the richest people in the city. He was vetted there by real estate developer, Clint Caldwell III, whose wife, a former top model, introduced me to Madison. But Dad knows I prefer to hang out where I can let loose, like the Top of the Standard or Soho House in the Meatpacking District. Maybe one day I'll be just like Dad, able to move between New York and the Southwest with ease, but I'm too New Mexican for that. It's in my blood.

But that doesn't mean I can't hang with the likes of Dr. Jeff Gardner when I'm in New York. I'm not just some simple woodworker from Taos. I'm Dax Drexel, the man behind Takeshi-Drexel Woodworking & Designs, with a showroom right on Seventh Avenue and a client list filled with the country's Who's Who. I'm also a man who can't let anything—or anyone—stop him. And until Harlow tells me she's pregnant with my child, I'm moving on.

Harlow

By the time I make it to New York three days later, it's almost midnight. Not wanting to bother Kathy, I check in at the Standard and get a room with a view of the Hudson River and the High Line, an almost two-mile long public park that used to be a rail track that ran from 34th Street to St. John's Park Terminal.

I have all these grand plans of taking a walk in the morning, maybe even a quick run and a stop at the Whitney Museum of American Art, but I'm so exhausted that I sleep for fifteen hours straight.

The next day, Kathy shows up after I check out to help me move a few of my things from my storage unit into the studio apartment she managed to talk her neighbor into renting to me. As long as I didn't mind the cat hair, it was mine.

I'm not about to complain, not when it comes fully furnished, and I need some place where Jeff can't find me while I meet with lawyers and plan my next course of action. And with Kathy next door, apparently I get home-cooked meals included, too, judging from last night's invitation to join her and her husband, Clyde, for dinner, and a refrigerator stocked with a week's worth of pre-cooked food. She tells me it's temporary, just enough to get me settled. I'm so touched by what she's done I give her a deep hug which surprises her.

"Everyone at the office is really happy to have you back," she says as she tightens her embrace.

"I'm sorry I haven't exactly been the best boss, Kathy," I murmur. "Thank goodness for Addy who is my total opposite."

"That and all the Filipino lumpia and pancit dishes her mother drops off every week and we're all off our diets," she says, chuckling as she pulls away to look at me. "But you're not her opposite, far from it. You're a good boss. You respect us and that's important. Why do you think we've been working for you all this time?"

I grasp her hand, squeezing it. "You're more than an office manager to me. You're my only friend. You always have been."

"You've got more friends than you think, Dr. James," she says, heading to the door. She pulls it open but doesn't step out right away. "Get some rest. Call me if you need anything."

I know now that I always had a friend in Kathy Pleschette, but I was too busy building walls up around me to notice. I cared more about being the best in my field even as my personal life crumbled around me. But I can't keep building walls anymore, not when I've seen what happens when you don't have such high walls around you, and when you allow yourself to be more open yet trust others to have your back. I saw it for myself around Dax and his family, and I want what he's got—people who genuinely love him.

But who am I kidding? I also want Dax.

The doorbell rings just as I'm about to attempt unpacking the second box of medical journals I'd retrieved from storage. I'm not expecting anyone—Kathy had just left an hour ago after helping me settle in. Curious, I peek through the peephole and break into a smile as I spot Addison's familiar face in the hallway.

"Addy?" I swing the door open to find my business partner and fellow doctor balancing a large paper bag and two cups of coffee in her hands. "What are you doing here?"

"Kathy texted me your new address." Addison Rowe breezes past me, her petite frame somehow commanding the space as she sets everything down on the small coffee table. "I figured you'd need sustenance after the move. My mother sent lumpia and pancit. She says you're still too skinny and need to eat more after your 'wilderness adventure.' Her words, not mine."

I laugh, genuinely happy to see her. While Kathy has been supportive from an administrative perspective, Addison has been my professional rock through this entire ordeal. As the nephrologist who manages our transplant patients' long-term care, she's had to field questions from concerned parents when the news about my "emotional instability" first broke.

"Your mother hasn't changed a bit, has she?" I say, taking the offered coffee. Mrs. Rowe has been trying to fatten me up since she first met me when Addison joined the medical practice, convinced that my slender frame was a sign of malnourishment rather than genetics.

"Never. She still talks about that Christmas party three years ago when you actually went back for seconds of her pancit. I think it was the proudest moment of her life." Addison shrugs off her coat, revealing her usual impeccable style—a silk blouse and tailored pants that make me feel underdressed in my jeans and sweater. "So this is home now, huh? It's... cozy."

I smile at her diplomatic assessment of the tiny space. "It's temporary. Just until the divorce is final."

Addison perches on the arm of the single chair and studies me with the same clinical assessment she uses on her patients. "You look different. Not just the hair..." She tilts her head. "You seem lighter somehow. Despite everything."

I busy myself with opening the container of Filipino spring rolls to avoid her perceptive gaze. Addison knows me too well to miss the changes in me. We've been friends since our residency days, and partners in our practice for five years. She's the extrovert to my introvert, the one who charms difficult parents while I handle the surgeries.

"Jeff was at the office yesterday," she says abruptly, watching my reaction.

My hand freezes midway to my mouth. "What did he want?"

"Officially? To consult on Penny Kingston's latest labs." Addison rolls her eyes. "Unofficially? To remind everyone within earshot that his ex-wife—that would be you—had a mental breakdown and ran off with some young carpenter to live in an eco-commune in New Mexico."

I nearly choke on my coffee. "He didn't."

"He did. And he made sure to mention it within earshot of the Stratton family. You know, the ones whose twins are both on the transplant list?"

I set down my cup, my appetite gone. "He's actively trying to sabotage our patients' trust."

"It gets worse," Addison says, her normally bright expression somber. "Someone from the Hamptons Magazine was sniffing around. Apparently, they're doing a piece on 'prestigious medical professionals behaving badly.' Three guesses who's feeding them information."

"Jeff," I mutter, sinking onto the bed. "Of course."

"They're framing it as a midlife crisis story. Respected surgeon abandons practice to shack up with boy toy half her age." Addison sighs. "I shut it down, but they'll find someone else to talk. Probably Frank."

"And you?" I look up at her. "This is affecting your reputation too, Addy."

She waves a dismissive hand. "Please. The practice can handle a little gossip."

"It's not just gossip. It's my life they're dissecting." I rub my temples, feeling a headache forming. "And for the record, Dax is not half my age. He's twenty-seven."

Addison's eyebrows shoot up. "So there is a Dax?"

I feel my cheeks warm. "Yes. But we weren't 'shacked up' for six months like Jeff is claiming. It was only a few days."

"Mmm-hmm." Her knowing look makes me squirm. "A few days that clearly left an impression."

I find myself smiling despite everything. "He did."

Addison studies me for a moment, then breaks into a wide grin. "Well, good for you! After what Jeff put you through, you deserve some happiness. And some great sex, which I'm assuming was part of the package, judging by that blush."

"Addy!" I throw a pillow at her, which she catches effortlessly.

"What? I've been living vicariously through fictional characters since Kevin and I split. At least one of us should be having a satisfying love life."

I'd almost forgotten about her breakup six months ago. "I'm sorry. I should have asked how you're doing with all that."

She shrugs, but I catch the flicker of sadness in her eyes. "It was the right decision. Seven years together and sex had become as exciting as watching paint dry." She looks away. "My mother still hasn't forgiven me. She had the wedding invitations designed already."

"She'll come around."

"Maybe when I'm forty and still single, she'll finally give up." Addison sighs dramatically. "Anyway, enough about my romantic disasters. Let's get back to business. I've been handling damage control at the office, but you should know there's talk about some of our referring physicians getting nervous."

The reality of my situation settles heavily on my shoulders again. "Do you think we'll lose patients?"

"Some, maybe." Addison's honesty is one of the things I've always valued about her. "But the ones who matter—the ones who know your work—they're standing by you. Senator Kingston has been particularly vocal in your defense."

I nod, grateful for his support. "And the hospital lawsuit?"

"Moving forward. Lionel Chambers called yesterday to update me. He thinks settlement is looking more likely than trial." She leans forward. "But Harlow, I need to know what your plans are. Are you coming back to the practice? Or..." She glances around the small apartment. "Is this just a stopover before you head back to New Mexico?"

The question catches me off guard, though it shouldn't. I've been asking myself the same thing since I left Taos.

"I don't know," I admit. "I love our practice. I love our patients. But..."

"But you also want Dax," Addison finishes for me.

My silence is answer enough.

She reaches across and squeezes my hand. "Well, whatever you decide, I've got your back. Professional reputation be damned. Though I should warn you—if you leave me alone with Mrs. Donovan and her endless questions about her son's sodium levels, I might never forgive you."

I laugh, feeling some of the tension leave my body. "Noted."

"Now eat your lumpia before it gets cold. Doctor's orders." She pushes the container toward me. "And then you're going to tell me everything about this Dax person. And I mean everything."

As I reach for the food, I realize how much I've missed this—Addison's straightforward affection, her unwavering support. No matter what happens with Dax, with my career, or with the lawsuit, I'm grateful to have people like her in my corner.

"Thank you, Addy. For everything."

She smiles, the warmth reaching her eyes. "That's what partners are for."

<hr>

I run into Jeff the next morning as I step out of the elevator after visiting my new set of lawyers at Chambers, Maynard & Lipman. He freezes, his eyes wide as he stares at me, his gaze moving down my body and then back up again. It's as if he's seen a ghost, or maybe it's the new me dressed in something other than the usual neutral colors I always wore underneath my white doctor's coat. Today, I'm wearing a teal ensemble complete with a loose scarf that drapes down my shoulders. Even my hair is different from how I usually wore it, no longer tied in a tight bun. Behind him, people mutter under their breath as they squeeze past him to get into the elevator.

He's called me so many times since I left Taos that

I've lost count. Strange, but he was even nice in his messages. There was no name-calling or threats. He only wanted to meet in person so we could discuss a few things, like getting back together.

"Jeff, what are you doing here?"

He glances at the elevator doors closing behind me before resting his fingers on my elbow and steering me away from the center of the lobby to a corner. "You know my lawyer's in this building, Harlow. I've got a meeting with them about our... our divorce. Didn't you get any of my messages? You had me so worried, baby."

"I did, but I was busy driving, Jeff. You know how you're not supposed to be distracted on the road, right?"

"You could have called me back," he says, his voice sounding almost like a caress and it makes my skin crawl.

"Jeff, you know we shouldn't be talking without our lawyers present." I gently peel my elbow away from him.

"That's why I've been calling you. I want us to talk like we used to, baby, about–"

"Please don't call me baby, Jeff. I'm not your baby," I say firmly, hating the way the word slides off his tongue.

Jeff studies my face for a few moments before nodding. He exhales. "Look, I just want us to talk about working on our marriage again. We can get counseling like you asked me so many times. I was so blind then, and I am truly sorry. I really am. I made a huge mistake, and I want to make it up to you."

"You do?"

"You know I do, Harlow," he says, his voice lowering as he takes a step closer. No, Jeff can't possibly be trying to sweet-talk me now, is he?

"How bad do you want to make it up to me?" I give him my best open expression as behind him, people go about their lives.

"Anything you want. I made a huge mistake with Lei... with her, and I want us to start over. I'll do anything, Harlow. *Anything.* We can be a team again, do great things again. *Together.* Isn't that what you always wanted?"

I don't answer him. His words bring back no solace; instead, all I feel is the pain and heartache of the past year settling deep in my chest, a reminder of how it broke me completely to watch him walk out of the delivery room even as I held Marcus in my arms, foolishly hoping that maybe my body heat would revive him.

"Why don't we sit somewhere, maybe do lunch and talk about it?" Jeff continues, smiling. "Remember when we used to discuss cases–"

"I want the Hamptons property." I blurt out, the haze of painful memories fading. I square my shoulders, my back straight. *New Harlow is in the house.*

"Are you out of your mind?"

"It's called equitable distribution, Jeff," I reply as he stares at me in disbelief. "You keep the Manhattan property you had me sign away my share of while I was grieving for our son, and I keep the Hamptons property you're always trying to bully me into giving up."

Jeff frowns. "I was grieving, too, Harlow."

In Leilani's arms, where you found solace all throughout my pregnancy, thinking I didn't know. But no, I'm not saying it out loud. It's what Jeff wants to see—me breaking down or losing it by getting personal—but I'm not giving him that satisfaction. The last time he lost his patience with me, I almost put a bullet through my brain. "But that's neither here nor there. You moved on a long time ago, so stop the pretense and tell me why you really want to talk to me."

Jeff takes a step back, surprised. Or is it shock? Then the corner of his mouth lifts and I see the Jeff that I've always known. "Look who's talking about moving on. You moved on pretty fast yourself, too. In fact, I met him, your new boy toy."

I feel all the color leave my face, my throat turning dry. What does Jeff mean, *I met him?* When?

"After Frank told me where he found you, I had to go see for myself and ended up all the way in the fucking desert." He chuckles dryly. "And guess who I find instead? Dex, right?"

Before I correct his pronunciation of Dax's name, I catch myself, the meaning behind his words sinking in. I can't show Jeff what he's waiting for, that moment when he gains the upper hand. And if I rise to his bait, he will. I just hope Dax didn't hurt him. Is that why Jeff kept calling me after I left Taos? Because he was at the Pearl? Which means Dax was there, too, if Jeff claims he met him? What happened? What did they talk about?

"Cat got your tongue, Dr. James? I can see why you like him. I bet he fucked you senseless with that big dick of his, huh? How long were you hiding up there all this time with your lovely toy? All the last six months? Is that how you nursed your grief? You recovered pretty quickly–"

My hand moves before my brain can stop it, my palm

slapping Jeff across the face. I don't even care that people have stopped to look at us, concern written on their faces though most of them keep walking, minding their own business. We're in a building filled with the country's top law firms of all places, and the last thing I need is an assault charge but Jeff hit too low this time, and new me or not, you don't recover from the grief of losing a child by fucking some guy in the desert. No, one night sitting next to a loaded gun and wondering how that bullet would destroy a human brain lost in grief did that.

"Did he get tired of you?" Jeff continues as he holds out his hand to one of the guards walking toward us. The guard stops and nods before returning to stand by the door. "Or is he the reason you want the Hamptons now? You guys thinking of moving in together or something?"

"No, Jeff, I want the Hamptons property because I own half of it. Plain and simple. Would you like to me to explain the meaning of equitable distribution to you? Or would you rather let my new lawyer define it for you at our meeting?"

He takes a step back. "What... what meeting? I don't know of any meeting."

"Your lawyer will be calling you today for a meeting so we can discuss the equitable distribution of marital property like rational adults, *and* with legal representation this time. Remember, you got to keep the Manhattan apartment, and that's something they'll take into consideration at the meetings to come. Equitable distribution of our assets whether you acquired it legally and not through intimidation while your wife was undergoing emotional grief from losing our son could very well mean that the Hamptons property is mine."

Jeff sputters angrily, but nothing coherent emerges from his lips.

"I'll see you at the meeting, Jeff," I say, squeezing past him and walking toward the exit. The moment I step outside, I don't stop. I keep walking, taking in deep breaths and willing myself to calm down. I flag a cab and slip into the back seat, telling the driver my newly memorized address.

As the driver slips in and out of midmorning traffic, I'm glad I didn't say anything about Dax. I don't want to give Jeff the satisfaction of knowing how much Dax means to me, even if I was the one who walked away from what we could have had together. I have so many questions about what Jeff was doing at the Pearl, and what went on, what they talked about, but I have to let it go. If there's one thing his admission tells me, it's that Jeff is still Jeff, ruled by the fear of failure and now, the realization that he'd been replaced by someone younger, gorgeous, and way better in bed than he ever was.

But I also know why he really wants a reconciliation, and it has nothing to do with wanting to be with me. Kathy told me the juicy details the moment she showed up at the hotel yesterday afternoon, and I can't believe that I felt sorry for Jeff. Leilani is pregnant, sure, but it's not Jeff's baby. If what Kathy says is true—and this she heard from Jeff's office manager—he broke a few patient privacy laws to find out. During one of Leilani's routine prenatal tests to check for certain conditions like Down's Syndrome, Jeff had somehow added a paternity test into the lab order, and the results told him the baby wasn't his. With the wedding off and the divorce still on, somehow Jeff thinks he can pick up the pieces of our marriage and start over when all he really wants is to save face.

"I can't believe I feel sorry for the guy," Kathy had added as we took the elevator up to my sublet. "Well, a bit."

"I'm sorry for him, too, Kathy, but he started screwing around with Leilani while I was pregnant with Marcus. I know I wasn't the perfect wife, but I guess for some people, karma has them on speed dial."

Even the hospital is feeling the heat from my return. But that's what happens when they get served with a notice that I'm filing a claim against them. I'm just glad that I have an excellent legal team representing me—thanks to Cole's recommendations.

The moment I get back to my tiny studio apartment, I undress and slip under the covers. It's still morning, and I should be out and about, but I need a break from what just happened even if it's just lying in bed naked. I focus on the little things first, like how Egyptian cotton sheets feel against my skin, the way it feels so liberating to sleep naked under the covers. I like this little apartment with its king-sized bed that's way too big for the place, but at the same time, so perfect. It feels like a cocoon, small and comfortable. The young woman who owns it took pride in everything she did to make her home look nice, from the paint on the walls to the trimmed moldings, and the well-read books that fill the built-in shelves. The setup is totally seventies, but I love it. It's like being in a time capsule, with a few modern touches here and there, like a flat screen TV and the softest Frette sheets.

I reach for my phone on the bedside table and scroll through my voice messages, searching for one that I received three days after I left Taos, during my last stop in Pennsylvania. I really shouldn't listen to it, but I know I will. Like having tasted something unpleasant, I need something else to cleanse my palate of Jeff, even if what I'm about to hear is bittersweet.

The moment Dax's baritone voice comes on the speaker, my breath hitches. I place the phone on the pillow next to me and close my eyes, imagining him in front of me, saying the words I'm about to hear.

"Harlow, it's me, Dax. I want to apologize for the things I said to you. They were cruel words, and I'm ashamed of myself for even thinking of such things. You didn't deserve them. You told me the truth after all. It's not like you walked away without telling me. You did, and but instead of talking rationally, I totally lost it, and I'm sorry. The only reason I didn't say anything about the gun or the note is because I trusted you'd know what to do. I... I don't know, but I just wish I could have apologized to you in person. It's the least you deserve. You're the most amazing woman I've ever known, Harlow, and please, never forget that. *Never*. I read your letter, and I understand you need to move on, and maybe you're right. What we had may have been just... just temporary to you, but you know what? It wasn't—not for me." He pauses, and in the background, I hear a deeper voice ask him if he's ready to get going to the airport. "Shit, I gotta go. I hope you're finally happy, Harlow. I really do. Good luck."

I don't know why I have to listen to Dax's message knowing how it rips at my heart every time I do so. But can't a girl dream, even if she has to sift through the details and pick only the parts that don't hurt? I love the way Dax says that I'm an amazing woman. It sounds like an affirmation I need to hear every day and most of all, tell myself and actually believe it.

I miss Dax so much, his infectious laugh, his mischievous gaze and that big heart he wears on his sleeve. But I also know that I have things to take care of, and I can't afford the distraction. I dropped the ball six months ago when I packed up the car and fled New York, telling myself I just needed to grieve over everything that I'd lost and come right back, good as new. Sure, I told myself I was going on a cross-country trip, but at the back of my mind, I always knew it was a one-way ticket, like Thelma and Louise driving off the Grand Canyon with my demons right behind me. The purchase of the gun in Texas proved as much, no matter how hard I tried to fool myself into believing otherwise.

I scroll through my phone calendar, going through my schedule for the week. I've got more meetings with Phoebe to work out every single detail of my divorce. There are also meetings with a team of lawyers led by Cole's father, Lionel Alan Chambers, of Chambers, Maynard & Lipman, who is overseeing my case against Miller General. He's not heading it, but as one of the major partners, he'll make sure that everything is done right. Thirty million dollars in future earnings, legal fees and compensation for damage to my reputation isn't anything to laugh about, and with Jeff and Peletierre named in the complaint, I know they won't be laughing either. I already know that the hospital will settle the case and give me back my job, but this isn't about the job. It's not even about the money. It's simply a statement that says, *Harlow James is back, and she's not taking shit from anyone.*

She's also damn amazing.

CHAPTER TWENTY-SIX

Dax

So much for moving on. I haven't gotten laid in the last six weeks and it's killing me. And it's not for the lack of trying. My phone's been buzzing with messages and I can't show my face at Larry's anymore without having a damn good reason why I'm not going home with Becky, Tina, or Allison for the night. Telling them I'm busy is no longer cutting it and even the guys are looking at me funny like they're wondering where the real Dax is.

And it's not like I can't get it up all of a sudden. My plumbing's just fine. In fact, it's on overdrive and it's driving me crazy. But I just can't. I can't stick my dick in just any pussy that shows up within a five-mile radius. Not anymore. There's only one woman I want and she's nowhere near Flagstaff. She's in New York City and she hasn't answered any of my calls—not that she can. Her cell phone number now goes straight to her medical office, and everyone who answers tells me that she's out on extended leave.

Sure, I left her that one message saying I understood

her need to move on, but my heart didn't get that memo, just like my brain ignored Dad's warning to leave Harlow alone and I finished the box, spent two more days completing the accent on top of it, packed it and had it delivered to her medical office. That was before all hell broke loose in her world, and I just hope my gift reminds her of the peace she found at the Pearl... and of me. I miss her, and I just want to know that she's okay. I need to hear it in her voice that she is okay. Hell, I just need to hear her.

Because as if being involved in an acrimonious divorce isn't bad enough, Harlow's also in the middle of a lawsuit involving the hospital that let her go after she lost her son, Marcus. Newspapers report that Miller General Hospital terminated her contract while she was on medical leave, their reasons citing "a record of poor performance." Their lawyers now say that the fact that she didn't fight the termination for six months proves the hospital's right to let her go. After all, if they were wrong, wouldn't she have fought the termination immediately?

All this makes Harlow's words about finding peace at the Pearl even more poignant knowing she drove home to a shit storm waiting for her. And stupid me, I let her.

Each day, whether I'm working at the warehouse, meeting with clients or searching for a particular slab of wood for a special order, my phone buzzes over some mention of her or Jeff in the news. Hell, it buzzes when I'm in the damn shower, too, every bit of gossip showing up in my notifications. The New York tabloids can't seem to get enough of the transplant surgeon and the thirty million dollar claim she intends to file against the hospital for lost future earnings, legal fees and compensation for damage to her reputation. It's bound to get settled out of court, but until then, people are painting her as a money-hungry bitch, emotionally unstable and, if anecdotal reports are to be believed, cold as ice.

Harlow? Cold? Are they all blind? Some days I want to get on the first flight to JFK and find her. I want to pull her in my arms and tell her she's not alone.

So what the hell am I still doing in Flagstaff?

But I also can't go ape-shit over the whole thing. That's what lawyers are for. And if Cole's firm is handling her case against the hospital, then Harlow's in good hands. They know what they're doing, and her silence is part of that strategy. If she does or says anything without legal advice or worse, against legal advice, it will only work against her. Just as it would do the same for me as well.

But even as Cole is a lawyer, he's also my friend. I'm just glad he's not directly involved with Harlow's case.

"It's a cluster-fuck, man. Just leave her alone for now," is all Cole says when I call him tonight, hoping for a few answers. He could have said fancier words, all legal mumbo-jumbo to my ears, but the word he chooses is enough for me to understand how bad things really are.

"Can you tell me one thing?" I ask as Cole groans. "Just one."

"It depends on what you want to know, man. My firm's representing her so I can't tell you much."

"Does she still have a career in New York after this... this cluster-fuck is over?"

Cole exhales. "Let me put it this way, Dax, although I

have to warn you that what I'm saying is strictly hearsay, nothing you've already read in the tabloids, and you and I know how reliable they can be, right?"

"I know you can't say anything official, man. But just humor me here, okay?"

"She had an offer for a Director position at New Haven Hospital, and they just withdrew it. What does that tell you?"

"She's done."

"Pretty much, if the tabloids are to be believed. It's unfair, but no matter what happens with the case, no one's going to touch her now. Not around here. Not right now. Again, hearsay."

"Did she know this before she filed the claim against Miller Gen?"

"She should have, but she also did it six months too late," Cole replies. "Look, man, I don't know what to tell you. I don't want you dragged into this thing any more than you already are being dragged into it."

"What do you mean?"

"This one's new, so you may not have heard of it yet, but you will soon. Gardner is now claiming that she'd been in Taos all this time... with some carpenter, no less. You. So don't be surprised if your swanky showroom's getting a bit more attention than usual."

My showroom has been getting more attention, and not from prospective customers as Miko, my manager, emailed me yesterday. She mentioned that there had been photographers outside, but she assumed that maybe I must have won some award that Dad forgot to include in the latest company email.

"That's a fucking lie, and you know it, Cole." I really should have killed the bastard when I met him at the Pearl and buried him in the property. I'm sure the Villier brothers would have volunteered to help me do the job, too. "Five days, Cole. I was with her for five fucking days, not six months."

"Does it matter how long you were with her, Dax? What is important is that Gardner is using the court of popular opinion against her. And I'm not talking Twitter here, or Facebook. I'm talking about their friends... colleagues, neighbors, even patients. He's not pulling any punches in that arena. He's using you to taint her reputation even more than he already did with her emotional instability when they were married, and after their kid was born. And even if people do check the facts and prove him wrong later on, the damage has been done. You know how the people are, Dax. Shoot first, ask questions later. But while all that doesn't mean anything in divorce court, add that to the talk that she was getting her kicks with you when she should have been defending her reputation back home, it's a death sentence for any career, no matter how impressive. But she'll bounce back–"

"What about him?" I ask, controlling my temper the best I can. "He had an affair and even set a wedding date before the ink was dry on their divorce. Hell, it wasn't even finalized."

"The wedding's off."

I don't even hear him, common sense taking over. "Of course, it's off! He's still married to Harlow!"

"Dax, calm down. It's off because the kid Leilani's carrying isn't his, and so he dumped her," Cole says, and his words stop me cold. *Kid.* Harlow could be carrying my child, and if she is, how is this court of public opinion going to treat her then?

"How come no one's talking about that? All they're doing is smearing Harlow's reputation all over the place."

"It's not in the news because he violated HIPAA to find out, and it's now up to the AMA to decide. That's the American Medical Association for you." Cole's voice is serious now. "So even if Gardner isn't playing fair right now by dragging your name into their mess, it won't look good for him in the long run either."

"And Dad? It's not just my name. It's his, too."

"Your dad's not happy, but he'll be okay. But just like your lawyers have advised you in any case you've been involved in, it's best to keep quiet and let us do the work. But really, do his clients care what the tabloids say? As long as he keeps making money for everyone and you do that thing you do and win your furniture awards, he'll always be part of the old boys' club... just like you and me some day." Cole exhales. "Crap, I shouldn't have told you anything–"

But while Dad and I surviving the court of public opinion is one thing, Harlow is a whole different matter. "One more question, and I won't bother you anymore."

"What is it?" Cole's tone is wary, but he's letting me continue.

"How is she doing? How is Harlow holding up?"

"That's two questions, man. But honestly, I can't tell you. I don't know."

If one night alone at the Pearl had Harlow come face to face with her gun, what about now? Who's got her back now that she's caught in this whole grand mess? She doesn't have any family. She doesn't have anyone, not in New York. Shit, I should have called her sooner. I should have insisted on seeing her. "Come on, Cole, throw me a bone here."

"I already did. I told you more than I should be telling anyone."

"How do I get a hold of her? I've tried calling her office, but it's like fucking Fort Knox over there. She's never available, or they're screening all her calls."

"I don't know, man. I can't–"

"Cole, come on. Please."

Cole is quiet for a few moments. "Wow. You're not even blackmailing me with the bath tub Millie ordered."

"It wouldn't have been fair, man. She ordered it, not you." I say although I pause, curiosity getting the best of me. Cole and I shoot the breeze every time I'm in New York, but that's about it. Guys being guys, we don't talk about things like love. "Can I ask you something personal?"

"Sure."

"How did you know Millie was the one for you?"

I hear Cole chuckle. "That's easy. I couldn't see myself with anyone else. Even when we broke up for a while. But your mom helped me make the decision when Dad and I visited you guys in Flagstaff just before she... well, before she passed away."

"What did she say?"

"'So what's it going to be, Cole? Fish or cut bait? That girl's not gonna wait forever,'" he replies, his voice going higher as he tries to imitate Mama. "You know how much she loved to go fishing, so it was no surprise coming from her. She'd have gone along on our deep-sea fishing trips if your dad had let her."

We laugh. "Nope, Dad saw *The Perfect Storm*, and that did it for him. He hates it when he can't control anything, and any body of water is his nemesis." Dad, ever the city man could never be a fisherman. Mom did a better job catching and cleaning whatever we caught. "You got Dad to a T, alright. But Mom loved him just the same."

We're silent for a few moments before Cole speaks. "You know he's not seeing anyone. Not even after five years."

"He has lady friends."

"Yeah, but he's all about his kids... especially you. He's very proud of you, Dax. I just wish my dad were like yours, though."

It's no secret that Lionel Chambers is tough on his only son, sometimes too tough for my taste. He's never praised Cole for anything, not even when he wins cases for the firm. There's always a case bigger than the one he'd just won, another chance to prove to dear old dad that he's good enough to earn the position of senior partner one day.

"He's proud of you, Cole. I see it."

"I'm glad someone does," Cole says wryly. "Well, back to your problem, man. I figured, after all, this time, you'd have moved on. You normally move on pretty quickly."

That's what I had thought, too, and God knows I did go out there and try to forget Harlow, hanging with the guys like I always did after work only to go home alone every night. It just didn't feel right. "Guess I've decided to fish."

"Kathy Pleschette," Cole says.

"Who the hell is Kathy Pleschette?"

"The next time you call Dr. James's office, Kathy's the one you need to ask for, Dax, my man. She's the gate-keeper of Fort Knox. *Your* Fort Knox."

It takes a few sparring rounds at the gym to work out all my frustrations, but it works. By the time I'm done, I'm a lot calmer and less likely to hurt anyone who crosses my path. Who I really want to beat up is Jeff, but I know better than to let my fists do the talking, the way I did with Frank.

The only reason Frank probably isn't suing is that he doesn't want to get dragged into the mess that his friend's already in. And while Dad can take care of himself, I'm worried about Harlow, and how she's faring with every-thing going on. Does she have anyone to turn to? What about the gun? Does she still have it? And as much as I've been telling myself that there's no way Harlow would do what Madison did, it's been six weeks since we slept together and I can't help but wonder, would Harlow know by now if she's pregnant?

Would she tell me?

CHAPTER TWENTY-SEVEN

Harlow

FIVE TEST RESULTS saying the same thing surely can't be wrong. Or can they?

I rest the pregnancy strip on a hand towel spread out on the bathroom counter next to the other four I just did, their results clear as day. I'm honestly out of morning pee to test for the presence of hCG, the pregnancy hormone, although at this point, I doubt I need to do it again. I've run the same test the last three days and each day, the results are the same. Even the ones from the dollar store came out positive. Pink line, blue line, single line, double lines—they all say the same thing, just as I'm sure the blood test I took at my doctor's office yesterday will say the same thing, too.

I'm pregnant.

That would make six weeks, and as I stare at my reflection in the mirror, one thing hits me. The one thing that I told myself would never happen—couldn't happen even if I wished it would—has happened. I'm pregnant without having gone through any hormone therapy or in-vitro fertilization procedures. No one artificially implanted this fertilized egg into my uterus. This time, it took just one man and countless enthusiastic sessions to do the job.

And a lie.

As much as I denied it, I recognized the signs immediately—tender breasts that had me finally giving in and getting new bras two days ago, the fatigue that has me constantly yawning at the office, and the many trips to the bathroom. And then there's nausea that continues to greet me at the oddest times during the day. It still does, though right now, as I slip back under the covers to collect my thoughts before getting dressed for work, I'm feeling fine. I just wish that everything else about my life was fine.

Even though my divorce is winding down and I get the Hamptons property as part of the settlement, my intent to file a claim against the hospital has blown up to epic proportions. And it's not even the case itself which is merely my intent to file one against them to contest the grounds for my dismissal. It's how it's affecting everything and everyone else in my life.

If I had thought then that being shunned by our friends when Jeff filed for divorce eight months ago was bad enough, it's nothing compared to how things are now. Burning bridges has never been more appropriate, although, in the professional world, it just means that fellow doctors are more wary of speaking with me now, and friends just don't want to be dragged into the mess even if they've called to make sure I'm fine. It doesn't help that Jeff is spreading lies about Dax and me, claiming that I'd been shacked up with him in Taos all this time. Jeff knows it's not true, but if it means that it will draw attention away from him and Leilani's betrayal, then he'll do anything.

I wish I could do something—say something—but I have to pick my battles. And right now, the best recourse against Jeff is silence, just as my lawyers advise me. Besides, I still have a medical practice to run. I still see patients; any scandalous talk about me is the least of their concerns. What matters to them is the welfare of their children, most likely on dialysis while waiting for their small bodies to have enough room to accommodate the donor kidney which in most cases, comes from an adult relative or match. I also have research papers to finish. Thank goodness the latest studies on cardiovascular risk factors in pediatric renal transplant patients don't stop for scandals either. As far as things go, this is my new normal.

Still, there's nothing normal about my new normal. I'm in uncharted waters, and while Old Harlow would have lost it a long time ago, her perfectly planned career going down in flames, New Harlow is unfazed. Well, almost. I finally started seeing a therapist on my own, twice weekly sessions that I now look forward to. I've kept everything bottled up for so long it feels good to let it out, even if my sessions are limited to an hour each time. I did take New Haven Hospital's withdrawal of their offer a bit hard, but not too hard. It didn't matter. Sure, it bruised my ego, but I'd always felt at the back of my mind that I wasn't going to be happy doing the same thing again. Or maybe it was because the Senator warned me of their decision ahead of time when I attended Penny's tenth birthday party in the Hamptons.

Thank heaven for little blessings, that she's been spared the news surrounding her favorite surgeon. As far as Penny is concerned, I'm still the angel who sat next to her after her surgery, holding her hand till morning because she asked me never to let go. I only let go when the Senator arrived the following morning, and from that moment on, he's treated me like part of their extended family. But his patronage can only go so far. When it comes to my legal troubles, Senator Leon Kingston has to steer clear. The only statement his office has released is that he and his wife had personally hand-picked me for their daughter's transplant over the leading surgeon, Jeff Gardner. "A personal choice based on Dr. James's exceptional skill set, her impeccable surgical record, and her compassion for her young patients," is the quote that the papers have chosen to run. And right now, that's good enough for me.

I can say this is all my fault. I should have remained silent and disappeared the way Jeff would have expected me to. But why should I? And why now after I'd found myself? So I got fired while I was on leave; so what? So I didn't fight the termination the moment it arrived in my mailbox while I was away; so what? So I allegedly have been shacked up in some off-grid New Mexico love nest owned by a carpenter all this time; so fucking what?

Only now, I'm pregnant with that carpenter's child.

I get out from under the covers and reach for a wooden box tucked under the bed. It's got some weight to it, not just from the piece itself, but from the little treasures I've placed inside since I received it a few weeks ago. I pull out the handmade box built using Japanese joinery or *sashimono* from its hiding place and rest it on the bed next to me. I really shouldn't hide it at all, not when it's the work of a master craftsman, but I also don't want it too far from my favorite place in this tiny apartment, my bed. In the craziness of my current life, I like having a part of Dax close by, even if it's just a box.

But it's not just any box. This one is pure perfection. Dax made it just for me and it's breathtaking. With my finger, I trace the sun and moon carved in relief on the lid. It's beautiful, and I'm so glad now that I didn't turn it away. Pride almost made me tell the petite Japanese-American woman who delivered it to my clinic to take it back. But my heart won over, and I accepted it and unwrapped it in the privacy of my office. Then I bawled my eyes out at the beauty before me, at the exotic woodsy smell that brought everything back, of the perfection of the entire piece with its gorgeous lid that slid down to conceal the box beneath it without me needing to push it down. It brought back all the memories of Dax and the feeling of home whenever I was in his arms.

As I lift the lid, I see the little mementos I collected during my long drive, though most of them come from New Mexico. There are small rocks I picked up during my walks around the Pearl, at Bandolier and the hot springs, even at Arroyo Seco where Dax said his mother taught them all how to fish, even his dad. There is also a smudge stick of sage and sweet grass that I bought from a shop at Taos Plaza, a reminder that the last six months of my life was a cleansing and a new beginning. Then there's the message that Dax burned at the back of the lid, words that I've memorized from the first moment I read it. I trace the letters with my finger, imagining him hunched over the wood as he wrote out the words, his brow knitted in concentration.

Did he mean every word?

I bring the lid back down on the box and roll onto my back. For the next few minutes, I let myself sink into my body, forcing everything else out of my mind. I let my hand drift down my belly, my thoughts shifting to the life that's stirring inside me. This time, I don't feel any guilt for having done what I did, even though it took me forever to admit it to myself then. I lied to Dax about being on the Pill, and now here I am, that lie blossoming into new life inside my belly.

At six weeks, though she's only the size of a pea, there's a heart that's already beating furiously, at about 100 to 140 beats per minute. And if she's like her father, it's a strong and resilient heart—a heart that I pray hasn't yet given up on me.

"You want to get something to eat?"

I look up from my laptop screen to see Kathy standing by the door to my office. It's one o'clock, which means I've been hunched over my laptop for the last four hours. Behind her, the staff is getting ready to break for lunch, deciding between pizza or Greek food. "I don't know, Kathy. I need to get this paper finished before my patients come in at three."

"But you also need to eat, Dr. James. You haven't been yourself lately, and I'm worried about you."

I close my word processing program and log out. "You're always worried about me, Kathy."

"I thought we could check out a new restaurant that opened up down the street. Maybe it'll cheer you up. Come on. My treat."

"Twist my arm now, why don't you?" The moment the words emerge from my mouth, the memories come. Dax had said those exact words to me first when I told him he could stay at the Pearl on the condition that he stay on his side, and I stay on mine. Of course, none of us followed that rule, choosing instead to use that king-sized bed as neutral ground.

I sigh. Oh, the perks of being pregnant, being melancholic and emotional which is exactly how I'm feeling at the thought of Dax and my pregnancy. I promised to tell him if I was pregnant and now I am. So why haven't I picked up the phone? Because I'm afraid, that's why. *What if, like the first pregnancies before Marcus, I miscarry?*

"Are you okay?" Kathy's worried face looms in front of me. "You're white as a sheet. Did you even eat anything today other than the banana nut muffin I brought in?"

Clearing my throat, I power down my laptop and get up from my chair. I need some fresh air. And no, I am not losing this baby. Her heart is strong, just like her father's.

"I'm just hungry, Kathy, that's all," I say as I grab my purse. "You ready?"

———

"So tell me about this Dax Drexel guy that Dr. Gardner can't stop harping about. You never talk about him," Kathy says halfway through our lunch at Santa Rosa Restaurant. The restaurant is only two months old, and already it's packed with millennials wanting their taste of *chilaquiles* and lunchtime margaritas. Or in my case, *chorizos con huevos y papas*. And after eating most of it and hoping pregnancy heartburn won't creep up on me while I'm seeing a patient, I'm in heaven. Well, almost. Heaven would be Anita Anaya's cooking and everyone sitting around that live-edge table laughing at something Dyami is saying.

"What do you want to know?" I try not to look too defensive, but at the same time, I'm not. Kathy has been there for me since I got back, and other than casual friends who call to say hello and find out how I'm doing, she's the only one I've allowed into my personal space. Heck, she got me my personal space.

Kathy shrugs. "Is it true that you were with him like Dr. Gardner says?"

"I was only with him for five days. Seven days, tops. Not six months. I spent a month in Albuquerque with Dr. Martin, remember?"

"Did you like him?" Kathy looks at me, her brow furrowed. "Do you like him still?"

I sigh. "I did like him... a lot. But it wasn't going to work out, not with my divorce still pending. The last thing I needed was another drama between Jeff and me."

"Drama came anyway, didn't it? Dr. Gardner made

sure of it by telling lies about you and this Dax guy. But your divorce is almost final. You told me it's now with the judge. So, what I want to know is, if Dax comes back, like if he were to be in town, would you have him? Would you see him again? Or is it all over between you two?"

This time, I'm starting to feel defensive. Kathy has always been blunt, and while I know she and everyone at the office have been dying to know if all the talk about Dax and me is true, she's held off asking. Until now. "Why are you suddenly so interested?"

"Dr. Gardner obviously feels threatened by him, and I don't blame the guy. Serves him right after the way he treated you. I looked up Dax Drexel, and he's a catch. He has a showroom on Seventh Avenue. Expensive stuff, too. Really expensive stuff, and I hear he designs them all." She arches her right eyebrow suspiciously. "You're also glowing."

I stare at her. "Excuse me?"

"You've got a glow about you that I've never seen before," Kathy says, leaning back in her chair. "You'd have gone ballistic with all this talk about Dax and you going at it like bunnies. You'd have sued Dr. Gardner for libel. But you haven't. You're calm. Too calm, for that matter. And the only times you've been this way were when you were..." Her voice fades, but I can feel her studying me. She can't say the word, and why would she? Every one of them didn't make it.

But I'll say it for her. "Pregnant?"

She nods. "You were always more careful with your emotions every time you were pregnant. Only this time, there's one more difference and this, you never did then."

"And what's that?"

"For the first time, you're pulling away from your career. You're cutting back on your schedule, and you're no longer putting so many things on your plate like you always did. No more research papers or rotations in other hospitals. You're also spending more time at home than you did back then. You're nesting."

I feel my face color. "It could also be your imagination, Kathy. All Jeff's talk about my sexcapades in Taos is getting to you."

She reaches for her purse and hands me an envelope. "This arrived this morning. I managed to sort it before anyone else did so no one has seen it but me."

I take the envelope from her hand, hating that I'd absently written down the office address when I blanked out and couldn't remember the simple details of my sublet. It's from Dr. Teves, my obstetrician, the same woman I've gone to for all my earlier pregnancies.

"How far along are you?" Kathy asks as she studies me carefully.

This time, there's no beating around the bush. Kathy knows. "Six weeks."

"Does he know?"

I don't answer right away, tearing open the envelope and taking out the slip of paper that will tell me what I already know. And it does, along with numbers that I don't expect at all. They make me do a double take as Kathy signals for the check. *It can't be.* I fold the paper and slip it back into its envelope.

"Are you going to tell him?" Kathy asks as I tuck the letter into my purse.

For a moment, I forget her question. "Um, of course, I will. But I think I want to wait until after the first trimester. You know how–"

"So he waits? Do you think that's fair?"

I frown. "This is none of your business anymore, Kathy."

Kathy rummages through her purse, retrieves a thick envelope that looks like a formal invitation and hands it to me. "This arrived for you while you were in your office. He hand-delivered it, but he knew better than to ask to see you. So he asked me to make sure that you received it. He seems like a nice man. Damn good-looking, too."

My hand shakes when I take the invitation from Kathy's hand. The envelope bears the name *Takeshi-Drexel Woodworking & Design* in gold-leafed lettering. My name is hand-written in the middle of the envelope along with a drawing of the sun and the moon, much like the drawing that he carved in relief on the box lid. As I open the envelope and pull out an invitation to a private event for tonight, I read the same message he wood-burned onto the back of the lid.

You are the moon and the stars to my sky, my lovely Harlow. And my world is dark without you.

I bring my hand to my mouth, fighting back the tears. I can see him writing the words. So intent, so focused, just like he always was with me, whether it was having a simple dinner of homemade pizza from across the table or making love to me. He looked at me like I was the only thing that mattered to him then. And maybe I still do, even after six weeks where I couldn't even honor him with a simple phone call.

"But what if I have a miscarriage like the others, Kathy? I'll just be telling him for nothing. It will just hurt him." The dreaded words spill from my lips before I can stop them and Kathy sighs. She reaches for my hand and squeezes it.

"He still deserves to know, Dr. James. The sooner, the better."

CHAPTER TWENTY-EIGHT

Dax

"I WISH you'd just wait until after her divorce is officially final before you do anything stupid."

Dad's words break through my thoughts as I sit on one of the benches at the Garden of St. Luke in the Fields. It's a tiny park in the heart of Greenwich Village, and right now, I'm trying to calm myself down after being mere feet away from Harlow. Knowing she was in her office was enough to make me throw caution to the wind and ask Kathy—beg her—if I could talk to Harlow right there and then.

But no, I could not do that. *Just drop off the invitation, Dax, and walk out that door. Kathy said as much that it was all you could do. It's exactly why she asked you to come over and drop the invitation at a specific time.*

Some days I wonder if I'm just being a fool, falling for a woman so hard after spending only five days with her. Every moment is stamped in my memory—every smile, every laugh, and even every single tear that I wiped from her beautiful face. But I threw all that away in a moment of anger, and here I am, lost in a secret garden in the middle of Manhattan. But I'm not really lost. Dad's driver knew exactly where I was going, and he must have called his boss to tell him where his son was.

"I didn't do anything stupid if that's what you're worried about."

"Sophie was quite disappointed that you left early last night. She was looking forward to spending more time with you," Dad says as he sits on the bench next to me. He's a regal looking man in his suit and glasses, and one day, I'll probably end up just like him if I didn't have too much of Mama in me. The artist, more comfortable in jeans and a t-shirt than what I'm wearing now, a suit that's slowly growing on me. I don't need to wear one, but I still do. It's the least I can do to look like a man whose skill is worth investing thousands of dollars on.

"Is this your idea of making sure I don't sneak out of your sight and find Harlow? By distracting me with booze and women?"

Dad laughs. "Distract you? Dax, this is no different than the last time you were here, and the time before that. And it didn't have to be me doing the plying. You did fine by yourself with your buddies. So no, I'm not doing all this so that you'll forget the lovely doctor."

"I told you this trip isn't like all the others, Dad, and I meant it."

"Doesn't mean we ignore the fact that everything's been planned for months. Other than the PR, the parties, the meetings, and the one-on-one consultations for new orders have all been on the calendar since the beginning of last quarter." Dad pauses. "But even with this self-imposed vow of celibacy that you seem to be taking, what if she says no?"

I shrug. "So she says no."

"It's been six weeks, Dax. Thank God, she's smart enough to stay away from you. It's not like her husband hasn't dragged your name through the whole mess as it is, and she's already been described as emotionally unbalanced. They say she lost it when her baby died at childbirth and drove off without telling anyone. They also say that she's frigid–"

"Would you want me to inform the press that they're wrong? That she's far from frigid, Dad? I'm sure someone will pay me five grand to say something, wouldn't they?"

Dad turns to look at me, looking not at all pleased. "You wouldn't dare."

"You're right. I wouldn't, but that doesn't mean I'm letting the tabloids tell me what to think about Harlow. They know nothing about her."

"And you do? Dax, this is ridiculous and you know it. You only knew her for five days."

"I know more about her in five days than I know about the very people I've known all my life, Dad, and right now, you're one of them. And it's not like you didn't fall head over heels over Mama when you first met her. You told me once that you would have proposed to her less than a month after you met her. So why are you giving me such a hard time?"

We don't speak for the next few minutes. We watch couples walk past us, hand in hand and lost in each other's eyes. I wonder if they're stealing moments together during lunch or maybe just spending the day together. After all, this little garden hidden behind brick walls is the perfect place to escape from the humdrum of Manhattan, although right now, Dad is ruining the experience. I just don't understand why he dislikes Harlow so much. So she's older than me. So what? It's not like I'm a kid and don't know what I want. I'm old enough to think for myself and up until Harlow, Dad's had no problems with the women I've chosen to share my bed.

But none of those women have my heart the way Harlow does. And maybe, until she says no and that we can't be together, my heart will finally get the memo, and I'll move on. But only until then.

"I don't hate her, Dax, if that's what you're thinking," Dad says slowly. "I just hate seeing you dragged into this whole mess that has nothing to do with you. Too bad Gardner thinks he can use you to destroy his wife's reputation."

"I can take care of myself, Dad. And I'm sure Harlow can, too."

"I also don't want you to get hurt. You care too much, Dax. You love too much, just like your mother."

"Call it a character flaw then, but that doesn't mean I don't know what I'm doing."

"It wasn't a character flaw with her, and it sure isn't with you," Dad says. "Look, I know you're not the same kid who punched the guy Claudia fooled around with in that bathroom. And God help me, but I'm just glad you handled meeting Gardner at the Pearl with grace. You didn't punch his lights out."

There's a hint of a smile on his face even though I glare at him. My temper can't be that bad. I may have almost killed a man in some bathroom because he told me he'd just fucked my girl, and she loved it, but I went through the court-mandated anger management courses and God knows, these days, I've been spending more time at the gym channeling my anger into a punching bag.

"Like I said, Dad, I can take care of myself."

"Good," Dad says, getting up from the bench. "Alright, anniversary man, I'm heading to the venue to make sure your party's going to be a hell of a success. I'll see you there at eight, then. Oh, and before I forget. Sophie's manager is bringing her over to the showroom, so you both can walk the press line together."

I watch Dad make his way past the flowering irises toward the gate. Of course, I'll be there. I may be just some carpenter lovesick over Harlow, but I'm still a businessman.

***

Two hours after the party officially starts, even I can say it's a success. Dad sure knows how to throw a party in the city. Only he knows how to snag one of the best venues in Manhattan and right now, we're on a rooftop garden overlooking St. Patrick's Cathedral and Saks Fifth Avenue. Who knew that this week marks the third year I won my first award out of the blue, for a stair design I made for a Montauk investor. It put my company on the map, and I've been swamped with orders ever since.

I'm glad Dad keeps track of these things. The PR company even notified the press, and there was even a press line at the entrance where guests posed for pictures that'll go on social media and local Lifestyle pages. Dad believes that an event like this will guarantee that my name is in the press for a good reason this time, instead of being attached to some scandal about me being a dick for hire for some frigid doctor.

I just wish Dad's idea of a party didn't include inviting every eligible woman under twenty-five within a five-mile radius. And right now, they're everywhere, and I can't even take a leak without someone following me to the bathroom and waiting till I come out. It's not like they don't know I've been tabloid fodder the last few weeks—or maybe that's why they're here. Maybe I'm more interesting that way.

Dad pulls me to meet more of his friends, and I busy myself with talk about bathtubs, and live-edge tables, much like the one I built for Nana in Taos. I have two on order, and today, there's one set up inside so guests can ask me how I construct them; how I start with a live tree, usually some hundred-year-old tree that's about to be cut down probably due to disease or the rise of some new development on the property, and then the cutting of the wood into long vertical slabs that showcase the beautiful grain. But first, I have to age the wood and for that, I have a few places where they're kept safe until I'm ready to use them.

Their eyes usually glaze over when I tell them those things, but it's the one or two guests who listen, enraptured till the very end, that matter to me. They're the ones who, in most cases, become lifetime customers. They're the ones I'm really here for, dressed in a Tom Ford suit so they don't think of me as just some carpenter lucky enough to have a father who knows all the rich people in the city.

As I excuse myself from Dad's company, I spot a few celebrities among the guests, and it doesn't surprise me. Like most of the guests, they started out as Dad's clients before becoming my customers. Unfortunately for them, I know them only through the pieces they order from me more than their movies or shows.

"Are you enjoying yourself?"

The woman asking the question is gorgeous with wide hazel eyes and high cheekbones. A runner-up in some modeling reality show that heavily featured my products in a media tie-in, Sophie Marsden was my prearranged companion last night at the dinner the PR firm organized at the Top of the Standard. It continued into the Boom Boom Room just before midnight, but that's when I begged off, telling Sophie that I had an early start in the morning. With the official pictures already taken at the press line and others that the guests were posting all over social media, my job was done.

"I'm having lots of fun," I reply as she hands me a beer. "Thanks."

"I figured, since you told me last night that you were more of a beer drinker, this will take the edge off. You look like you wish you were miles away from here, and with someone else."

"It's not that obvious, is it?" I say, chuckling wryly. "I'm sorry, Sophie. I was actually thinking of how to explain to people what Japanese joinery is and why I still do it when modern technology and 3D modeling is taking over the world."

She giggles. "Liar."

I grin. "You're right. I just hope you're having a great time even if your date is basically moping."

"I am, but can I say something?" Sophie's brow furrows and I nod. "It *is* true, isn't it? All the talk about you and that doctor? I can see it. You haven't stopped watching the door since the party started. Is she coming?"

"I hope so."

"I won't keep you away from her, Dax, when she shows up. But you still need to socialize a bit. It's your party, remember?"

I glance at the door again, wondering when Harlow is coming. *If she's coming.* It's already ten and by all accounts, it would be rude for anyone to come this late to an event. But if it's any consolation, the photographers are all gone, except for two who work for the PR company. But I also can't be standing in the same spot staring at the door all night. I take a deep breath and nod at Sophie, then we turn away, toward the direction of the reflecting pool and the garden. Maybe Dad is right. Maybe I'm just being foolish about all this, unwilling to wait until all the talk about Harlow and her claim against the hospital dies down. Maybe that's why she didn't come.

From the corner of my eye, I see Dad watching me. He's talking to Clint Caldwell III, the man whose wife introduced me to Madison years ago. His wife, Paige, is here, too, standing with a group of former models like her, now trophy wives to some of New York's richest men. Is that how Dad wants me to be, too? Does he want me to find someone like Sophie and together, we can live just like he and Mama lived during the beginning of their marriage? But that was before she had enough of it and returned to Taos when she was pregnant with me. And she never returned to Manhattan, not permanently.

By the time we reach the other end of the pool, we're joined by a few more people eager to congratulate me. I lose sight of Dad, seeing only Clint with Paige standing next to him. Ever the savvy businessman, Dad's probably working the event, making sure everyone's comfortable because God knows I just don't think of those things, not when all I can think of is why Harlow isn't here.

But she *is* here, dressed in a red dress that highlights her dark hair and those gorgeous doe eyes. She's standing at the door leading to the garden and she's looking around. *Looking for me.*

"She's here." I pull my arm away from Sophie's grasp. I don't even care if someone was in the middle of some story about a club we should all go to and meet up after this is over. Harlow is here, and that's all that matters.

I hurry toward the double doors, slowing down only to tell someone trying to get my attention that I'll be right back. One of them grabs my arm and pulls me aside to talk about the staircase he wants me to build in his Hamptons estate. It's the Montauk investor that put my name on the map, and I'm fucked because I can't ignore him. By the time I'm done promising to squeeze him into my schedule during the week so we can discuss the specifications of what he wants me to build for him, it's too late. Harlow is gone, and in the place where she stood just minutes earlier stands Dad.

My heart is beating a mile a minute and as I frantically look around, I have a sinking feeling that Dad just told her to go away. I don't want to blow up, not when I've come so far in all my anger management exercises. Either I beat that punching bag at the gym to a pulp or I build things to channel that anger elsewhere, but right now, all I can do is stay as calm as I can. "Where is she? She was just here!"

"You should have known better than to invite her, Dax. Thank God she had the foresight to come late and miss the press line. What if the press saw her?"

"I don't give a flying fuck if they saw her, Dad. Why'd she leave? What did you say to her?"

Dad's expression is all business, his eyes cold. "I didn't say anything she didn't already know, Dax. I told her that until her divorce is final, it's in everyone's best interest that she stay away from you."

I shake my head, my hands balled into fists by my side. "It's to your best interests, you mean? To your business?"

"I'm only thinking of your future, son."

"No, you're not. You still see me as that kid on the playground who got teased because I couldn't read, and they were right. I couldn't, not then. But guess what, Dad? That kid grew up and these days, he reads just fine. He reads every detailed report you send him. He even makes his own decisions," I say as I make my way toward the elevator, doing my best not to punch the *Down* button in my anger.

"Dax..."

"We'll talk about this later," I say as I feel Dad stand next to me in front of the elevator doors, the numbers creeping up on the monitor. "If Harlow will have me, I'm staying with her, so apologize to the guests for me, will you?"

CHAPTER TWENTY-NINE

Harlow

"No offense, Dr. James, but I hope you'll understand if I don't allow you to see my son. This party is the only one we hold every year and I want him to get the recognition he deserves as an award-winning craftsman, not as some dick for hire your husband has painted him out to be. Why are you even here?"

"Your son invited me, Mr. Drexel." He didn't even need to introduce himself before he launched into his tirade. Dax has his deep blue eyes and baritone voice.

He scoffs. "It doesn't even matter if Dax invited you. He hasn't been thinking straight since he met you and now, you being here will only bolster the rumors that your husband was right. What are you going to tell him? That after all this time, all the talk about you must have died down so you and Dax can be together again?"

No, I was going to tell him that I'm pregnant. But it will be a cold day in hell before I tell anyone but Dax that fact. "Dax is old enough to think for himself, Mr. Drexel. He was old enough to decide for himself when he first met me, and he's old enough to decide now where he wants our relationship to go."

"Relationship? What you have is no relationship, Dr. James. What you did have was a fling. *A fling*."

"With all due respect, Mr. Drexel, but even if it were, I'd rather hear that from your son than from you. He's also not a boy whose future you can decide on your own. He's a man."

"Of course, I know he's a man, Dr. James. His mother raised him to be one. But can't you see how damaging your presence will be to his reputation tonight? Now that your husband has ruined yours, are you so intent on destroying Dax's, too? And to think that even all this is just a piece of theater for everyone concerned courtesy of our PR company, just so no one will laugh at him for being your boy toy, or whatever it is your husband has painted him." Daniel exhales, exasperation written on his face. "Did you know how hard it was for Dax to grow up hearing kids make fun of him for being dyslexic? Oh, yes, he was. Could barely read a word right. They called him stupid, a moron, and a retard. But look who's laughing now? None of them can hold a candle to what Dax has achieved with his craftsmanship, and I'm not about to let you destroy everything he's worked hard for."

He's right, of course. Any talk about Dax and me may have died down in the tabloids, their attention focused on someone else more exciting, someone who'd respond to their allegations and not hide behind her office doors or rent some tiny studio apartment. But that doesn't mean my presence here wouldn't resurrect it back again.

Behind Daniel, I spot a photographer making his way toward us, a camera with a long lens cradled in his hands.

"If you really cared for my son, you'd leave now, Dr. James."

I don't wait to hear any more, not because I'm letting Dax's father bully me into leaving, but because I want Dax to get all the attention he deserves. Do these people even know the masterpiece he built in Taos? That beacon of hope in the middle of nowhere that saved me?

I turn around and head to the elevator, knowing I came here without thinking things through. I simply let my emotions get the best of me. Surely, Old Harlow would have considered how her presence would impact Dax's career—and whatever was left of hers. Like Daniel Drexel, Old Harlow would have known just how important one's reputation is in today's world.

I'd been lucky enough to have missed the press line at the lobby, a red carpet in front of a backdrop featuring the Takeshi and Drexel Woodworking & Design logo. I actually have the least likeliest of people to thank for my tardiness, for she'd been waiting for me outside the office and I did not have the heart to turn her away, even if she was the woman Jeff left me for.

Leilani is a pretty little thing, and now on her second trimester, she's showing big time. I had to beg Kathy to give us some privacy so I could hear what Leilani had to say. But if I had thought Leilani had come to apologize, I was wrong, even though an apology was unnecessary. My marriage had crumbled long before she came.

Jeff had gotten someone else's test results, she told me. *The baby is his. Just talk to him, please. Or his lawyer. Tell him I never... I never cheated on him.* Then she handed me an envelope from her doctor's office, begging me to give it to him, although it was Kathy who took it from her hand. The poor woman couldn't stay away and I'm glad she stepped in. Old Harlow would have ripped that envelope to shreds in front of Leilani and told her to go to hell, but I'm pregnant now, and hormones are making me soft. Besides, it's not unusual for test results to get switched up at the doctor's office; I had called Dr. Teves twice to confirm my own. For Leilani's request, all I have to do is pass the envelope to my lawyer to pass to Jeff's, and the rest would be up to him. Besides, right then, I had problems of my own, like being late for Dax's party. I'd been in such a rush the moment I got home to shower and change into something that fit that I even forgot to put on any jewelry.

But it's too late to worry about such things. There were no photographers at the press line and right now, the only one left in the lobby is the doorman, and he nods at me as I hurry toward the door, the tears threatening to fall. But I manage to keep it all in until I reach the sidewalk, and like a dam breaking, the tears come. But I need to take hold of my emotions for I can't let anyone see me falling apart like this. So I keep walking, deciding to go back to being Old Harlow again with that armor that kept everyone away.

But there's also something I can't deny. Something happened on the outskirts of Taos where I almost ended it all. It's where I was able to let the pain of losing Marcus go, even though he'll always be with me until my last breath. It's where my life began again, and where new life was born. It's also where I fell in love with a young man who's far from the boy everyone thinks him to be. Even me.

But I'm not too proud to admit when I'm wrong.

I don't hear Dax's voice until he's right in front of me, out of breath yet looking gorgeous in his tux. He's removed his bow tie, and his shirt is unbuttoned, revealing that hollow at the base of his neck that I loved to kiss, and the hint of curling chest hairs I'd trace with my fingers until he'd grip my wrists to stop me because it tickled... and turned him on.

Dax runs his fingers through his hair, blowing air through his lips as he stares at me. "Harlow, you look absolutely beautiful."

His words make me blush even though his presence makes my heart pound and I can barely breathe. How can he say I look beautiful when the dress can barely fit me? It's tight around the waist and for crying out loud, it's like I gained five pounds just from eating that *chorizos con huevos y papas* for lunch.

"Whatever my dad said, I apologize. He shouldn't have even talked to you." Dax closes the distance between us and cups my face in his hands. I can smell his cologne, mingled with that of his own man-smell. I don't even care which pheromones they are anymore. He just smells so good.

"But he's right, Dax. Me being at your party could have damaged your reputation. You're already infamous as it is."

He chuckles, shaking his head as his thumb caresses my cheeks. Then he holds my face up toward him, his smile replaced with a frown. "I don't care about fame, Dr. James. Or infamy, for that matter. All I care about right now is you. And being with you."

"I'm pregnant," I blurt out.

Oh, great! I can't believe socially inept Harlow struck again and without warning. Why couldn't I have just said it while we were alone? Instead, we're out here in the middle of Fifth Avenue, blurting out secrets better left reserved for another time. Preferably alone.

"I'm pregnant," I continue, figuring it's too late to back out now. He might as well know right here. "Six weeks. Going on seven."

It takes Dax a moment to recover from the news but he grabs me and kisses me. Then he laughs right in the midst of the kiss, our breaths intermingling. His beard scratches my face, but I love it. I've missed it. I cling to him as he kisses me again, his tongue slipping between my lips and I love how he tastes, smells and feels. All man... and all mine.

Cars honk around us and pedestrians snicker, some saying, *Get a room!* But I don't care. I've stopped caring about a lot of things lately, mostly about what other people thought. It used to be the only thing that mattered to me, even if it left me miserable inside. But I can't live like that anymore. I want to be happy... really happy... with Dax.

I want to wake up every morning next to the man I love. I want to go on hikes with him amid the piñon trees and breathe in clean New Mexico air. I want him to teach me how to fish the way his mother taught him, cuddle up with him as we watch old movies, and then make love till morning. I want to watch our children grow up, knowing they'll have to settle for peanut butter and jelly sandwiches until I learn how to cook as good as his grandmother. I want Dax Drexel. No, I love Dax Drexel.

And even though rational me would argue and say I don't need a man, I do. I need *this* man like the air I breathe—although, at this moment, I'd gladly trade all the car exhaust of Manhattan for Taos.

I pull away. "You wanted to know if I was or I wasn't, and that's why I came–"

He frowns. "Is that the only reason you came to the party? To tell me that?"

I run my hand along his beard. How I've missed doing this. "No, I wanted to thank you for the box in person. And..."

"And?"

"I want us to be together again, Dax. But I want you to be with me because of me, and not just because I'm pregnant. I know how important family is to you, but–"

Dax traces my cheekbone with his index finger; his gaze is pained. "Oh, Harlow, can't you see? I'd stay with you even if you weren't pregnant. I know it must scare you being pregnant like this, but no matter what happens, I'll be with you. Good or bad, I'll be right here. I'm not leaving you ever again." He pauses. "Well, unless you say no, then that would be considered stalking."

I laugh, his words bringing fresh tears to my eyes and a giggle. How words can hold so much power, both to wound someone and then heal them, too. And in Dax's case right now, even make me laugh all in one breath.

"I don't care if people say it's too soon for us to be

together, or that what I'm about to say to you is not real. But nothing has been more real than this... you and me together," Dax continues. "I'm not a child. I'm a man, and right now, I know what I want. I know *who* I want. *You.* It doesn't even matter if I've only known you for five or seven days, or whether we started out on the wrong foot. What is important is that we want to be together. Don't we?"

As I nod, I see him frown. "What's wrong?"

"Where is the gun? Do you still have it?"

"I returned it when I got to Texas, where I bought it," I reply, pausing as I remember the words he'd said to me just before he walked out of the Pearl that day. "You were right, Dax. I needed help, and I am getting help. I've been seeing a therapist since I got back. Twice a week. It's why I never contacted you all this time. I needed to sort out my own stuff before... before anything else."

Dax sighs, leaning his forehead against mine though he doesn't say anything. He just closes his eyes and breathes deep, as if he's inhaling the air between us, taking whatever he can. Pheromones maybe, but really, I don't care. "I can't be an island anymore, Dax," I add as he opens his eyes and gazes at me.

"I felt like an island without you, Harlow, and I hated it. It's lonely."

"I'm sorry."

"I love you."

I stare at Dax, soaking in the words he just spoke out loud even though he said them long before this moment, taking the form of words he carved on the box he made for me. This time, I don't even think twice. There's no reason for me to analyze anything else, not when it comes to what my heart wants.

"And I love you right back, Dax Drexel. And I don't care what the world says, whether you're too young for me or I'm too old for you, or whether all this is happening too fast. I love you."

Dax draws a ragged breath and without saying another word, he pulls me into his arms. I feel the beating of his heart as I rest my head on his chest, feeling my body melt against him. Up until this moment, nothing has ever felt so right, the future I've been searching for right here in his arms. And just like the first time when Dax held me at the Pearl, when all the armor that was Dr. Harlow James, the transplant surgeon, fell away, all that's left of me is Harlow James, the woman.

And a very happy one at that.

CHAPTER THIRTY

Dax

I DON'T REMEMBER how we got from that sidewalk to Harlow's new apartment, but I'm not complaining. We're in bed, and I'm wearing only my boxers and nothing more, my dick tenting the sheets every chance it gets. And Harlow's not helping. She teases me with her fingers tracing circles on my chest and abs. Absence has made my heart grow so much fonder for her. It's also made my abs rock hard from all the workouts where I've channeled my pent-up frustrations from missing her. But she's here now in my arms, and I'm not letting her go ever again. I want to make love to her, but there's still so much we have to say to each other.

"Who was that girl with you? It was on Page Six," Harlow says as I pull her closer. She rests her chin on her hand as she leans on my chest.

"Sophie's a runner-up for a modeling reality TV show. My company's PR firm arranged it, thanks to Dad. It's his idea of a first-aid kit against all the talk about you and me, but if you're worried about–"

"She's young."

"Does it bother you?" I ask as I push a lock of hair from her face. She doesn't answer right away, but I know the age difference between us bothers her. It's in her eyes.

"One day you'll look around and see these beautiful young women–"

"And you're not? You're absolutely beautiful, Harlow, inside and out, and that's why I'm here with you. If the last six weeks told me one thing, it's that I don't want to be with anyone else but you." I caress her cheek with the back of my finger. "I love you, and no matter what Dad thinks about all the drama and his fear it will affect my company's bottom line, it won't matter to me. Just like your patients choose you for your skill, my clients pick me for my expertise, not my personal life."

Relief floods her face, and I kiss her, my lips brushing against hers tenderly. The sensation of her lips brushing against mine sends a blast of heat down my body, settling right in my solar plexus. It tells me that what I'm doing is right, even if I ended up abandoning my guests. Besides, they're long gone now, for it's raining, a late night downpour that's perfect for snuggling under the softest covers I've ever felt before. I lie back on the pillows as Harlow rests her head on my chest. Underneath the sheets, she's wearing only an oversized t-shirt, her legs bare and rubbing against mine lazily. The sheets tent again, and I force myself to think of other things. *Focus, Dax. F-O-C-U-S.*

"How's the divorce going?"

"It's with the judge now," she replies. "Phoebe says

the judge will, most likely, rule the Hampton's property to be mine while Jeff keeps the Manhattan apartment. The quitclaim deed I had signed before I left was invalid because of my emotional state, but it makes for an equitable distribution of assets if he demands nothing else."

"I'm glad he's not getting away with all your joint property. It was joint for a reason."

"I know, but it's almost over," she says.

I kiss the top of her head, loving the scent of rose oil. It brings back the first time we officially met outside the Pearl, of her and her finger making a dent on my chest. It brings back the range of emotions I saw on her face, of surprise, followed by anger, and later, when Harlow finally let her guard down, her grief. "Harlow, I'm sorry about Marcus. And I'm sorry you have to go through all this with Jeff. But whatever drove you to rent the Pearl, I'm not exactly sorry about that, not when it brought you to me."

"Maybe it was simply meant to be, even if I had no clue then what an Earthship was. It just felt like home the moment I walked in there with Anita."

"That's because it *is* home, Harlow, and one day maybe it will be a home for us if you want it to be."

"Home is anywhere you are, Dax. I know that now," she says, tracing the hairs on my chest. "Even here in this tiny studio apartment." Suddenly, she pulls away from me, reaching for an envelope from the bedside table. "Oh, speaking of home, there's this."

"What is it?" I ask as she resumes her spot next to me under the covers and as I hold the envelope with one hand, Harlow takes my other hand and rests it flat on her belly, just above her pubic bone.

"The fetus..." She pauses, rolling her eyes as she catches herself saying medical terms again. "Well, the baby, that is, is six weeks going on seven. And right now she's the size of a pea."

"A sweet pea," I grin. "But how do you know she's a she?"

She pouts. "Because I don't want to call her an 'it.'"

"What if I want to call her a 'he'?"

"Then we'll have to fight for it," Harlow says, giggling. "Anyway, so the baby is sitting right here, where your hand is."

I trace the C-section scar with my index finger. "That low?"

"But as she grows bigger, she'll fill this space." She takes my hand and slides it higher, toward her belly button, suppressing a giggle as I dance my fingers over her skin. Then she slides it higher still, halfway between her belly button and her sternum. "All the organs have to scoot up just a little."

"Just a little? That doesn't look like a little to me, Harlow. Is that why they say pregnant women get heartburn?"

"Pretty much, and I already get it. Just be fore-warned." She lets go of my hand and pulls out the piece of paper from the envelope I'm still holding. All I see is her name along with a bunch of numbers that mean nothing to me. But I see the letterhead.

"Who's Dr. Teves?"

"My obstetrician," she replies. "These are the test results that tell me the hCG levels in my blood."

"What's hCG?"

"It's the pregnancy hormone. Human chorionic gonadotropin–"

I laugh. "Okay, pregnancy hormone, then. So what do the numbers mean exactly?"

"Usually, at six to seven weeks, the range is generally about 2,400 to 4,800."

I peer at the series of numbers under the results. "But this one says 88,000. Why's that?"

Harlow doesn't answer right away, though she's grinning. "A higher range could mean multiples, like twins... or more."

It takes a few seconds for her words to settle in, for a fog seems to have descended on me. *Did she say twins... or more?* I take the paper from her hand and study the results again. 88,000. I look at Harlow in amazement, and she's grinning like a Cheshire Cat. "Harlow, does this mean you're... we're having–"

She exhales. "Well, we *could* be having twins, but I want to wait a few more weeks to be sure."

I set the paper aside and pull her to me, kissing her. I've never loved a woman this hard before, and it feels fucking amazing. Scary, but amazing.

"But, Dax, we really should be practical about this." She pauses, then takes a deep breath. "What if I lose–"

"Harlow, no." I draw away from her, what she told me when we were on the Gorge Bridge returning to me, about the miscarriages. "I can't promise you a perfect pregnancy, not when I'm in no position to know what will happen tomorrow or next week, or next month. But what I can promise you is that no matter what happens, I'll be right here with you the whole time."

She looks at me, the fear in her eyes fading as I continue. "And once everyone knows about this, hell, my family will be with us, too, unless you don't want them there–"

"Oh, but I do, Dax. I want all of you. Even the whole package. Nana, Dyami, Sarah, Benny, Gabe. Even your dad, if he ever softens up toward me."

"Eventually," I say, pulling her closer. "But I'm serious, Harlow. I'll be with you. You hear me? I don't know about New York, but we could live wherever you want to live. We'll make things happen. We'll make us happen like we did back at the Pearl."

I rest my forehead against hers, breathing hard. My heart is racing, my pulse drumming in my ears. I must be delirious, promising her the world but I've never felt this happy before. And while I'm still reeling from the news (damn, but I've got some good swimmers), I feel like running outside in the rain and shouting out the good news to the world.

"Come here." I pull her back on the bed next to me, her head cradled on my shoulder. I'd give Harlow the world if I could, but right now, all I can give her is me, one hundred percent of me and whatever future awaits us. We watch the rain outside in silence; the only other sound is a clock ticking somewhere. It's reassuring, a reminder that no matter what happens, we'll make use of all the time we have together. And damn if I don't want forever with Harlow. After the last six weeks without her, I don't want to be away from her ever again.

A few minutes later, she rubs her legs against mine, her movement slow this time. Deliberate. Then she takes my hand and rests it over the same spot again, just above her pubic bone. There's a playfulness to her voice this time when she speaks. "Did you know that while all that stuff is going on for the baby, you know... pregnancy stuff?"

"Yes?"

"There's a little side-effect," she murmurs, biting her lower lip as she eyes me mischievously. "You see, all that blood rushing down here often makes me feel... horny."

She whispers the last word like it's forbidden, but she's being playful, reminding me of the Harlow I know with all the sex positions she wanted to try out at the risk of my dick breaking off. I turn to face her and press my hand against her mound.

"That's a terrible predicament, Harlow. I'm glad to know I wasn't alone with the same problem. Well, not the pregnancy part."

"So, do you think you can remedy my predicament, Mr. Drexel?"

I kiss her, my hand slipping inside her panties to find her already wet. Fuck, Harlow James is going to be the death of me. "How much time do we have, Dr. James?"

My question implies so much more than it sounds, only because I want everything from her. I want all of Harlow James just as she gets all of me in this life, and beyond.

She pulls me toward her, our foreheads touching, our breaths intermingling. "Forever, Dax Drexel. We have forever."

EPILOGUE

Harlow

Hard to believe that nine months ago, I stood right here, thinking my fairy tale was over, and almost blew my brains out.

Thank God, I was nowhere near as drunk as I thought I was, for somewhere inside that inebriated surgeon, a voice said, *no, you're not going down like this. You're not fading away like you always allowed yourself to disappear behind the facade of the surgeon and the researcher who was more comfortable hiding behind her credentials. You're definitely not going down believing yourself the wife of a man more accomplished than you... or something like that.*

Instead, I laughed at my weakness then (drunk people tend to do that besides crying into their wine), and the next morning, collided with a man who made me feel things I hadn't felt in a long time. Beautiful, wanted, and special. Most of all, he made me feel like a woman again.

Dax Drexel.

Sure it was fast... love at first sight usually is. And it's not for everyone, even as I imagine them scoffing about the craziness of it all. *Come on!* Who falls in love with someone after spending only five days together? How can I, a normally sane transplant surgeon, fall for someone so fast? How can Dax? But I'm also not about to live the rest of my life according to unspoken rules that no longer apply to me, all the "you should's" and "you're supposed to do it this way or that way" crap established by people who have no idea who I am or what I've been through. People honestly would prefer to see me unhappy so that I fit into the image they've created in their minds about how I should be—the woman who can juggle it all. Only I couldn't, and it almost broke me when I tried.

No, wait! It did break me.

So, been there, done that, and except that one night when I almost blew my brains out, everything else is written in the tabloids for all to see. Well, according to Jeff, that is.

Jeff Gardner.

The mere thought of my ex-husband makes me sad. I shouldn't be thinking of him, not today of all days, but in many ways, he made this day possible. Without him, I wouldn't have ended up at the Pearl.

I just hope he's happy, wherever he is. He's still Director of Transplant Surgery at Miller General, his violation of patient privacy settled with a simple fine and a slap on the wrist. What can I say? Sometimes, people don't get the karma we think they deserve but who am I to say if Jeff's not getting it right now? I heard the real reason he dumped Leilani was not because the test results said the baby wasn't his, but that they showed a

98.7% chance that the fetus had trisomy 21, another name for Down syndrome and he was certain that no baby of his would ever have that condition. I heard that they've reconciled since then, and they even got married although it was a small affair this time, and are living in the apartment Jeff and I once owned together. He kept it as part of the final divorce settlement while I got the Hamptons property outright.

We could have lived there, but the Pearl is home for me. I have Dax and his family, and with them, a whole new future. I'm crazy mad in love with him and I don't even know what I must have done right in a previous life, but he loves me just the way I am, even with all my fears —like growing older faster than I'd like (when you're thirteen years older than the man you love, there's no doubting that), or that one day, I'll wake up and realize this life is just a dream. Maybe I did pull that trigger after all.

But of course, I didn't.

What I did do that night was lay the memory of Marcus to rest along with all the regrets I'd carried with me for so long, from my imperfect childhood to my outwardly perfect career that hid an empty life. I also let go parts of Old Harlow along the way, even if sometimes she reappears just for fun, and Dax has to remind me to lay off the medical jargon whenever we go at it like bunnies.

The sound of crunching gravel behind me brings me back to the present, and I turn to see Kathy make her way toward me. Her eyes crinkle around the corners as she smiles although I know she's been crying. Tears of happiness, I hope, with some bittersweet ones mixed in. I never realized how much she had missed me when I left New York that first time and how relieved she was when I finally returned.

But leaving New York for the second time was a whole different matter, and this time Kathy knew I was leaving for good. As soon as my divorce from Jeff was finally granted, I sold the Hamptons property in a heartbeat while letting Chambers, Maynard & Lipman handle my lawsuit against Miller General. When we settled the case for an amount commensurate with lost earnings and the damage to my reputation thirteen months later, it proved the end to the last of my ties to New York although my name is still on the door of the medical offices I share with Dr. Rowe. I still consult remotely on certain cases although my life now lies right here in New Mexico.

Sometimes you wake up.

"I don't blame you for living out here," Kathy says as she stands next to me and clasps my hand between hers. "It's beautiful... well, in a desert kind of way."

We both giggle. I know exactly what she means. You can take the girl out of New York, but you can't take New York out of the girl. That's Kathy for you—a true blue New Yorker, originally from Brooklyn. As for me, I had six months of getting New York out of my system. But then, our lives weren't exactly alike. While Kathy spent her life with her husband, Clyde (and he's back at the Pearl, one of the guests testing out the Pearl's maximum occupancy limitations), mine was spent working too much and coming home to an empty apartment, even when Jeff was home.

"Did you see the stars last night?" I ask. It's one of the perks of living out here and Dax and I often spend nights lying underneath the sun-shaped skylight gazing at the stars. He even bought these giant floor pillows that I love to take naps on, surrounded by the indoor plants and everything else that I love about the Pearl.

"Did we ever!" she exclaims, shaking her head in disbelief. Some nights, the clouds cover up the stars, but last night, there wasn't a cloud in sight, and it was glorious. "I thought such things didn't exist, seeing that many stars, Harlow. It was just gorgeous. Mark my words. We'll be back again."

I squeeze her hand. "You and Clyde are always welcome here. We've already marked that guest bedroom as yours."

"You know, I have to tell you. Nana cooks a mean hominy stew!"

"*Posole*, you mean?" I say, laughing. "And that's not all she cooks."

"I probably gained five pounds the last two days alone. I loved that green chile stew she cooked that first night." She smacks her lips together. "I need to snag that recipe because Clyde couldn't get enough of it. He's threatening to move next door to Nana unless I get those recipes."

For the next few minutes, we don't speak. We look out at the vast expanse of sagebrush in front of us, the landscape dotted by Earthships just like the Pearl in the distance. At night, it's total darkness with not a single lamppost in sight, and it's just the way I like it. Besides, it's never really quiet inside the Pearl anyway, not since five weeks ago.

"Senator Kingston sends his regards, by the way," Kathy says. "I'm sure he told you himself, but he and Penny dropped by the office just before I flew out here three days ago."

"He and Penny called this morning. They sent flowers, too. One day, Penny wants to visit, and they're already making plans."

Kathy chuckles. "I hope you have room for the security detail."

"They have their own place in Santa Fe."

"Oh, that's right."

Behind us, the door opens, and I hear someone clear his throat. It's Sawyer. Dressed in a white button-down shirt and jeans, he nods quietly before stepping back into the Pearl.

Sawyer sure cleaned up nicely since I first met him when I came back to Taos with Dax almost a year ago. Ever since he got rid of his mountain man look, with his unkempt beard now trimmed and his long hair cut and styled, he could easily be mistaken for Dax's older brother except for his eyes. While Dax has sky-blue eyes, Sawyer's eyes are hazel-green.

"Guess it's time," Kathy says as we make our way back to the Pearl, the interior all aglow with festive lights. "That Sawyer sure is one handsome man, just like that man of yours. I could find myself a young man like you did, but then I doubt Clyde would approve."

We pause as we reach the door and for a few seconds,

I center myself, taking deep breaths and exhaling from my mouth. I feel my cheeks color as Kathy fusses at my hair, arranging the loose waves around my face. The door opens, and Sarah slips outside, handing me a bouquet of sunflowers. *God, it's happening.* I fight back the tears that threaten to roll down my face.

"No crying, missy, or you're going to get us all bawling our eyes out and messing up our makeup. And you know I rarely wear it," Sarah reprimands me with a stern look although I see her face start to crumble, too. I force a smile, knowing if I don't, I really will start crying my eyes out. And happy tears or not, it won't look pretty.

As I fan my face with my hand to stop myself from crying, Sarah arranges the hem of my dress. It's a simple sheath dress, with a layered top to help camouflage my swollen breasts. It's functional, too, with secret panels sewn in to accommodate other duties besides giving me that hourglass figure that Dax loves, sewn just for me by one of Gabe's aunts the day before. She took my measurements in the morning, draped the smooth fabric over my body, pinned, tucked and began cutting the fabric right then and there. By evening, there was a dress all perfectly molded to my body. No pattern paper needed; just a sharp eye, a tin full of pins and three decades of sewing quinciñera gowns for all the girls in town.

Inside, the voices lower to a hush and I hear the strains of a piano and a guitar playing, courtesy of two of Gabe's cousins who volunteered to provide the music.

"Well, I guess this is it, Dr. James," Sarah whispers, grinning. "We better get started before, you know, they wake up."

"Oh, and just in case I get a tad emotional, just ignore me," Kathy says just before she and Sarah slip back inside, leaving the door slightly ajar.

I take another deep breath. I've only been outside for all of ten minutes, yet it feels like an eternity to be away from everyone. And it's not like they can't see me through the glass panel in the door. I can see all of them watching me although I don't see Dax for guests are standing in the way.

Dyami waves excitedly. Apparently, that's my cue to start. I square my shoulders back and holding the bouquet of sunflowers and baby's breath in front of me, I take a step inside. There's a collective sigh in the air, and I have to chuckle and roll my eyes. It's not like they haven't seen me before this moment. We were enjoying a nice party just half an hour earlier. My stepping outside was simply the formality everyone needed to get everything ready. I'm just glad Gabe's cousins aren't playing, *Here Comes the Bride.*

As I make myself down the makeshift aisle, someone has scattered a trail of rose petals on the floor. So much for a simple affair. How a proposal turned into a wedding in less than 48 hours is beyond my scope of understanding at the moment, even with my years of medical training. But it's happening, and I'm not complaining. It's one of the pluses of having a big family like Dax's. There's always someone who can cook enough food for twenty people on the fly (Nana and Gabe's mother), put up decorations indoors and also outside where they're going to move most of the festivities so the Pearl can be relatively quiet (Sarah, Benny,

Gabe, and Todd), and even officiate the ceremony (Sawyer, of all people).

All Dax and I have to do is show up.

As gracefully as I can, I make my way forward just as I remember seeing brides on TV do it. But I stop worrying about the way I'm walking the moment I see each person's face beaming back at me. Every one of them is a stitch in the tapestry that is my life, holding it together. Anita, Sarah, Benny, Dyami, and Gabe. Kathy and Clyde. Dr. Addison Rowe, my colleague whom I suspect is pregnant but she's not saying it out loud—at least, not yet. Todd and Sawyer. Cole and Millie. And then there's Daniel Drexel towering over everyone else, grinning from ear to ear. Although he started out grudgingly accepting me as the woman his son loved when Dax officially introduced me to him days after the party in New York, he's my biggest supporter now and one of my staunchest defenders. He may even move back to Taos for good. The Pearl, after all, is over 6,500 square feet with two separate living areas.

When I see Dax standing in front of the indoor garden that separates both sections of the Pearl, I catch my breath. Flanked by Gabe on one side and Sawyer on the other, he looks gorgeous in his suit. Who knew that out of billions of people in this world, I'd find the one meant for me when I thought myself lost. Turns out, I was right where I was supposed to be.

We both were.

"Fancy meeting you here, Mr. Drexel," I whisper giddily as Dax takes my hand, his thumb brushing the top of the diamond of his late mother's engagement ring.

Then he brings my hand to his lips, his beard tickling my skin. He shaved it once, to surprise me, and it's something he's never doing again. Dax is a gorgeous man with or without his beard, but he's devilishly sexy with it.

"Te amo, mi amor," he murmurs. "Mi vida." *My life.*

I don't need a dictionary to understand what those words mean just as I don't need anything else to know what Dax's eyes tell me each and every day, that he loves me with everything he's got—mind, body, and soul. It's corny, but it's true, and it's everything I could ever ask for, though he's given me so much more.

"Alright, dude, let's do this before they wake up," Dax tells Sawyer, cocking his head at the portable crib behind Gabe where our five-week-old twins, Anita Pearl and Dax Nathaniel Jr. are fast asleep. Anita-Pea, as Dax calls her, is the one with the temper while Dax, Jr., the mini copy of his dad, is the mellow one.

"Yes, please," I chuckle, my breasts aching at the thought of the twins waking up. They're due for their feeding, and if Sawyer doesn't get started, my breasts are about to spring a leak any minute now. As it is, they also look like they're about to pop out of my dress.

As Sawyer begins the ceremony, I can't help but think how the Pearl has proven to be the perfect place for us. Dax moved his base of operations from Flagstaff to Taos as soon as we arrived from New York nine months ago. Even Nana has her own bedroom so she can help take care of the twins, spoiling them with kisses and hugs. And because we're cloth diapering (for the environment), she often brings the twins' laundry home so we can save on the water deliveries for the Pearl's reservoir.

She doesn't have to, but she does anyway. It's also something Todd and Sawyer are working on—learning how to design Earthships to meet the demands of pooping babies since they never considered it before.

It's a perfect life for Dax and our growing family off the grid, even if it's the last place anyone would have thought I'd find happiness. I still catch myself sometimes wondering when the fairy tale will end, but Dax is quick to remind me that what we have is no fairy tale—it *is* the real thing.

Fate led Dax to me the night I almost ended it all, just as I was meant to fall in love with the man who'd do more than just help me find my way back to the things that mattered. Love, family, and this... us.

And as he slips the wedding ring around my finger and the twins finally wake up demanding their dinner, Dax also helped me find my way back home... to me.

BONUS: PLAYING HOOKY

Dax

A few months later...

"So which of you two did it? Because I don't need to take a peek under the hood to know that one of you did something, but it will make my job easier if you just told me. So who did it, huh? Was it you?" I narrow my eyes at the blonde with the killer smile. "Y tu?" This, to the brown-haired ladykiller who definitely takes after me.

The two of them look up with their big blue eyes and giggle. They giggle! *How dare they?* I roll my eyes just as the door behind me opens and a man wearing a gas mask walks in. He's holding a container of wet wipes in one hand and a pair of bright yellow gloves in the other.

"Okay, I think I'm ready," the masked man says, his voice muffled as I grab the wet wipes from his hand and pull out a few sheets.

"Sawyer, it's not *that* bad. I can't believe you're being such a prima donna about this." The only reason I know it's Sawyer is because he's got the most arresting blue eyes

I've ever seen on anyone. And it's not like I check other guys' eyes or anything, but when you end up passed out drunk one night and wake up to see a pair of eyes glaring back at you and demanding you get your shit together or else, you simply don't forget. It can scare any man sober, and man, did I ever need that wake-up call after Mama died and I almost drank myself to death. As soon as I got myself cleaned up and sober, Sawyer helped me build the Pearl.

"It's bad, man. I don't know what you guys feed them, but it's bad," Sawyer mutters. I can't believe he's doing this. He's going to get into trouble if Harlow sees him like this. He's probably pulled the same act on the twins before because they just gurgle happily, not the least bit scared although one of them is more preoccupied by her toes.

"Homegrown breast milk, what else? And there's more where that came from," I reply. "Any more questions?"

He gulps. "Um, nope."

The door opens again and Harlow walks in. She frowns when she sees Sawyer in his headgear and he sheepishly pulls it off his head, revealing a clean-shaven face. He abandoned his crazed mountain man look the moment Harlow came back with me from New York over a year ago although he maintains a neat trimmed beard now and then. "Is everything okay in here?"

"Yes, ma'am," Sawyer replies.

I hand him the container of wet wipes. "You still want me to do the honors or you think you can handle it? It's only one of them. I don't think both of them pooped."

Harlow sniffs the air. I don't get how it doesn't faze her in the least but then she's probably smelled worse things in the operating room. Still, Sawyer is right. Some days, it does smell toxic, especially when Harlow's eaten anything with cauliflower or Brussel sprouts in them. "I think they both did. When one goes, the other usually follows. Why don't I do it? It will be faster anyway."

Sawyer and I do our best to tell her that we can handle it like the big boys that we are, but Harlow kicks us out of the nursery anyway, and we walk out of there to the chuckles of Nana and Sarah standing in the hallway.

"You took too long, *mijo*," Nana says as Sawyer and I follow her to the living room.

"It's my fault. I had to bring in extra gear." Sawyer brings up his gas mask as Nana and Sarah shake their heads in mock disapproval.

"It's only poop, you know, and once upon a time, you must have done the same," Sarah says.

"Alright, alright. Can we talk about something else besides the obvious?" I ask, stopping by the front door where I had set the two weekend bags. I'd been on my way to the truck but volunteered to change the twins' diapers while Harlow was in the office. It's usually a quick affair but with an Earthship filled with friends and family out to distract me today, it proved to be a challenge. I can barely pay attention with everyone talking all at once.

It's not as if we're going away for a long time. It's only for two days. Harlow's got a conference in Santa Fe and I'm tagging along. Tomorrow, she stands onstage with a colleague to do an important presentation. But work or no, it's also the first time for us to get away since the twins' arrival four months earlier. It's why everyone is here to take care of them while we're gone. Not that I need a whole cavalry to do it, but the moment Sawyer and Todd—who is out in front checking the solar panels with Benny and Dyami—heard that Nana was bringing her famous barbacoa, they've found reasons to come by. Even Gabe is on his way.

"You two have a great time, okay?" Sarah says as she follows me outside to the truck and I store the bags in the back seat. "Tell Harlow not to worry about the twins."

"I'll try, but you know how she is," I say as I shut the truck door and we make our way back into the Earthship.

"You're starting to worry as much as she does." Sarah smiles. "The twins will be fine with us, Dax. It's only two days."

"I know, but she's never been away from *them* before." Harlow's also nursing and she's worried about her milk supply. So I've made sure that we have everything she needs in that department for this trip. Breast pump – check. Those little bags to store milk in even if she's supposed to toss it out in case she decides to have a glass of wine or two – check. Cooler with tons of ice packs even though I reserved a 2-bedroom suite with a refrigerator in case Harlow decides not to dump her breast milk — check.

Funny how life changes in a blink of an eye; I would never have thought twice about such things a year ago. Now, Harlow and our babies are all I think about. Well, and my work, of course. Except for a brief lull when I had to move my base of operations from Flagstaff to Taos, I've never been this prolific with my custom designs. I even get to give Harlow and the babies twenty kisses each before I leave the house for the office a few mornings a week. It usually takes about twenty minutes, maybe more especially when Anita P and Dax Jr. grab my beard and there's nothing like babies gurgling happily as they drool all over you.

"They'll be alright, *mijo*. We'll see you soon before you know it," Nana says as she folds one of the twins' onesies and places it on a pile next to her.

While the Pearl is ideal for medium sized groups of people, it had never been tested for its use around babies —specifically pooping babies. While Taos has more than enough sunlight to help with the drying of the colorful cloth diapers Harlow bought online, water is a big problem. With the region hardly experiencing rainfall throughout the year, we've had water trucked in every week although Nana manages to sneak some of the laundry back to her home and then bring them back washed and neatly folded. Still, that's the whole reason I built the Pearl even if the twins prove to be a challenge. It's an ongoing lesson in sustainability.

My phone beeps to remind me of check-in time. We're also supposed to meet her friend and fellow doctor, Addison Rowe, at the lobby before the meet-and-greet. "Let me go get Harlow."

I find her giving the twins tummy kisses, the usual twenty I give them every day. Raspberries, by the sound of them as the twins squeal with glee. If there weren't a whole cavalry outside of the nursery making use of the Pearl's maximum capacity features, I'd be giving the twins kisses of my own, too, and we'd never leave the earthship.

I stand behind Harlow and wrap my arms around her waist. She's always been self-conscious about her post-pregnancy body, and there's now a treadmill in the part of the Pearl that's become her office where she's manages to write her papers while walking on it. Despite her misgivings about the changes in her body, I love every-thing about Harlow, even the stretch marks that she constantly worries about, applying lotion to them morning and night hoping they'd go away quicker. Once she told me that she'd read about how breastfeeding changed a woman's breasts.

At the rate I'm nursing the twins, they're going to sag down to my knees one day, Dax, she said.

And I'll love you just as much as I love you now, Harlow, I'd told her then. *Besides, my balls would prob-ably sag all the way down there, too.*

She laughed. *God, I sure hope not. At least, there are breast lifts for women, but scrotal lifts?*

You mean ball lifts.

Okay, okay, she'd paused, shaking her head as she chuckled. She's yet to get over all the medical jargon. *Ball lifts? No, I don't think so.*

Now you're breaking my heart, Dr. James.

As I lean my chin lightly on her shoulder and gaze at the twins on the changing table, I can tell Harlow is nervous. I don't blame her. I'm nervous, too, and I'm not even the one who'll be standing onstage tomorrow morn-ing, talking about immune suppression therapies among pediatric patients post-kidney transplant... or something like that. She's the one with the big words while I just say things as they are.

"We need to get going, mi amor," I murmur in Harlow's ear as she sighs, her hands resting over mine.

"I know."

"They'll be okay."

"You're right. I've only been agonizing over this moment because it's one of the things I do so well. Worry." She lifts Dax, Jr. in her arms, gives him a kiss and turns to look at me. "But I'm also looking forward to be alone with you, Mr. Drexel. We've got a lot of catching up to do in the bed department. Something about new positions I've discovered online."

Oh no. Harlow and her sex positions... not that I'm complaining. I've done my fair share of research, too, because I sure as hell don't want to pull a groin muscle the next time we get adventurous.

"Well, I have been working on my yoga poses so I won't pull a muscle." I scoop Anita Pearl in my arms before turning to look at Harlow. "But whether we try those new positions or not, I can't wait to be alone with you, too, Dr. James. I've missed us."

During the drive to Santa Fe, we talked about the twins and her presentation at first, before conversation shifted to the things we wanted to do after she finished her presentation and networked with her colleagues. A dip in the hot tub, a couples Thai massage, and a walk around the area to explore the latest art.

By the time we arrive in Santa Fe, Harlow is relaxed. The hotel right off the Plaza is a grand place, and right now, it's teeming with doctors and surgeons from the world over, all here for a conference. This one had been planned more than two years earlier, right before Harlow started her road trip. She'd actually assumed the organizers had removed her from the roster of speakers in light of her lawsuit against Miller General and, of course, the fact that Jeff was also one of the speakers. So she never gave it any thought until she received the conference schedule eight weeks ago which just about sent her into a panic. She hasn't seen him since she left New York. That's why also I'm here. I'm not about to leave her alone with that man in any capacity.

Two hours later, we've checked in, met Addison in the downstairs lobby for tea and even ran into three of her colleagues on our way to the elevator. Now we're back in our suite freshened up and dressed for the cocktail hour, or as Harlow calls it, the moment of truth where her colleagues get to see how she's *really* doing after Jeff.

I watch her pace the hotel room, her brow furrowed as I slip on my watch. I'm wearing a dark blue dress shirt that Harlow says highlights the sky in my eyes and trousers she swears showcases my ass. She looks stunning in her linen pink and white top and matching white pants that's further complimented by a long billowy scarf. But perfection aside, I want nothing more than to walk right over to her, kiss her and take off every piece of clothing before dragging her into bed for the rest of the day.

Play hooky.

But I don't. Maybe she's collecting herself for her appearance among her peers, the same group of men and women who questioned her professional ability when word got out that she'd allegedly shacked up with a man thirteen years her junior. Suddenly her credibility went down the toilet, a new job position was withdrawn, and people looked away when she'd enter a room. Yet she stood firm on her decision to come home with me to Taos and become the wife and mother she'd always wanted to be.

I adjust the collar of my shirt, leaving the top two buttons undone since it's supposed to be an informal affair. I could probably get away with wearing one of my favorite fitted t-shirts but I also know I have to make a good impression. If not for myself, for Harlow.

I bring my hand to my face, rubbing my beard absently. I shaved it off a few weeks ago, wanting to surprise her but that backfired royally. Even the twins couldn't stop staring—and crying—probably wondering where their Daddy went. Worse, Harlow didn't like it one bit and made me promise never to shave my beard off again, not even for 'trimming' purposes.

"Hey," I murmur as I approach and she finally stops and faces me. "I've got an idea."

Her face brightens. "What is it?"

"Do you really want to go down there?"

"I don't know. I mean, it's not like I won't see them tomorrow," she says, sighing. "But outside of Addy, I also haven't seen them in over a year, Dax, not since I left New York... with you."

My breath hitches in my chest. How can I forget the

night I told the woman I'd only been with for five days that I loved her? I stayed one more week in Manhattan then, seeing customers during the day and spending every night with her in that tiny studio apartment, loving every moment we spent in that king-sized bed with Frette sheets. We snuggled under the covers talking about anything we could think of. Every secret she'd held back was out in the open and I loved her even more for it.

She told me about growing up without anyone there for her and learning how to fend for herself in the end. She told me about wanting children more than anything in the world because then, she could show them the things she never experienced—love and family.

I helped her pack up everything she owned after that week. Some things went into storage and others to Taos. I did my best not to feel so bad for Kathy, her office manager, who couldn't believe Harlow was really leaving New York when she just got back. But it hasn't been as bad as Kathy initially thought; she's flown in four times in the last eight months alone, and she loves the break from New York more and more every time.

"You must miss all this, being with your peers," I say.

"In a way I do, but it's not like I abandoned them," Harlow says. "I still write my papers, study and analyze results like I used to, and just like before, via email or phone. I mean, I haven't exactly left that life behind, Dax. I just changed my scenery for something better. And then there's the office. I'm still technically part owner of the practice."

"There you go," I say. "Yet you're nervous right now."

"Jeff might be there tonight," she says. "He's one of the key speakers this weekend."

"You're one of the key speakers, too, Harlow. You and Addison," I remind her. Addison co-authored the research paper they've been asked to present. I just hope the organizers were tactful enough not to put Harlow and Jeff onstage at the same time. At least, their divorce is final. It only took another year to get every demand countered until even Jeff's lawyer had to concede that they were all running around in circles. Harlow kept the Hamptons property while Jeff kept the Upper East Side apartment.

Since then, I haven't followed any news about her ex-husband although I know he's supposed to come back to Santa Fe for another presentation, a smaller one, and fortunately, Harlow isn't part of that one. Still, just the mere thought of him and the hell he put Harlow through before—and after—I met her makes me want to punch something. It's why I still punch the bag at the home office and go a few rounds with the guys at the gym. Though Harlow doesn't talk about it, I know that Jeff still hasn't given up on making her life difficult—her professional life most of all.

"Addy told me that he'll be in a different hall the whole time. The organizers made sure of that," Harlow says, breaking through my thoughts. "But not at the cocktails tonight. It's social hour and knowing Jeff, I'm sure he'll be there."

"So what if he's there? I have a feeling he's just jealous." I force a smile. "What's that saying? Success is the best revenge?"

"Yes, and that's something he can't take away from me."

I tilt her chin so she's looking up at me. "You want to know what's an even better form of revenge, Dr. James?"

"What?"

"Happiness" I reply. "I'd like to think you're happy with me. With us."

Harlow kisses me lightly on the lips, my beard grazing her lips and chin. "I am. I'm very happy."

"May I make a suggestion then?"

She nuzzles her face against my neck. "Hmm... of course. The suggestion box is open."

This time, I don't speak. I'm more of a hands-on type of guy anyway, and it's just the way Harlow likes it. I kiss her, pulling her closer, the feel of her breasts pressed against my chest driving me crazy. I want to lift her in my arms and toss her on the bed. I want to have my way with her right now; I've only been holding myself back ever since we left the Pearl. When you have newborn twins demanding all of your waking time, making love sometimes ends up at the back seat. That and another C-section incision that needed more time to heal. So yes, I'm fucking horny right now.

Harlow pulls away, pouting playfully. "It's a great idea, but we're going to be late."

"I thought you weren't too thrilled to do the meet-and-greet, to be honest. You wanted to come here, show the audience you're still as good, if not better than you were before, and leave them in the dust. And that's exactly what you're going to do... tomorrow." My hands stroke her back, stopping to rest just above the curve of her buttocks. Then I give her perfect ass a squeeze and she squeals, laughing.

"You're right. I really didn't want to go downstairs, but that was before Old Harlow stepped in and said, *you have to show them, Dr. James.*" She pauses, laughing. "But you're right, Dax. I can show them that Old Harlow never left tomorrow." Her hand slips down from my neck and slips between our bodies down to front of my pants. Her eyes widen. "Dax, you're hard."

"Of course. It's only been three days since our last quickie. And it *was* a quickie."

She rolls her eyes. "Half an hour is not a quickie. Not by a long shot."

"Oh, too long? So you've been timing it?"

She swats my chest playfully with her hand. "No, I was not timing it, but you said so yourself then, Dax. 'We only have thirty minutes before Nana comes back with the twins.' So no, thirty minutes was not a quickie," she pauses, her hand leaving my crotch and I groan. "Did you know the average length for sex is about seven minutes?"

"Seven minutes?" I look at her incredulously. "I wonder how they went about testing that hypothesis."

"They have their methods. But get this, about 43 percent are completed within two minutes," she adds, emphasizing the word *two* like it's a challenge. She's a veritable treasure trove of information, important facts like the average length for sex being seven minutes and trivial facts like Michael Fassbender getting married in Ibiza.

"Two minutes is even worse than seven, mi amor. Too bad the researchers didn't poll us. We could have told them the average length of sex is thirty minutes." *But only when the twins are spending time at their grandmother's house.*

Harlow giggles. "Oh, and did you know that ten to thirty minutes was considered *too long* by many of the respondents?"

"Then they have the wrong partners," I say, narrowing my eyes as Harlow starts unbuttoning my shirt. "So does that mean I take too long?"

She pulls my shirt open, sliding it off my shoulders. "Oh no, Mr. Drexel. As a matter of fact, you're perfect." She starts to unbuckle my belt. "So perfect you have me wanting to prove every single one of those people surveyed wrong."

"Really?"

She kisses me lightly on the lips before pulling away, our breaths intermingling. "We've got thirty minutes."

"Aren't you afraid we're going to disappoint the experts by going 'too long?'" I ask. "You know, in case we make it to thirty."

"Screw the experts," Harlow says, laughing. "They haven't met you."

Minutes later, our clothes are strewn all over the hotel room floor and we're on the bed. I'm in the middle of a meeting with the only expert I trust to judge my sexual skills, and right now, we're beginning with my lingual skills on her body, starting from her mouth down to her swollen breasts and then lower still to her belly and the liquid heat that awaits me between her legs.

She's my goddess, my Queen and right now, she's muffling her cries in the pillows as I lick and suck her slick folds. Before long, an orgasm rips through her body and Harlow gasps, her body trembling before me as she lifts her hips off the bed.

"Oh, fuck! Dax!"

I keep going, waiting for her to beg me to stop and fuck her and when she finally does, after two more orgasms force her to cover her face with the pillows, I crawl over her body and toss the pillow aside. Gasping for breath, she pulls my head down toward her, our mouths and tongues meeting, sparring, tasting each other as her hand drifts lower to wrap around my cock. She strokes me, her palm rubbing along the sensitive head of my dick that my breath emerges in ragged gasps and I rest my forehead against hers.

"Fuck me," she whispers as she guides the head of my cock toward her slick center.

I love it when she talks dirty and takes charge. Hard to believe there was a time when she couldn't even say the word, not when Dr. James was always at the helm, never giving the woman underneath all the credentials and licenses to emerge. But somewhere along the way, professional and personal Harlow must have struck a deal because not only can she talk dirty with all her medical terms and jargon that turn my head around, but she can talk real dirty in bed, too. The kind of dirty I like.

"I want your cock inside me, Dax," she whispers. "I want you to fuck me hard."

Like that.

I thrust my hips, sinking deep into the throbbing heat between her legs, her pussy tightening around my cock. Hell, I don't even know if I'll last thirty minutes because I can't remember if our informal rebuttal of the findings started from the time we landed on the bed or the moment of entry. If it's the latter, then I'm in trouble.

"Dax..."

I pin her arms on the bed, my face buried in the crook of her neck and giving her a good case of beard burn she won't be able to hide from her colleagues. Her legs wrap around my hips. "What?"

"I think we're good on time," she whispers playfully between gasps perfectly times with my movements.

"Please don't tell me you've been watching the clock," I groan before nibbling the skin between her neck and shoulder blade. She can hide the mark with one of her silk scarves tomorrow.

"We're not going to make the meet and greet," she says between gasps. "They can meet... and greet me tomorrow."

I raise my head and look at her. Heavily lidded eyes gaze back at me, her lips swollen from my kisses just minutes earlier. I haven't stopped fucking her although at that moment, I bury myself deep inside her, my mind intent on multitasking because I'll be damned if I'm going to stop now to talk. She feels too good for me to make any intelligent conversation.

"Good, because you' won't be able to walk a straight line after this anyway. I've got other positions in mind for the rest of the evening, just like we planned," I say, our breaths mingling in the little bit of space between our faces. I love everything about her, from the scent of French roses in her hair, the sounds she makes, the moans and the whimpers as I speed up, her pussy walls pulsating around my cock as her orgasm nears. Her fingers dig into the skin of my back as my balls tighten. She's close.

Fuck, I'm close, too.

Her pussy grips me, its intimate walls fluttering around my shaft. She's there. "Come for me, Harlow."

And she does, no longer muffling her cries with pillows or sheets this time. We don't care if we wake up the guests next door. They can put headphones on, or ear plugs. We need this. We want this.

When my release comes, it hits me hard, waves of pleasure starting from my balls radiating all the way to the tips of my toes. I cry out Harlow's name before claiming her mouth with mine. It's a connection like nothing I've ever felt before, to be so close to the one person who makes me whole.

I never thought of myself as a love-at-first-sight guy until the day I fell for her outside the Pearl, when I found myself unable to think of anyone else but her and her smile, her eyes, and the way she allowed herself to be vulnerable with me—and she still does. Or the way she looked with daggers in her eyes that first day we officially met face to face, even as she tried to poke a hole in my chest with her finger accusing me of being the courier of bad news. How I loved seeing that fire inside her, especially when she's angry. Ah, but when she loves, she loves deeply. Such things don't happen to a guy like me everyday.

"Te amo, mi amor." The words tumble from Harlow's lips to mine and I smile, kissing her again. Soft kisses that start from her lips to her chin, her cheekbones, and her eyelids before moving down her neck to that place behind her ear that leaves her trembling as she clings to me. She knows the words that make me melt, too, and I kiss her again, feeling her breasts rise and fall beneath me, her skin flushed and gleaming with light sheen of sweat.

Time seems to stand still and I couldn't care less about the survey, or whether it's two minutes or ten... or thirty. In the end, it didn't matter. What matters is this, moments of vulnerability and connection where we're both left catching our breaths as we search for a foothold back to reality that sometimes isn't so kind... or considerate, given the meet and greet downstairs that we're blowing off.

"I love you, Dr. James. Mi amor. Mi vida," I murmur as I gaze at her. *My love. My life.*

She smiles, a blush creeping along her cheeks. "I love it when you talk dirty to me, Mr. Drexel."

I chuckle as I roll onto my side of the bed and she rests her head on my shoulder. "So did we prove the experts wrong?"

"I think we did."

I look at her. "You did not look at the clock."

"I didn't."

A few minutes later, I have a feeling that she did. Harlow James is all about data. "Liar."

"Thirty-nine minutes," she whispers, grinning. "Forty-two if you count the kissing part."

I pull her to me, kissing her temple. "Why don't we shoot for fifty minutes after dinner? Three positions."

"Okay. If you can last that long."

"Is that a challenge, Dr. James?" I ask. "Or are you

finding a way out because you do have a big presentation tomorrow."

"No, just being realistic," she says and there's a mischievous glint in her eyes. "For *your* sake."

"Oh no, you didn't just say that." I tickle her and Harlow shrieks just as the hotel phone on the bedside table rings and her eyes widen with that, oh-no-it-must-be-a-complaint-that-we're-too-noisy look before I reach of the receiver.

"Are you guys done yet?" asks a familiar voice on the other line.

"It's Addy," I whisper as I hand the receiver to Harlow.

Her eyes widen. "Crap! I forgot to tell her that we were not making the cocktail hour. She's probably down-stairs." She takes the phone and brings it to her ear. "I'm so sorry, Addy. I forgot to text you that we weren't going to make it."

"I figured as much," I hear Addison say, laughing. I'm not eavesdropping but since I'm still on top of Harlow mid-tickle, I can hear everything. From what I remember, Addison hadn't been keen on going to the meet-and-greet, not when she'd just flown in from New York and she's also in her second trimester. It was a big surprise, her deciding to be a single mother, going to a sperm bank instead of finding herself a man the old-fashioned way.

"I'm sorry." Harlow covers her eyes with her free hand as I nuzzle against her neck. "It's not like me to bail on these things."

"I know it's not, but it's okay. Really. I'm binge-watching *Breaking Bad.* That series that's set in Albuquerque? Figured I'd find out what all the fuss was about this show while I am in New Mexico," she says, laughing. "And it's not like I'm not spending the whole day with you tomorrow and after this, I'm staying at your place. Besides, sounds like you guys are busy..."

"I'm so—" Harlow says again, freezing as I raise my head. "Wait. What do you mean, *sounds like?*"

"Oh, I thought you knew about the room arrangements," Addison says. "I'm right next door to you, guys..."

Thank you so much for reading **Everything She Ever Wanted**.

Check out exclusive artwork based on Dax and Harlow as well as my inspiration for the Earthship here: lizdurano.com/inspiration

Loved your time in Taos?
Stay here for Sawyer's story, a second chance romance about healing and risking love after loss in **Breaking the Rules**

Curious about Gabe?
See what happens when ten years of friendship turns into a weekend that could change everything in **Where She Belongs**

Go back to where it began
with Sarah and Benny in **Other Side of Love**.

*If you prefer to follow the series chronologically (or the order I released them because I was clueless then about release order within a series), the next book would be Addison Rowe's **Falling for Jordan**, a surprise baby romance set in New York.*

Want to know when the next book in A Different Kind of Love series drops?

Sign up for my newsletter at https://lizdurano.com/esew/

NANA'S RECIPES

Nana's Green Chile Breakfast Burritos

Ingredients:

> 6 eggs, beaten
> 2 tablespoons oil or butter
> 3 potatoes, shredded OR 2 cups Southern
> style diced hash browns
> 1 medium onion, chopped
> 1 garlic clove, minced
> 1 can diced tomatoes, drained
> 2 cups sausage or chorizo
> 1 cup mild cheddar cheese, shredded
> 1 jar Hatch green chile sauce (or make it
> from scratch like Nana does!)
> 8 large flour tortillas, warmed

Directions:

1. In a bowl, beat eggs and set aside.
2. Heat a medium sized pan over medium high heat; add oil.
3. Add chorizo and cook until heated through,

about 5 - 7 minutes or until no longer pink.
Drain and set aside.

4. In the same pan, add onion and garlic and stir
   for one minute. Stir in potatoes, patting the
   mixture down to cook evenly and scraping up
   the lightly browned bits and patting down
   again. Cook for about 5 - 8 minutes.

5. While potatoes are cooking, in a separate
   skillet over medium high heat, add egg
   mixture and cook without stirring until edges
   and bottom begin to set. Gently turn to
   scramble and continue cooking until eggs
   are set.

6. Add the crumbled sausage to the potatoes.
   Add the eggs to the sausage and potatoes, and
   mix until blended.

7. Divide the potato, chorizo, and egg mixture
   among the tortillas. Top with shredded
   cheese and green chile.

8. Roll each burrito and arrange seam side down
   on a plate or on a square of foil wrap to go. If
   serving on a plate, you can also spoon
   additional green chile sauce over each burrito
   and sprinkle with cheese.

Nana's Green Chile Sauce

INGREDIENTS:

> 2 teaspoons vegetable oil
> 3/4 cup onion, minced
> 2 cloves garlic, minced
> 2 tablespoons flour
> 2 cups roasted and diced mild to medium
> green chile (I like using Hatch green
> chile if I can get it)
> 1 to 2 cups of hot water (depends on how
> thin or thick you want the sauce)
> Salt and pepper, to taste
> Garlic powder and Oregano, to taste

DIRECTIONS:

1. In a sauce pan, heat oil over medium heat.
2. Add minced onion and minced garlic. Stir until soft, about 3 - 4 minutes.
3. Sprinkle flour over mixture to create a roux and stir for about 1 minute.
4. Add chiles and water or broth.
5. Add salt, pepper, garlic powder and oregano to taste and heat to boil.
6. Lower heat and simmer for 15 minutes.

ACKNOWLEDGMENTS

thank you...

This book is a labor of love born from friendships, near and far, of family, and places that have stayed with me.

To Sara Jane Crow, for your friendship and creativity, and the days of magic in your little casita in the South Valley. Thank you for all the love, the talks, the art, and for being the beautiful soul that you are.

Dearest Tsuya Chinn, thank you for your friendship and kindness during times when I needed it the most; I miss your beautiful face and your laughter.

To the people of New Mexico who made every visit magical, my eternal gratitude. I can't wait to see you again.

My eternal gratitude to Brendan James, whose song planted the seed for this story from the first moment I heard it up to now. Your gift is something I'll always treasure.

Thank you so much, Franggy Yanez, for being the perfect Dax Drexel on the original book cover.

I'd like to thank the many people who beta-read this baby for me on Wattpad and also answered all my questions: Alexia Montibon-Larsson, Michelle Jo Quinn, Amanda Lenore Acheairs, Leah Liburd, Beth Carpenter, Ana Simons, Mary Fahey, Michelle Morrow, Janet

Sevonukun, Laura Shaw, Cherry Shrestha, Helen Graul, Lou Ann Rice, Robert Alvarez, and J.C. Gunn.

To Donna Gibbs, thank you for sharing your life with me. You are an inspiration to me always. To Paul and Pat Sinclair, Lisa and John Stancin, and Lantz and Victoria Simpson, thank you for listening to all my stories.

Thank you to Jackie Velez for dragging me away from my laptop for those weekly walks. I treasure our friendship so much!

Thank you to my family for their support, to Lucas who one day will be old enough to read this book (but until then, no, you can't bring it with you on the bus for extra credit), and Matt who understand my creativity and craziness. Most of all, eternal gratitude to my brother, Paul. Thank you for believing in me.

ABOUT THE AUTHOR

Liz's start in storytelling got its rocky start in 8th grade when the "play" she was writing landed her in the principal's office for being a bit on the NSFW side. Since then, she's done penance by writing romance and chick lit– with a dose of naughty on the side if you look hard enough.

She lives in Southern California with her family, a chihuahua mix rescue Truffles, and way too many books and handspun yarn.

Let's Connect!
Lizduranobooks.com
lizduranobooks@gmail.com

facebook.com/LizDuranoBooks

instagram.com/lizdurano

bookbub.com/authors/liz-durano

amazon.com/author/lizdurano